Shade

Also by Jeri Smith-Ready

Wicked Game

Bad to the Bone

Shade

JERI SMITH-READY

Simon Pulse
New York   London   Toronto   Sydney

SIMON PULSE

An imprint of Simon & Schuster Children's Publishing Division
1230 Avenue of the Americas, New York, NY 10020
First Simon Pulse hardcover edition May 2010
Copyright © 2010 by Jeri Smith-Ready
SIMON PULSE and colophon are registered trademarks
of Simon & Schuster, Inc.
For information about special discounts for bulk purchases,
please contact Simon & Schuster Special Sales at 1-866-506-1949
or business@simonandschuster.com.
The Simon & Schuster Speakers Bureau can bring authors to
your live event. For more information or to book an event contact the
Simon & Schuster Speakers Bureau at 1-866-248-3049 or visit
our website at www.simonspeakers.com.
Designed by Mike Rosamilia
The text of this book was set in Adobe Caslon Pro.
Manufactured in the United States of America
2 4 6 8 10 9 7 5 3 1
Library of Congress Cataloging-in-Publication Data
Smith-Ready, Jeri.
Shade / Jeri Smith-Ready. — 1st Simon Pulse hardcover ed.
p. cm.
Summary: Sixteen-year-old Aura of Baltimore, Maryland, reluctantly works
at her aunt's law firm helping ghosts with wrongful death cases file suits in
hopes of moving on, but it becomes personal when her boyfriend, a promising
musician, dies and persistently haunts her.
ISBN 978-1-4169-9406-0
[1. Ghosts—Fiction. 2. Trials—Fiction. 3. Musicians—Fiction.
4. Supernatural—Fiction. 5. Baltimore (Md.)—Fiction.] I. Title.
PZ7.S6634Sh 2010   [Fic]—dc22   2009039487
ISBN 978-1-4424-0640-7 (eBook)

To Jimmy, whose future
shines as bright as ghosts in the dark

Acknowledgments

Thanks to my loving family, who have always let me be myself and make my own mistakes. Not that they had much choice.

To my "first readers": Lauren Becker, Patrice Michelle, Jana Oliver, Cecilia Ready, Tricia Schwaab, Jimmy Smith, Rob Staeger, Marcia Tannian, and Elizabeth Wein. Especially Jana and Patrice, who braved that heinous first draft and weeks of insane babbling— I mean, brainstorming.

To my dearest author friends: Adrian Phoenix, who held my virtual hand through that nail-biting day; Stephanie Kuehnert, who inspires me to dig deep even if it hurts; Ann Aguirre, who inspires me to shut up and write; and Victoria Dahl, who just plain cracks me up. Special thanks to P. C. Cast, for every XOXO, OMG, and exclamation point—in e-mails and in person.

To the amazing folks at Simon Pulse—Bethany Buck, Mara Anastas, Lucille Rettino, Paul Crichton, Bess Braswell, Anna McKean, Cara Petrus, Katherine Devendorf, Jennifer Klonsky, Valerie Shea—for turning the dream of *Shade* into a reality. I'm still pinching myself. Ow.

To my indescribably awesome agent, Ginger Clark, for her faith that I could do this, and for finding *Shade* a perfect home. Her humor and enthusiasm keep my crazies at bay. To my phenomenal editor, Annette Pollert, who cheered me on at every step and made me justify every word. I'm a better writer because of her.

Thanks most of all to my husband, Christian, for his love and patience and for giving me forever.

The boundaries which divide Life from Death are at best shadowy and vague. Who shall say where the one ends, and where the other begins?

—Edgar Allan Poe, "The Premature Burial"

Chapter One

"Y ou can hear me, can't you?"

I punched the green print button on the copier to drown out the disembodied voice. Sometimes if I ignored them long enough, they went away—confused, discouraged, and lonelier than ever. Sometimes.

Okay, almost never. Usually they got louder.

No time to deal with it that day. Only one more set of legal briefs to unstaple, copy, and restaple, and then I could go home, trade this straitjacket and stockings for a T-shirt and jeans, and make it to Logan's before practice. To tell him I'm sorry, that I've changed my mind, and this time I mean it. Really.

"I know you can hear me." The old woman's voice strengthened as it came closer. "You're one of them."

I didn't flinch as I grabbed the top brief from the stack on the conference room table. I couldn't see her under the office's bright fluorescent lights, which made it about one percent easier to pretend she wasn't there.

Someday, if I had my way, none of them would be there.

"What an intolerably rude child," she said.

I yanked the staple out of the last brief and let it zing off in an unknown direction, trying to hurry without *looking* like I was hurrying. If the ghost knew I was getting ready to leave, she'd spit out her story, no invitation. I carefully laid the pages in the sheet feeder and hit print again.

"You can't be more than sixteen." The lady's voice was close, almost at my elbow. "So you were born hearing us."

I didn't need her to remind me how ghosts' ramblings had drowned out my mother's New Agey lullabies. (According to Aunt Gina, Mom thought the old-fashioned ones were too disturbing— "down will come baby, cradle and all." But when dead people are bitching and moaning around your crib at all hours, the thought of falling out of a tree is so not a source of angst.)

Worst part was, those lullabies were all I remembered of her.

"Come on," I nagged the copier under my breath, resisting the urge to kick it.

The piece of crap picked that moment to jam.

"Shit." I clenched my fist, driving the staple remover tooth into the pad of my thumb. "Ow! Damn it." I sucked the pinpoint of blood.

"Language." The ghost sniffed. "When I was your age, young ladies wouldn't have heard such words, much less murdered the mother tongue with . . ." Blah blah . . . kids these days . . . blah blah . . . parents' fault . . . blah.

I jerked open the front of the copier and searched for the stuck paper, humming a Keeley Brothers song to cover the ghost's yakking.

"They cut me," she said quietly.

I stopped humming, then blew out a sigh that fluttered my dark bangs. Sometimes there's no ignoring these people.

I stood, slamming the copier door. "One condition. I get to see you."

"Absolutely not," she huffed.

"Wrong answer." I rounded the table and headed for the switches by the conference room door.

"Please, you don't want to do that. The way they left me—"

I flipped off the light and turned on the BlackBox.

"No!" The ghost streaked toward me in a blaze of violet. She stopped two inches from my face and let out a shriek that scraped against all the little bones in my ears.

Cringing? Not an option. I crossed my arms, then calmly and slowly extended my middle finger.

"This is your last warning." Her voice crackled around the edges as she tried to frighten me. "Turn on the light."

"You wanted to talk. I don't talk to ghosts I can't see." I touched the BlackBox switch. "Sucks to be trapped, huh? That's how I feel, listening to you people all day."

"How dare you?" The woman slapped my face, her fingers curled into claws. Her hand passed through my head without so much as a breeze. "After all I've been through. Look at me."

I tried to check her out, but she was trembling so hard with anger, her violet lines kept shifting into one another. It was like trying to watch TV without my contacts.

"Those shoes are beyond last year," I said, "but other than that, you look fine."

The ghost glanced down at herself and froze in astonishment. Her pale hair—gray in life, I assumed—was tied in a bun, and she wore what looked like a ruffle-lapelled suit and low-heeled pumps. Your basic country-club queen. Probably found her own death positively *scandalous*.

"I haven't seen myself in the dark." She spoke with awe. "I assumed I would be . . ." Her hand passed over her stomach.

"What, fat?"

"Disemboweled."

I felt my eyes soften. "You were murdered?" With old people it was usually a heart attack or stroke. But it explained her rage.

She scowled at me. "Well, it certainly wasn't suicide."

"I know." My voice turned gentle as I remembered to be patient. Sometimes these poor souls didn't know what to expect, despite all the public awareness campaigns since the Shift. The least I could do was clarify. "If you'd killed yourself, you wouldn't be a ghost, because you would've been prepared to die. And you're not all carved up because you get frozen in the happiest moment of your life."

She examined her clothes with something close to a smile, maybe remembering the day she wore them, then looked up at me with a sudden ferocity. "But *why?*"

I ditched the patience. "How the hell should I know?" I flapped my arms. "I don't know why we see you at all. No one knows, okay?"

"Listen to me, young lady." She pointed her violet finger in my face. "When I was your age—"

"When you were my age, the Shift hadn't happened yet. Everything's different now. You should be grateful someone can hear you."

"I shouldn't be—this way—at all." She clearly couldn't say the word "dead." "I need someone to make it right."

"So you want to sue." One of my aunt Gina's specialties: wrongful death litigation. Gina believes in "peace through justice." She thinks it helps people move past ghosthood to whatever's beyond. Heaven, I guess, or at least someplace better than Baltimore.

Weird thing is, it usually works, though no one knows exactly why. But unfortunately, Gina—my aunt, guardian, and godmother—can't hear or see ghosts. Neither can anyone else born before the Shift, which happened sixteen and three-quarters years ago. So when Gina's firm gets one of these cases, guess who gets to translate? All for a file clerk's paycheck.

"My name is Hazel Cavendish," the lady said. "I was one of this firm's most loyal clients."

Ah, that explained how she got here. Ghosts can only appear in the places they went during their lives. No one knows why *that* is, either, but it makes things a lot easier on people like me.

She continued without prompting. "I was slaughtered this morning outside my home in—"

"Can you come back Monday?" I checked my watch in ex-Hazel's violet glow. "I have to be somewhere."

"But it's only Thursday. I need to speak to someone now." Her fingers flitted over the string of pearls around her neck. "Aura, please."

I stepped back. "How do you know my name?"

"Your aunt talked about you all the time, showed me your picture. Your name is hard to forget." She moved toward me, her footsteps silent. "So beautiful."

My head started to swim. *Uh-oh.*

Vertigo in a post-Shifter like me usually means a ghost is turning shade. They go down that one-way path when they let bitterness warp their souls. It has its advantages—shades are dark, powerful spirits who can hide in the shadows and go anywhere they want.

Anywhere, that is, but out of this world. Unlike ghosts, shades can't pass on or find peace, as far as we know. And since they can single-handedly debilitate any nearby post-Shifters, "detainment" is the only option.

"I really have to go," I whispered, like I'd hurt ex-Hazel less if I lowered the volume. "A few days won't matter."

"Time always matters."

"Not for you." I kept my voice firm but kind. "Not anymore."

She moved so close, I could see every wrinkle on her violet face.

"Your eyes are old," she hissed. "You think you've seen everything, but you don't know what it's like." She touched my heart with a hand I couldn't feel. "One day you'll lose something important, and then you'll know."

I ran for the car, my work shoes clunking against the sidewalk and rubbing blisters on my ankles. No time to stop home to change before going to Logan's. Should've brought my clothes with me, but how could I have known there'd be a new case?

I'd wussed out, of course, and let the old woman tell my aunt her nasty death story. The ghost was angry enough that I worried about what she'd do without immediate attention. "Shading" was still pretty rare, especially for a new ghost like ex-Hazel, but it wasn't worth the risk.

The leafy trees lining the street made it dark enough to see ghosts even an hour before sunset. Half a dozen were loitering outside the day care center in the mansion across the street. Like most of the buildings in the Roland Park area, Little Creatures Kiddie Care was completely BlackBoxed—its walls lined with the same thin layer of charged obsidian that kept ghosts out of sensitive areas. Bathrooms, military base buildings, that sort of thing. I wish Gina and I could afford to live there—Roland Park, I mean, not a military base.

I stopped for a giant Coke Slurpee and guzzled it on my way toward I-83, wincing at the brain freeze. I usually prefer to use the spoon end of the straw, but after ex-Hazel's intake session, I desperately needed the massive caffeine-sugar infusion that only pure, bottom-of-the-cup Slurpee syrup could provide.

The long shadows of trees cut across the road, and I kept my eyes forward so I wouldn't see the ghosts on the sidewalks.

Lot of good it did. At the last stoplight before the expressway, a little violet kid waved from the backseat of the car in front of me. His lips were moving, forming words I couldn't decipher. An older girl next to him clapped her hands over her ears, her blond pigtails wagging back and forth as she shook her head. The parents in the front seats kept talking, oblivious or maybe just unable to deal. *They should trade in that car,* I thought, *while that poor girl still has her sanity.*

The on-ramp sloped uphill into the sunshine, and I let out a groan of relief, gnawing the end of my straw.

After almost seventeen years of hearing about grisly murders and gruesome accidents, you'd think I'd be tough, jaded. You'd think that ghosts' tendency to over-share would eventually annoy instead of sadden me.

And you'd be right. Mostly. By the time I was five, I'd stopped crying. I'd stopped having nightmares. I'd stopped sleeping with the lights on so I wouldn't see their faces. And I'd stopped talking about it, because by that point the world believed us. Five hundred million toddlers can't be wrong.

But I never forgot. Their stories are shelved in my mind, neat as a filing system. Probably because I've recited many of them on the witness stand.

Courts don't just take *my* word for it, or any one person's. Testimony only counts if two of us post-Shifters agree on a ghost's statement. Since ghosts apparently can't lie, they make great witnesses. Last year, me and this terrified freshman translated for the victims of a psycho serial killer. (Remember Tomcat? The one who liked to "play with his food"?)

Welcome to my life. It gets better.

I pulled into Logan's driveway at 6:40. I loved going to the Keeleys' house—it sat in a Hunt Valley development that had been farmland only a few years before. Newer neighborhoods had way fewer ghosts, and I'd never seen one at the Keeleys'. At the time, anyway.

I checked my hair in the rearview mirror. Hopelessly well-groomed. I pawed through my bag to find a few funky little silver skull-and-crossbones barrettes, then pinned them into my straight dark brown hair to make it stick out in random places.

"Yeah, you look totally punk in your beige suit and sensible flats." I made a face at myself in the mirror, then leaned closer.

Were my eyes really that old, like ex-Hazel said? Maybe it was the dark circles underneath. I licked my finger and wiped under my brown eyes to see if the mascara had smeared.

Nope. The gray shadows on my skin came from too little sleep and too much worrying. Too much rehearsing what I would say to Logan.

As I walked up the brick front path, I heard music blasting through the open basement window.

Late. I wanted to hurl my bag across the Keeleys' lawn in frustration. Once Logan got lost in his guitar, he forgot I existed. And we really needed to talk.

I went in the front door without knocking, the way I had since we were six and the Keeleys lived around the block in a row home like ours. I hurried past the stairs, through the kitchen, and into the family room.

"Hey, Aura," called Logan's fifteen-year-old brother Dylan from his usual position, sprawled barefoot and bowlegged on the floor in front of the flat-screen TV. He glanced up from his video game, then did a double-take at the sight of my Slurpee cup. "Bad one?"

"Old lady, stabbed in a mugging. Semi-Shady."

"Sucks." He focused on his game, nodding in time to the metal soundtrack. "Protein drinks work better."

"You bounce back your way, I'll bounce my way."

"Whatever." His voice rose suddenly. "Noooo! Eat it! Eat it!"

Dylan slammed his back against the ottoman and jerked the joystick almost hard enough to break it. As his avatar got torched by a flame-thrower, he shrieked a stream of curses that told me his parents weren't home. Mr. and Mrs. Keeley had apparently already left for their second honeymoon.

I opened the basement door, releasing a blast of guitar chords, then slipped off my shoes so I could walk downstairs without noise.

Halfway to the bottom, I peered over the banister into the left side of the unfinished basement. Logan was facing away from me, strumming his new Fender Stratocaster and watching his brother Mickey work out a solo. The motion of his shoulder blades rippled his neon green T-shirt, the one I'd bought him on our last trip to Ocean City.

When he angled his chin to check his fingers on the fret board, I could see his profile. Even with his face set in concentration, his sky blue eyes sparked with joy. Logan could play guitar in a sewer and still have fun.

Logan and Mickey were like yin and yang, inside and out. Logan's spiky hair was bleached blond with black streaks, while Mickey's was black with blond streaks. Logan played a black guitar right-handed, and his brother a white one left-handed. They had the same lanky build, and lots of people thought they were twins, but Mickey was eighteen and Logan only seventeen (minus one day).

Their sister, Siobhan—Mickey's actual twin—was sitting cross-legged on the rug in front of them, her fiddle resting against her left knee as she shared a cigarette with the bassist, her boyfriend, Connor.

My best friend, Megan, sat next to them, knees pulled to her chest. She wove a lock of her long, dark red hair through her fingers as she stared at Mickey.

The only one facing me was Brian, the drummer. He spotted me and promptly missed a beat. I cringed—he was sometimes brilliant, but he could be distracted by a stray dust ball.

Mickey and Logan stopped playing and turned to Brian, who adjusted the backward white baseball cap on his head in embarrassment.

"Jesus," Mickey said, "is it too much to ask for a fucking backbeat?"

"Sorry." Brian twirled his stick in his thick hand, then pointed it at me. "She's here."

Logan spun around, and I expected a glare for interrupting—not to mention leftover hostility from last night's fight. Instead his face lit up.

"Aura!" He swept the strap over his head, handed his guitar to Mickey, and leaped to meet me at the bottom of the stairs. "Oh my God, you won't believe this!" He grabbed me around the waist and hoisted me up. "You will *not* believe this."

"I will, I swear." I wrapped my arms around his neck, grinning so hard it hurt. Clearly he wasn't mad at me. "What's up?"

"Hang on." Logan lowered me to the floor, then spread my arms to examine my suit. "They make you wear this to work?"

"I didn't have time to change." I gave him a light punch in the chest for torturing me. "So what won't I believe?"

"Siobhan, get her some clothes," he barked.

"Choice," she said. "Say please or kiss my ass."

"Please!" Logan held up his hands. "Anything to keep your ass in the safe zone."

Siobhan gave Connor her cigarette and got to her feet. As she passed me, she squeezed my elbow and said, "Boy thinks he's a rock god just because some label people are coming to the show tomorrow."

My mind spun as it absorbed my biggest hope and fear. "Is she kidding?" I asked Logan.

"No," he growled. "Thanks for blowing the surprise, horse face!" he yelled as she slouched up the stairs, snickering.

I tugged on his shirt. "Who's coming?"

"Get this." He gripped my shoulders. "A and R dudes from two different companies. One's an independent—Lianhan Records—"

"That's the one we want," Mickey interjected.

"—and the other is Warrant."

I gasped. "I've heard of Warrant."

"Because they're part of a major, major, *major* humongous label." Logan's eyes rolled up in ecstasy, like God himself was handing out record contracts.

"We'll use Warrant to make Lianhan jealous," Mickey added. "But we're not selling out."

Logan pulled me to the back side of the stairs, where the others couldn't see us. "This could be it," he whispered. "Can you believe it? It'd be the most amazing birthday present ever."

I steadied my breath so I could get the words out. "Hopefully not the best present."

"You mean the Strat from my folks?"

"Not that, either." I reached up under the back of his T-shirt and let my fingers graze his warm skin.

"Is it something you—wait." His eyes widened, making the silver hoop in his brow glint in the overhead light. "Are you saying—"

"Yep." I stood on tiptoe and kissed him, quick but hard. "I'm ready."

His gold-tipped lashes flickered, but he angled his chin to look at me sideways. "You said that before."

"I said a lot of things before. Some of them were stupid."

"Yeah, they were." His eyes crinkled, softening his words. "You know I'd never leave you over this, either way. How could you even think that?"

"I don't know. I'm sorry."

"Me too." He traced my jaw with his thumb, which always made me shiver. "I love you."

He kissed me then, drowning my doubts in one warm, soft moment. Doubts about him, about me, about him *and* me.

"Here you go!" Siobhan called from the stairs, a moment before a clump of denim and cotton fell on our heads. "Oops," she said with fake surprise.

I peeled the jeans off Logan's shoulder and held them up in salute. "Thanks, Siobhan."

"Back to work!" rang Mickey's voice from the other side of the basement.

Logan ignored his brother and gazed into my eyes. "So . . . maybe tomorrow night, at my party?" He hurried to add, "Only if you're sure. We could wait, if you—"

"No." I could barely manage a whisper. "No more waiting."

His lips curved into a smile, which promptly faded. "I better clean my room. There's like a one-foot path through all the old *Guitar Worlds* and dirty laundry."

"I can walk on a one-foot path."

"Screw that. I want it to be perfect."

"Hey!" Mickey yelled again, louder. "What part of 'back to work' is not in English?"

Logan grimaced. "We're switching out some of our set list—less covers, more original stuff. Probably be up all night." He gave me a kiss that was quick but full of promise. "Stay as long as you want."

He disappeared around the stairs, and immediately Megan replaced him at my side.

"Did you make up? You did, didn't you?"

"We made up." I sat on the couch to remove my stockings, checking over my shoulder to make sure the guys were out of sight on the other side of the stairs. "I told him I'm ready."

Megan slumped next to me and rested her elbow on the back of the sofa. "You don't think you have to say that to keep him, do you?"

"It's something I want too. Anyway, who cares, as long as it works?"

"Aura . . ."

"You know what it's like, going to their gigs." My whisper turned to a hiss. "Seeing all those girls who'd probably pay to get naked with Mickey or Logan. Or even with Brian or Connor."

"But the guys aren't like that—well, maybe Brian is, but he doesn't have a girlfriend. Mickey loves me. Logan loves you."

"So?" I slipped on the jeans. "Plenty of rock stars have wives and girlfriends, and they still screw their groupies. It comes with the territory."

"I find your lack of faith disturbing," she said in her best Darth Vader impression, forcing a smile out of me.

I unbuttoned my white silk blouse. "What should I wear?"

"Same stuff as always, on the outside. That's the way he likes you." Megan snapped the strap of my plain beige bra. "But definitely do better than this underneath."

"Duh," was my only response as I slipped Siobhan's black-and-yellow Distillers T-shirt over my head. I'd made a covert trip to Victoria's Secret weeks before—the one way up in Owings Mills, where no one would recognize me. The matching black lace bra and underwear were still in the original bag, with their tags on, in the back of my bottom dresser drawer.

"The first time doesn't have to suck," she said, "not if you go slow."

"Okay," I said quickly, in a deep state of not wanting to talk about it.

Luckily, at that moment Brian tapped his sticks to mark time, and the band launched into one of their original tunes, "The Day I Sailed Away."

The Keeley Brothers wanted to be the premier Irish-flavored rock band in Baltimore. Maybe one day go national, become the next Pogues, or at least the next Flogging Molly, with a heavy dose of American skate-punk 'tude.

As Logan began to sing, Megan's face reflected my bliss and awe. With that voice leading the way, the Keeley Brothers didn't have to be the next anyone.

Two record labels. I closed my eyes, ignoring the way my stomach turned to lead, and savored the sound that Megan and I would soon have to share with the world.

I knew then that everything would change the next night. It was like time had folded in on itself, and I could remember the future.

A future I already hated.

Chapter Two

O oh, that's a new one."

Megan pointed across the school courtyard at the tall, lean man's violet outline. In the sunshine he would never have been visible, but heavy clouds made the afternoon look like evening.

The ghost circled the fountain, stopping every few feet to peer into the water.

"No, that's ex-Jared," I told Megan. "He graduated from Ridgewood nine years ago. Died in the war."

"What's he looking for in the fountain?"

"Go ask him."

"No way."

"He's not mean or anything. But if he starts in about his uncle Fred, change the subject. Unless you want to see your lunch again."

Megan grimaced as a pair of seniors walked right through ex-Jared.

"I hate that," she whispered. "I can't wait till we're seniors and everyone will be like us."

"Except the teachers. And the janitors. And the librarian and the secretaries." My butt hurt on the iron bench, so I uncrossed my legs and recrossed them the other way. "Face it, when everyone is like us, we'll be old."

She frowned and twisted the emerald pendant Mickey had given her for her sixteenth birthday. "So how much are you dreading this assembly?"

"Let's just say I'd rather take the PSATs again than hear some government worker bee tell us how we can serve our country by locking up ghosts."

I jabbed my thumb at the trio of white vans pulling into the school parking lot. Each bore the logo of the federal Department of Metaphysical Purity.

Megan said, "I heard the DMP has a special forces unit, the Obsidians. They're like Navy SEALs. They're the ones who, you know, take care of the shades." She made a slashing motion across her throat.

"Aunt Gina would kill me if I did anything remotely anti-ghost." Back before the Shift, Gina was one of the few people who could see and hear the dead. Now she can't, but she still has a thing for them.

Megan bit the cuticle of her thumb. "Still, I bet the uniforms are cool."

The phone in my hand buzzed. Logan had just texted I LOVE YOU—

so cute how he never abbreviated it. It had been more than a year since his family moved out to Baltimore County, but I still missed him like crazy during the school day.

The sun broke through the clouds, warming the top of my head and dimming the screen. Ex-Jared faded in the full light of day.

As he disappeared, my eyes refocused on a boy I'd never seen before, chatting with my history teacher, Mrs. Richards, across the courtyard.

"Who's that?"

Megan gasped and grabbed my arm. "Scottish exchange student. In my homeroom."

"But it's the middle of October. I thought exchange students came at the beginning of the year."

"The more important question is, who did we exchange him for, and can Scotland keep them?"

I nudged her side with my elbow. "Aw, I'm telling Mickey."

"Go ahead." Megan pulled her sunglasses from her bag. "This clearly falls under our Look-Don't-Touch policy." She put on her shades. "Speaking of looking, he's staring at you."

The boy stood alone now, hands on his hips, examining me. A breeze blew a splash of dark bangs across his forehead, and his posture made his faded blue T-shirt stretch across his broad chest.

I stared back, and he tilted his head as if surprised. Guys are like ghosts that way—when they check you out, they expect you to glance away all meek and flirty-girly. Yeah, right.

Despite the chilly air, he wore long khaki shorts and a pair of sandals. Sandals on feet that were now walking straight toward us.

Megan grabbed my wrist under the open binder on my lap. "Here he comes," she said, as if I could've missed it.

He stopped in front of us and nodded at Megan, who dug her nails into my arm. Then he turned the purest green eyes to mine. "Excuse me. Are you really Aura?"

I didn't notice the "really," because my ears had heated at the sound of my name spoken that way, his tongue curled around the *r* like it was a piece of candy.

"What?" I said eloquently.

"Aura," he repeated, pronouncing it *Ooora* (again with tongue curl). "That's you, aye?" *You* like a female sheep. Wow, it's true what they say about Scottish accents.

"Um. Yeah, I'm—" I couldn't speak my name without sounding lame and American. "That's me." I cleared my throat. "Why?"

"Mrs. Richards said you were studying ancient astronomy for your thesis."

"Uh-huh." Too bad I'm an idiot savant, emphasis *not* on the savant. "Sort of."

He shook his head, a dark wave of hair lashing his left cheek. "Incredible."

Another *r*, but his skepticism broke through my haze. "Why, because girls can't be astronomers?"

"Of course they can, but the girls I know who like science aren't—" He cut himself off and looked away, dragging a hand through his hair. "I just met her," he muttered to himself. "I'll no' say *that*."

"Cut the crap," Megan said. "Zachary Moore, this is Aura Salvatore, and yes, she's into science even though she's pretty. Shocker. Get over it." She turned to me. "Show him how you can walk and chew gum at the same time."

I rested my elbow on the back of the bench and inspected Zachary in what I hoped was a casual way. "You don't look much like a science geek either," I told him.

He lifted one brow while twitching a corner of his mouth. I realized how my words sounded—that I thought he was pretty too.

Unfortunately, I did. Not that it was a matter of opinion, except maybe to the legally blind.

"Where's your kilt?" I asked him.

Zachary looked over my head, and I got the feeling he was trying not to roll his eyes. Then he moved closer, put his hand on the back of the bench near my shoulder, and leaned deep inside my personal space. "How about this," he said in a low voice, "you don't ask me about haggis and bagpipes, and I won't ask you about garlic and *Goodfellas*."

Megan laughed out loud. My fingers tightened on the edge of the bench to keep from hitting him. Not that he didn't have a point.

"Okay, no stereotypes," I said. "Deal."

"So do you have a kilt?" Megan asked him. When I glared at her, she said, "What? He only said *you* couldn't ask." She looked at him. "So do you?"

Straightening up, Zachary rubbed the back of his neck and smirked. "I might, I might."

God, he was gorgeous. And Scottish. But maybe kind of an ass.

I cleared my throat again. "So what do you want?"

"Oh." He shifted his books under his other arm. "Mrs. Richards said you needed help with your thesis."

My mouth dropped open.

Megan snorted. "Uh-oh."

"I don't need help with anything," I told him.

"But everyone else has a partner for—"

"Everyone else is researching easy topics like the French Revolution or the Boer Wars. I'm working on—" I pulled my binder to my chest. "Something important."

"Megaliths," he offered. "Like Stonehenge. I know a bit about them."

I frowned. No way his "knowledge" would have anything to do with the answers I was seeking. I'd specifically told Mrs. Richards I wanted to do my research alone. Any partner would think I was crazy for investigating whether the megaliths were connected to the Shift.

"Are you a Droid?" Megan asked him. "Like the ones who built it?"

Zachary's cheeks dimpled as if he was trying not to laugh. "You mean a Druid. No, I'm afraid not."

"Besides," I told her, "Druids didn't build Stonehenge. It's way older than them. They just say they built it so they can have their little festivals there. It's total bullshit."

Megan cocked her head at Zachary. "Sure you're man enough to work with this girl?"

"She'll tell me if I'm not." He winked at her, and I felt weirdly jealous.

Megan shaded her eyes to peer up at the clock tower. "Aura, assembly's in ten, and I gotta pee like crazy. Save you a seat?"

"Thanks."

She sent me a sly glance over her shoulder as she walked away. Zachary took her spot beside me.

"So what do you know about megaliths?" I asked him. Ugh, I had to clear my throat *again*. I probably sounded like a pack-a-day smoker.

"Well, before I moved here last week? I never lived more than an hour's drive from standing stones."

The back of my neck tingled at the thought. "Wow. In Scotland?" I realized how stupid that sounded, but he saved me.

"Right, and Ireland, Wales, England. Other places I've lived."

"Are the stone rings—you know, creepy?"

"You mean magical?"

I nodded, encouraged by his serious face. "Do you ever get used to it? Is it ever like seeing, I don't know, a garbage truck?"

"A garbage truck?"

"Ordinary. Or do the stones have all this weird energy zinging off them?"

"It depends." Zachary pulled one foot onto the bench and rested his elbow on his bent knee.

"Depends?" I tried not to check out his cute ankle peeking through his sandal. (What kind of dork notices ankles?) His face was just as distracting, so I focused on an imaginary point over his left shoulder. "Depends on what?"

"Their arrangement. The time of day. The weather. At sunrise or just before a thunderstorm, they almost look alive. Like they're waiting for something to happen, you know?" Zachary rubbed his chin, then spread his fingers as he looked at me through his thick, dark lashes. "But mostly it depends on your mood."

My neck warmed at the way his lips puckered with the *oo* sound, and then the way his tongue tagged the *d*. This was Bad with a capital Hell No. Logan was the only guy who'd ever made me feel like this, like I had a caffeine overdose and a second-degree sunburn. *Get a grip, Aura. It's just the accent.*

"Have you never seen any, then?" he asked me.

"Just pictures." I twisted the zipper at the end of my jacket sleeve. "I've never been out of the country, except to Italy for my great-grandmother's funeral."

"Oh, you should go someday. Especially since the stones are so important to you."

A sudden chill flowed over me, like I'd been stripped naked. "They're not important to me."

"Then why did you pick this topic?"

"I just think they're cool, okay?" I slapped my binder shut. "And I don't need help studying them."

"Mrs. Richards said you'd say that. She also said to tell you that you have no choice." He whipped out his phone like he was drawing a weapon. "Give me your number. How's Sunday?"

I didn't hide my groan of dismay, but exchanged my information for his and opened the calendar app on my phone. "Sunday I have my first meeting with my adviser at College Park." For our theses, we were required to have expert guidance from someone outside our school.

"Brilliant. I'll go with you. Pick me up at noon? I can't drive here yet, and this city's public transport is crap."

I hesitated, wondering if I should be alone in a car with this strange guy. I decided to check him out with Mrs. Richards. If he seemed the least bit serial killer-ish, I'd ask for a new partner.

"You're just here to help," I said. "I've already started this project, and I know where I want it to go."

"And where's that, Aura?" Zachary met my glare with a cool gaze. "What do you hope you'll find?"

"That is not your business." I stood and snatched up my bag before he could see the flush on my face.

"You'll need my address to pick me up."

"Give it to me at the assembly." I stalked toward the double doors under the peaked stone archway. "We'll be late."

"I'm no' going to the assembly."

I stopped and looked at him. "I thought you were a junior."

"I am, but I was born pre-Shift." He slid off the bench, his long legs unfolding in a fluid motion. "Only by a minute, though," he said as he passed me.

My bag slid out of my hand and thudded onto the pavement. Zachary kept walking.

I sat in the auditorium, clutching my seat's armrests, as the DMP agents—or "dumpers," as we call them—led what should have been the most boring lecture of my life.

The blonde in the stark white uniform pointed her remote at a laptop on the projector, taking us to the second PowerPoint slide. Then she continued her spiel.

"As far as we can tell," she said, "the Shift took place during that year's winter solstice. December twenty-first, oh-eight-fifty Universal Time. That would be three fifty a.m. local time."

I glanced at Megan beside me, slouched in her seat, jacket shrugged up to her ears. She was one of the few people who knew that *that* was the moment of my birth.

Somebody had to be first, right? Why not me? And somebody else had to be last, before the Shift. Zachary. There were probably hundreds of others around the world born during our minutes. It's not like I was the first-first, or he was the last-last.

Still, what were the chances we'd meet here? We're not exactly on top of an alleged mystical vortex like Stonehenge or Sedona, Arizona. This is Baltimore. Home of steamed crabs and big hair. Even Edgar Allan Poe's ghost never hung out here, and he died right down on Fayette Street.

A folded piece of paper jabbed my arm. I took Megan's note. (Low-tech, I know, but the BlackBox screws with electronic signals, so texting and cell phone calls inside school are pretty much out.)

What's up, Pup?

I wrote, *Zachary was born one minute before me,* and passed it back.

Megan scribbled, *LIAR!!*

She meant him, not me. But why would he say that unless it were true, and/or he knew when I was born and wanted to mess with my head?

Could there be a deeper answer, something that would unlock the mystery of who (and why) I was?

I smoothed out the wrinkles near the seams of my faded jeans, trying to calm my careening imagination. Zachary probably didn't know anything about me. The fact that he looked like he could star in a James Bond Jr. film just made him seem more exotic than the average guy.

The agent switched off the projector, darkening the screen. She sat on the edge of the table and leaned forward, as if she were about to tell us a secret. More like give the closing sales pitch.

"A year and a half from now," she said, "the first class of post-Shifters will graduate. The Department of Metaphysical Purity needs you—as translators, engineers, investigators . . . the list goes on. With us, you could have any career track you want. And here's the kicker: We'll pay for your education."

Most of my classmates sat up straighter at the mention of free college. Our families already had a mountain of debt from private-school tuition. But my aunt would rather have a whole mountain *range* of debt than let me be a dumper.

Megan poked my arm. She turned her notebook to show me:
YOU & ZACH = SECRET TWINS?!?

I scowled, and her eyes went wide as she realized she'd stepped into *that* subject. She scratched out the words and wrote in bigger letters, *SORRY.*

I curled my arms around my waist, feeling cold. Ex-Hazel's words came back to me, about how I'd never lost anything important. Since I was barely three when my mother died of cancer, everyone thinks I don't miss her. But sometimes I wish that if she had to die, she would have done it suddenly, so that at least I could've known her ghost. There's so much I would've asked her.

And it's not like I'd never thought about what would happen if my aunt or grandmom died and then haunted me. Part of me even wished my father's ghost would show up one day.

Because at least then, I'd find out who he was.

Chapter Three

The Keeley Brothers' gig was at a northwest Baltimore County community center. Not the world's most cutting-edge venue, but it had an actual stage, and an actual *back*stage that led to a private exit, which would add to the mystique, Logan said. The band members could leave the building without meandering through the crowd like mere mortals.

Megan and I got dinner at the mall food court, but we only had enough appetite to split a salad and a yogurt. I was so nervous for Logan, my stomach was leaping and diving like a kitten on speed.

I sipped my iced tea and watched a woman in her twenties bring a stroller to a stop outside the window of Baby Gap. She spread her hands in frustration at the selection, and I knew what she was thinking. Ninety percent of the clothes were red this season, just as they'd been every season since we realized the dead hate that color. Unlike obsidian, it's not foolproof, but it's better than nothing. Megan and I never wore red to any place important, like a club or even the mall. No way we would advertise the fact that we were only sixteen.

While we ate, we talked about everything but the gig, and tried to avoid the attention of ghosts, barely visible in the shadowed corners.

They never spoke among themselves and, as far as I could tell, didn't know that other ghosts existed. Another mystery, this one a tiny branch off the Big Question of why the Shift happened in the first place. If I knew that, I'd make it unhappen.

"So what are you giving Logan for his birthday?" Megan asked me.

I checked my purse to make sure it was shut, hiding the wrapped gift. "It's personal."

"I already know about the sex. What's more personal than that?"

With me and Logan? Music. I'd bought him an autographed copy of Snow Patrol's *Eyes Open* CD off of eBay, but I wanted to give it to him alone. Mickey and Megan had this thing about "sellout" bands— as soon as an artist had a Top 40 hit, they were eternally uncool. But all Logan and I cared about was how the music made us feel when we were together.

"Have you seen my baby?" a violet woman asked us. She stood so close to our table she was practically a part of it, but in the light we could barely see her shimmering outline.

"No, sorry," we mumbled, focusing on our food.

"How do you know?" The ghost's voice sharpened. "I haven't even told you what he looks like."

I set down my spoon. "Did you try your home?"

"Of course I did, but they went and moved. I know I should've stayed away, but I couldn't. I made him cry just by sitting on the end of his bed." When we didn't react, the woman moved into our table, standing between us. "I'm his mother, how could he be scared of me? *I* pushed him out of the way of that car, and now he goes running to that whore for comfort. Calls her 'Mommy' now. Ungrateful little beast."

"I'm sure he's grateful," I told her, "or he will be someday. But you're dead. You're not part of our world anymore. Once you deal with that, you can move on."

Megan slurped the last of her drink, then set her cup down in the middle of the ghost. "Come on, we gotta get ready."

The gig wasn't for two hours, but I nodded and picked up my bag. We headed for the exit without another word for the ghost, even as she shrieked behind us, "I don't want to move on. I want my son!"

Heads turned our way—not all of them, just the post-Shifters'. A freshman girl from my debate team gave a sympathetic wave, which helped ease the knot in my neck as I braced for the inevitable tantrum.

"Don't you walk away from me!" the ghost snarled.

A toddler in yellow overalls burst into tears. His mom picked him up, looking exasperated at his change in mood.

"Shut up!" the ghost shrieked at the child. "You still have your mother, so—Shut! Up!"

The toddler wailed louder, and Megan and I hurried toward the bright light of the exit.

Outside, we were alone as soon as the door closed behind us. I guess the ghost never used that entrance when she was alive.

"Jesus, Aura," Megan said. "An intervention in the food court?"

"I can't help it sometimes."

"It's less cruel just to ignore them."

"I don't know, maybe." One theory said that "engaging" ghosts actually made them hang out in our world longer. The longer they stayed—and stayed unhappy—the more likely they were to become shades.

But I couldn't help imagining how it would feel to be trapped here with no body, no way to change anything. How lonely it would be for no one to hear or see you, except little kids who cried when you talked to them, or people me and Megan's age, who just wanted to be left alone.

I looked back at the mall entrance and saw the ghost watching us from inside the darkened doorway. The mother with the screaming child walked right through her.

Megan and I got to the community center in time to change and find a spot up front. We'd missed the sound check on purpose, since it usually consisted of Mickey yelling at Logan, who would respond with silent obscene gestures (to save his voice).

Before long, the place was packed and sweaty, most people already bouncing to the recorded music on the speakers.

We boosted our butts up to sit on the edge of the stage so we could scan the crowd.

"What do recording label people look like?" I asked Megan. "They wear suits?"

"Not the indie guy, I bet," she said. "He'll probably look hipper than us."

"Easy, in my case." My aunt wouldn't allow non-ear piercings or funky dye like the green streak in Megan's red hair, and my clothes had designated no-rip zones.

I couldn't hide hair or piercings, but clothes could be changed. Hence my sleeveless black Rancid T-shirt with the long diagonal razor cuts across the front and back. It looked like I'd been swiped by the claws of a twenty-foot cougar. White cami underneath, because I'm not a total skank, and besides, I wanted Logan to be the first to see the new bra.

I swung my legs, knocking together the insteps of my black pin-stripe creepers. I wanted to dance, but even more, I wanted them to get that first song over with. When they nailed it, the rest of the night was heaven. When it tanked—well, let's just say Cain and Abel had nothing on Mickey and Logan.

The recorded music faded as the house darkened. We jumped off the stage, into a throbbing mass of humans. There couldn't have been more than a thousand people, but their roar seemed to make the walls pulse.

Brian lumbered onstage alone and casually picked up his drum-sticks. He flipped one of the sticks, end over end, then rattled off a steady, superfast beat, stoking the crowd into a frenzy.

The tension in my shoulders loosened. I could tell by Brian's rhythm that he was sober.

Connor and Siobhan came on next, taking their sweet time pick-ing up their bass guitar and fiddle on opposite sides of the stage, while Brian broke into a serious sweat.

When they were in position, Brian hit the snare to signal them to start. Siobhan dove into the intro to the Pogues' "Streams of

Whiskey." Connor's tall, thin frame bobbed in time, his bass giving her melody a thrumming backdrop. The tempo was even faster than the album version, and I prayed Logan had done his tongue warm-ups.

The Keeley brothers themselves swaggered onstage, arms around each other's shoulders, the energy between them crackling. They gave the crowd a quick fist-wave, then Mickey picked up his white Fender from its stand.

Logan leaped straight for the microphone. The first song was always vocals only—partly to calm his nerves, but also to mark his territory as the front man. He sent me a brief smirk, as if he knew I was even more scared than he was. Then he began to sing.

He clutched the mike and stared straight ahead during the rapid, tongue-twisting verses. Logan told me once that singing this song was like trying to run while tied to a car bumper—one misstep and there's no recovering, just gravel up your nose.

But Logan let loose on the choruses, bounding across the front of the stage like his high-top Vans had springs in them, waving the crowd to sing along. With just a little less conviction, he would've looked like a complete asshat. But he sold it, and they bought it, lapped it up, and begged for more.

Me, I didn't dance or even clap. My fingernails dug into the black drapery tacked to the front edge of the stage. Every muscle was frozen except my heart. It throbbed in sync with the song until I thought I'd pass out.

When it was over, Logan raised his fists to the screaming crowd, then winked at me, sharing my relief.

As he turned and knelt to pick up his gleaming black guitar, I thought I saw him cross himself—either to say, *Thanks, God, for not letting me screw up* or to ask forgiveness for the song choice. His parents hated when the boys "exploited the drunken Irish stereotype," as if there were a huge selection of Celtic music *not* about alcohol.

But Mr. and Mrs. Keeley were currently on a cruise to Aruba. So Logan could sing what he wanted—and later, with me, do what he wanted.

"Thank you," Logan said into the microphone, eyes gleaming at the volume of the shrieks. "Best crowd ever. Thank you." He soaked in their attention another moment, giving Mickey a chance to trade his own guitar for a mandolin. "We're the Keeley Brothers, and this is one of ours."

Brian counted off, and they slammed into "The Day I Sailed Away." I forced my fingers to let go of the stage.

"They've got it tonight," Megan yelled in my left ear. "Come dance!"

"I'm too nervous!" I clasped my hands behind my head and turned back to the stage, my elbows blocking out everything but Logan.

As always, he wore the wristband with the black-and-white triangles—the one I bought him last year during my pyramid obsession. In the white stage light, the wristband blurred gray as he strummed the Fender Strat with a new ferocity. His calf muscles twitched and stretched as he kept time with his heel.

Sweat streamed down my back, tickling my spine. Around me, people bounced and swayed, but I kept still, as if I could shatter the pulsing perfection by breathing too hard.

The set continued. The band was like a thundercloud of chain lightning, each musician's energy feeding off the others' until it felt like the stage couldn't hold them. I thought the strings of Siobhan's fiddle would catch fire, and for a brief second, that all three guitars were doomed to be slammed into Brian's drum set.

But even Mickey's brilliant solos couldn't steal the focus from my boy. Logan's voice switched from a growl to a scream to a seductive whisper from one song to the next. As each new tune began, his face lit up, as if it was the first time he'd heard it. He looked like he was having a religious experience, one he wanted us all to share.

Was it because the A and R guys were watching that he had such intensity? Or was it something else?

All I know is that I was ecstatically, painfully in love with him, waiting for him to slip away, leaving me with my palms singed from clutching a blue-hot star. No matter how many times his eyes found mine, or how brilliantly he smiled at me, I could still taste the bitterness on the sides of my tongue. Because he loved the crowd more than he loved any one person, even me. He always would.

After the last song, Mickey and Logan bowed together. Then Mickey shouted into the mike, "Happy birthday to my little brother!"

That was our cue. All of us up front reached under the black drapery and brought out the plastic shopping bags we'd hidden there. Then Mickey held Logan in place as we pelted him with handfuls of multicolored birthday candles. Connor and Siobhan tossed them back into the crowd so we could hurl them again.

Once all seventeen hundred candles had been thrown (most of them two or three times), the band waved and dragged Logan away.

Megan and I and a few other friends scrambled onto the stage to collect the candles. The view from behind Logan's microphone showed a darkened room ablaze with cell phones and lighters—and along the edges, more than a few ghosts.

The Keeley Brothers came back for an encore, a cover of blink-182's "Dammit," with Mickey singing the chorus. Then their own "Ghost in Green," which gave everyone a chance to solo while Logan crowd-surfed, and ending with Flogging Molly's "Devil's Dance Floor"—the hottest, fastest song yet, as if to prove they had the stamina to start over and go all night long.

Finally they took one last bow, then sprang offstage, this time with their instruments.

Megan pulled me into a long, tight hug. "Aura, they did it, they really did it. That was their best show ever by a hundred times."

Over her shoulder I got a glimpse of Logan backstage. He waved at me, then flashed both palms wide to signal *ten minutes*. Then Mickey walked up and spoke in his ear. Logan's smile widened, then he signaled to me *twenty minutes*.

"The label guys." I let go of Megan, sweat making our shirts stick together. "This is it."

"Don't worry, they can't sign anything until they're all eighteen, or Mr. Keeley will disown them. No car, no college, no food."

I watched Logan fade into the darkness, his golden hair catching the last shred of stage light. Adrenaline crashed through my veins, making the blood pound in my ringing ears. The last song ran through my head, backward and forward.

I knew Logan would give up cars, college, and food for a chance to be a rock star. He'd sell his soul and wouldn't miss it for a second. Because until everyone in the world loved him, he'd have no use for that soul anyway.

My boyfriend's onstage invincibility was a pale preview of his birthday party.

The news was good—both recording labels wanted to sign them, and they were willing to wait until the Keeleys (and Brian's parents, since he was a minor too) could call their lawyers. I was glad the boys and Siobhan had played hard to get. I'd heard stories about bands getting crappy contracts that would never make them money no matter how many records they sold.

The reps' attention gave Logan enough ego juice to act like he was turning seven instead of seventeen that night. He seriously proposed to Mickey and Siobhan that they finish off the night by making a music video in the local graveyard.

"I'm telling you, it'll be huge." Standing in the downstairs hallway, Logan looped an arm around each of their necks, barely holding himself up. "For 'Ghost in Green,' right? I got it all planned out. We go up to Sacred Heart, okay, and just shoot the video like regular." He flapped his hand in my direction. "Aura and Brian can let us know when the ghosts show up, and tell them to jam with us. Like, not for real or anything, 'cause they can't hold instruments. I mean dance along. It would be"—his gaze roamed the ceiling, looking for the perfect word—"tremendous."

"Yeah, tremendous," Mickey said, "and we still wouldn't be able to see them, even on film."

"That's not the point, dumb-ass." Logan flicked the side of Mickey's head. "Post-Shifters'll see them. You gotta think forward."

I snagged a blue corn chip from Siobhan's paper plate. "But ghosts don't hang out much in graveyards," I told Logan, "We'd find more inside the church itself."

"Aw, yeah! Let's do it! Father Carrick would go for it, right?"

"Sure he would." Mickey patted Logan's hand. "How many drinks have you had?"

"None." Logan shook his head emphatically. "None drinks. Officially."

I held up a half-empty pint of Guinness. "Officially this is mine, even though it's never touched my lips."

"She's lying," Logan told them. "Never trust a girl who hates Guinness."

"And how many of those have 'you' had?" Siobhan asked me, with air quotes.

"This is his fourth—I mean, my fourth."

"Right." Mickey snatched the glass from me. "You're cut off."

"Thank you." I took Logan's hand and tried not to yank him in my annoyance. "Come dance with me."

Siobhan sidled over to the stereo. "I'll switch to something slow so he doesn't puke on you."

Logan took the lead, guiding me through the scattered partyers to the center of the living room floor, where he wrapped his arms around me. The music's beat dropped to a slow throb.

He gave a warm sigh into my scalp. "This is better."

"Much."

"Let me know when I get too obnoxious."

"'Too'?"

"Okay, okay." Logan kissed my forehead. "This is such an amazing night, Aura. We did something spectacular on that stage. I never felt that kind of energy before."

"I know."

"But it wouldn't mean shit without you there."

My heart thudded. I wanted him to promise he'd always feel that way. But I couldn't ask that of him, and even if he said it, I wouldn't believe.

"Wow," he whispered. "I'm suddenly sober."

I tugged one of the black streaks in his spiky blond hair. "You are not."

"Feels like it." Logan slid his hand over my waist, following the curve of my ribs. "I'm nervous. I'm afraid I'll do something wrong again tonight, like I did a couple weeks ago."

"You didn't do anything wrong then. It's supposed to hurt a little the first time. I shouldn't have wussed out and made us stop."

"It was my fault. If I knew what I was doing, maybe it would've been easier for you."

"I was probably just worried Aunt Gina would come home early." I rested my cheek against his warm chest and watched Megan and Mickey dance, their bodies in perfect sync. "I just want to get it over with."

"Don't say that." Logan pulled away a few inches, blue eyes bleary but determined. "I won't be able to go through with it if I know you're dying for it to end."

"Logan, just shut up. It'll be fine. It'll be great." I tried to coax my mouth into a convincing smile.

He looked strangely vulnerable. "You wanna get out of here?"

One last heart-slam. "Definitely."

We headed for the stairs, making sure no one was following.

"Hey, birthday boy."

Brian Knox stood in our path, flanked by Nadine Ross and Emily McFarland, girls I recognized from Logan's school here in Hunt Valley. Brian held two glasses of a clear drink.

Nadine took one of the glasses and pressed it into Logan's hand. He held it up to the light.

"What the hell is this?" he asked Brian.

"My new invention." The drummer bowed. "I call it Liquid Stupid."

Nadine giggled. "Liquid Stupid."

"Guaranteed to lower your IQ twenty points with the first sip." Brian put the other glass in my hand. "Aura, why don't you take five sips and come down to our level?"

"Who'd be dumb enough to drink something called Liquid Stupid?" I turned to Logan, who was downing the first half of his glass. "What are you doing? You don't even know what's in it!"

Logan swallowed, then whooshed out a hard breath. "What's in it?"

Brian counted off on his fingers. "Grain alcohol, Aftershock, and uh, some other stuff. Guess I should've written it down before I drank some."

"You like it?" Nadine brushed her hand over Logan's arm in a way that made me want to bite it off.

"Tastes like Fireballs and battery acid," he said.

"The second half is better, after it kills your taste buds." She lifted Logan's wrist toward his mouth.

"Easy now." He gently removed her hand. "I want to remember this night tomorrow."

"I bet you do." Brian threw a greedy glance over my body.

"Hey." Logan stepped between us and poked Brian in the chest. "Don't make me lose those sticks of yours up your ass."

Brian barked a laugh. "If anyone here has a stick up their little diva ass, it's—"

Logan shoved him against the wall, knocking off his cap. The thud of Brian's shoulder blades caught everyone's attention.

Brian lifted his hands in surrender, even though with his beefiness, he could've slammed Logan into the floor. "Dude, I'm kidding."

"About what?" Logan snarled.

"Everything. Anything. Whatever." Brian seemed amused but a little worried, and I sensed something was going on that I wasn't aware of, that maybe I didn't want to know. Emily looked as confused as I felt, while Nadine watched the guys like they were characters on her favorite reality show.

I put a hand on Logan's back. "Come on. Let's get something to eat."

He blinked at me. "Right." He let Brian go with another slight shove. "Sorry, man."

"S'okay." Brian picked up his cap, avoiding my eyes.

I led Logan through the kitchen.

"You still hungry," he said, "after all that pizza?"

"No, but you need a time-out."

"I'm not a little kid."

"Yeah?" Without looking back, I walked through the side hallway toward the stairs. "Come prove it."

"I wrote a song for you." Logan picked up his acoustic guitar and sank onto his bed with a *whump!* that made the instrument hum. "For tonight."

I sat beside him. "A private performance. I feel so privileged." I didn't mean it as sarcastically as it came out.

He strummed quietly with the pick, then adjusted the pegs. I twisted my hands in my lap, knuckles scraping my palms, wishing simultaneously that the night would end Now and Never.

Logan's room was spotless—at least as far as I could see in the warm, dim light from his desk lamp. The Irish flag hung on one wall, a smaller version of the one in the basement. (The Keeleys' ancestors left Dublin in the 1840s, but they acted like they just hopped off the boat last week. Their wet bar had a slow-pour keg tap specially designed for Guinness, and Notre Dame football was a second religion.)

Another wall was all shelves—CDs and music books. There was no obvious order, but Logan could always find what he needed in two seconds. In the far corner, his battered skateboard sat abandoned. I thought I could see a layer of dust on it, but that might've just been the angle of the light.

On the wall above his bed hung posters of his two heroes—the entire lineup of the Baltimore Ravens, and the Pogues' front man, Shane McGowan. His parents didn't approve of the second—anybody who could get kicked out of an Irish punk band for drinking too much was a bad role model, they said.

After a minute or two of tuning, Logan shifted his position and gave me the shy smile I hadn't seen since we were ten. "Ready?"

As soon as he hit the first jangled chord, we knew something was wrong.

"Huh." Logan flexed his fingers, then did another quick strum. "My hands are tingly." His speech was slower than usual. "Maybe worn out from the show. Sorry about that."

"Just play what you can. It doesn't have to be perfect."

"Yes, it does." His voice gained a hard edge, obliterating the slur. "I promise tomorrow night it will be. The song, I mean." He switched on the CD player with the remote control. "Go pick something while I put this away."

I fished out the first nonpunk CD I could find, one from a new Danish band with fuzzy guitars and a lumbering beat that echoed in my gut. The music made the room feel like it was on a different planet from the rest of the house. I closed my eyes for a moment and let the wall of sound soothe my mind.

Logan snapped the catches on his guitar case, then stood, wavering as his knees straightened.

"I have a present for you." He glanced down at his body. "And you get to unwrap it."

Ew, I thought.

Then his eyes widened. "No, I don't mean that!" he said. "Well, yeah, that too, but not yet." He took my hands and placed my fingers on his shirt's top button. "Ready, go."

I tried to keep my hands from shaking as they unbuttoned his shirt. His lips folded under his teeth, and I knew he was as nervous as I was.

I reached up to push the shirt off his left shoulder. That's when I saw it.

Over his heart, a tattoo with four letters written in a Celtic font: AURA.

My hand froze. "God."

"Do you like it?"

I couldn't breathe. It felt like I'd never breathe again. "When did you get this?"

"Last week. It was my birthday present to myself. And no, I don't expect you to get a matching one. Your aunt would have a stroke. After she finished killing me."

I traced the smooth black lines where my name met his flesh. "Does your mom know?"

"No one knows, except me and you. My dad'll probably have a heart attack when he finds out, but that's why we have the defibrillator."

I didn't laugh. Mr. Keeley had had too many close calls. This cruise had been on his cardiologist's orders.

"I know you're worried," Logan said. "You think the second I sign a deal, I'll turn into some kind of man-slut." He put his hands over mine, pressing my palms against his chest. "You've always been the only one, and you always will be."

I knew I should step away, tell him he was crazy, that we were too young to talk like that. But I wanted this crazy more than anything.

"I love you, Logan." I breathed in his scent, sweet and heady as hot cider. "Happy birthday."

"So far, yeah." He bent over, picked me up, and stumbled to the bed. He knocked his shin against the frame, and I spilled out of his grip. I was laughing before my face hit the pillow.

By the time I flipped onto my back, he had crashed next to me, arms and legs everywhere. "Sorry," he said. "I suck at this."

I couldn't stop laughing, mostly at myself for being so afraid. This was Logan, after all, the boy I'd thrown snowballs at and chased ice cream trucks with. Not Logan the rock star.

He stretched out beside me, his eyes sharper now. "Don't tell me no this time, Aura. Please. Don't make me stop."

As my laughter died, my thumb traced a trembling line along his bottom lip. "I won't."

Logan kissed me, before and after removing my shirts, and told me I was beautiful. Unlike the last time, he was slow and patient, and when his fingers brushed my skin, I melted instead of freezing. I could feel our happiness radiating off each other in waves, like the music pulsing from Logan's speakers.

But then his touch grew heavy and his kisses sloppy, making me squirm.

"What the hell?" he muttered as he fumbled with my bra clasp.

"I think you twist it. The lady at Victoria's Secret said it was easy." I examined it in the dim light, trying to remember how I'd put it on.

But Logan was staring at his hand, not at the clasp.

"What's wrong?" I asked him.

He wiggled his fingers. "I can't feel my face."

"Oh my God, are you sick? Should I get Mickey?"

He laughed. "No, no, no—definitely no." He slumped back onto his pillow. "I'm just wasted. It's really hitting me." He looked at the ceiling, then shut his eyes hard. "Wow."

"How wasted?"

He spoke slowly. "I have absolutely no feeling in my extremities."

A horrible thought hit me. "All your extremities?"

Logan gave me a guilty look. "Sorry. I guess that's why they call it Liquid Stupid." His lashes fluttered. "Man, this is hard-core." He laughed again—high-pitched, like a stoner.

"How could you do this to me?" I sat up, afraid I would punch him if I didn't get out of range. "I was ready. Yeah, I was scared, but I was ready, Logan. And now you can't even—"

"We can try again tomorrow." He touched the half-empty glass on the nightstand. "Hey, you should have some too, get floaty with me." His voice drifted off. "I bet this is better than sex."

"Well, I wouldn't know, would I?" I kicked his foot. "They don't call it Liquid Stupid because it *makes* you stupid. It's what you have to be to drink it in the first place."

"Said I was sorry." After a moment, Logan's eyes opened wide, like he was forcing them. "I have an idea. Help me up."

I pulled his arm until he was sitting on the side of the bed.

"I'll take a shower," he slurred, "wake myself up." He pushed himself to his feet and staggered to the dresser. "I'll make it all better. We are not done here yet."

"Do you want me to come with you?" I asked, hoping he'd say no.

"No! I mean, it'll be a cold shower. Not fun for you." He withdrew something small from his top drawer, which he slipped into the front pocket of his baggy shorts.

"What's that?"

"Nothing. New shampoo, sample pack." He ruffled his hair. "Supposed to be good for getting all this spiky gel crap out."

Logan was always trying new hair products. He had more styling goops than most salons.

"Lock the door after me," he said.

I stood behind him as he opened the door slowly and peeked out. The upper hall was empty, and so was the bathroom halfway down on the left.

Logan kissed me, then turned away. The soles of his shoes scraped the carpet.

I touched my lips. His kiss had been clumsy and cold.

Down the hall, Logan slowed, fingers trickling along the wall to stop his momentum. With what looked like a great effort, he turned, shuffled back to my side, and carefully cupped my chin.

This time when he kissed me, his lips were still cool, but they felt like his again.

He whispered against my mouth. "Wait for me, Aura."

As soon as he was gone, I shut the door and locked it. Then I sat on the bed, crossing my arms over my chest.

Now what? I felt kind of silly sitting there in my bra. I wondered if I should get dressed again. Or maybe undressed, wait for him under the covers. No, he probably wanted to help with that. Besides, then he wouldn't see my matching underwear.

So I paced, rubbing my arms to keep warm, and every time I

passed the nightstand I looked at that half cup of Liquid Stupid. On the tenth lap I picked it up and took a swallow.

It burned everywhere—my nose, throat, chest.

When I finally stopped coughing and gagging, I heard shouts coming from the hallway. I muted the stereo and listened for Logan's voice in the crowd.

Instead, I heard his name, shrieked by Siobhan, followed by the word "defibrillator."

"Oh God." I grabbed my shirt and cami from the floor and yanked them both over my head in one movement. My face was lost inside as I tried to find the right hole and not shove my skull through a sleeve.

My head popped through, and I screamed.

Logan was standing at the foot of his bed, his shirt open and his hair rumpled, just as he'd been a few minutes before.

But now he was violet.

Chapter Four

I tried to say Logan's name. Nothing came out but a squeak, and then the tears flooded my eyes, blurring his image so that he looked like any other ghost.

"I'm sorry," he whispered. "I did something stupid."

"No!" I ran through the mirage. Had to find the real Logan.

The door was locked. My cold, sweaty fingers slipped over the slick brass switch.

"It's too late," he said behind me.

I unlocked the door and jerked it open.

In the hallway outside the bathroom, Mickey was screaming at someone lying on the floor.

I stopped at the threshold. That wasn't the real Logan either. It didn't matter that the feet were wearing his blue-and-black-checkered Vans, or that the chest Siobhan was compressing bore the AURA tattoo.

"Goddammit!" Mickey crumpled his hands in his jet-black hair. "Don't leave us. Don't you dare leave us."

Siobhan paused in her compressions, keeping her hands on the motionless chest. "Breathe now."

"Come on, Logan." Pinching the body's nose, Mickey bent over and breathed twice into its mouth.

I took a shaky step forward, then another, then stopped and grasped the railing overlooking the foyer. One more step and I would crumble into a hundred million pieces.

At the other end of the hall, Dylan burst out of the master bedroom, clutching the portable defibrillator against his chest. "I got it! Where do we—" He saw me and slid to a halt, almost falling backward on the plush carpet. He uttered an incoherent noise as the defibrillator fell from his hands.

Siobhan and Mickey looked up at him, then back at me. Their eyes bulged wild, confused, while Dylan's bore enough pain for the three of them.

Slowly, so I wouldn't shatter, I turned and looked over my shoulder. Logan's ghost stood there, staring at his former body. He lifted his gaze to meet his younger brother's. "I'm sorry," he croaked. "I'm so sorry."

"Dylan, come on!" Mickey waved his arm. "Bring it over before it's too late!"

"It's too late," Logan and Dylan said.

"Oh God." Siobhan sank back on her heels. "You can see him? He's here? He's a—"

"No!" Mickey folded his hands on the body's chest and started pumping, counting under his breath. "Siobhan, breathe."

She moaned, then bent over and brought her mouth to the life-less lips. After two breaths, she stroked what used to be Logan's hair. "Come back. Please come back."

"I can't," Logan whispered behind me, his voice twisted in pain. "Aura, tell her. Make them stop."

I crammed my hands over my ears and sank to my knees. *This isn't happening. The Liquid Stupid is making me hallucinate. Logan and I are going to wake up and laugh about this, and then we're going to kill Brian.*

I rocked back and forth, hoping the motion would knock me out of the nightmare.

"Aura, come on," Logan pleaded. "I can't watch this."

I shook my head. *Not happening. Not happening.*

NOT.

HAPPENING.

Then came the screams.

The foyer below was filling with the other partygoers, many of them staring and pointing at Logan's ghost. Some were crying, and some were pulling phones out of their pockets.

"Siobhan, breathe!" Mickey seized his sister's shoulders. "Don't you dare give up. We were supposed to take care of him!"

The stairs thumped with rapid footsteps. Megan stopped on the landing when she saw Logan's body at the top. "Oh my God."

"Don't say it." Mickey turned his tear-streaked face to her. "Don't say it. Don't say he's dead."

Megan's hand trembled as it pointed at Logan's ghost. "But he's—"

"Don't say it!" Mickey wiped his nose with the back of his wrist.

"Don't say it." He went back to doing CPR, shutting out the world with his muttered count.

Siobhan buried her face in her knees, swaying and sobbing. Dylan stood there staring at Logan, slack jawed, like he'd never seen a ghost before. The cord of the fallen defibrillator still dangled from his fingertips.

I dug my nails into the carpet, to keep the earth from slipping out from under me.

Megan crept up the rest of the stairs. "What's that on the bathroom sink?"

"Shut up," Mickey growled.

She shouted, "Logan, what the hell were you thinking?"

He raised his hands. "It was an accident. I wasn't trying to kill myself." Logan reached to touch me, then pulled back. "Tell them what I just said."

I repeated his words with a nearly numb tongue, then said, "Kill yourself with *what*, Logan?"

He spoke to Mickey and Siobhan. "I know you turned yours down, and so did I. But when he offered again later, I—I didn't want to piss him off. I was just trying to be nice. I swear I was gonna flush it, but when we got home, people were in all the bathrooms, so I just stuck it in my drawer."

"Stuck *what* in your drawer?" I was yelling now, but Logan stayed silent while Dylan repeated what he said in a halting voice.

Siobhan covered her face with her arms. "But Logan, why did you take it?" she shrilled.

"Because I was drunk and stupid, okay? I was trying to wake

myself up so I wouldn't pass out on—" He glanced my way, then curled his arms over his chest. "Never mind."

Dylan recited Logan's words slowly, as he realized their implications.

All three siblings turned to look at me with the eyes of judge, jury, and executioner. The house had fallen silent as the screams below became sobs. Someone had switched off the music.

When Megan drew me into a tight hug, I clung to her with arms I could barely feel. One piece of my body after another seemed to be following Logan into the cold, dark oblivion.

Then she whispered, "Your shirt's inside out and backwards."

I slipped my hand between us to touch the front of my neck. The tag was sticking out, telling the world the whole story of Logan's death, a story I didn't understand.

I lurched to my feet.

"Aura, don't!" Logan called, but no one else tried to stop me as I stumbled to the bathroom. Gripping the doorjamb, I peered inside.

No blood stained the white tile floor or pale blue walls. The only thing out of place was a fallen hand towel. The monogrammed letter *K* winked up at me in silver thread.

But on the shiny marble sink, one line of white powder said it all.

"You're such. A fucking. Idiot!"

Mickey was shaking Logan's body by the shoulders. The head lolled to the side on a rubbery neck.

"How could you do this to us?" he shrieked. "How could you do this to Mom and Dad?"

Logan's ghost watched Mickey's meltdown with wide round eyes. "I didn't mean to. Swear to God. Please don't—"

"Stupid. Asshole!" Mickey's mouth twisted in a silent howl. He pressed his forehead to his brother's chest, then his arms snaked around the limp body until he clutched it in an embrace. *"Why?"*

Siobhan kept sobbing. Dylan kept staring. I just tried to keep breathing.

Megan went to the railing and said, "Everybody go home. Now."

I felt four tight walls emerge within me, thick and soft as cotton, muting the noise and pain. Safe in my cocoon, and knowing it wouldn't last, I turned to comfort Logan.

But he was gone.

The paramedics made everyone but Mickey sit downstairs in the living room, out of sight but not quite out of earshot.

On the other side of the wide, empty space where an hour ago I had danced with Logan, Siobhan sat curled up in Connor's arms, her tears staining his maroon T-shirt. Connor stroked her back and stared at the floor, which was still strewn with beer cups.

Brian paced beneath the wide archway leading to the dining room, crumpling his baseball cap in his hands, then unfolding it and putting it back on his head.

Instinct told me to keep my mouth shut instead of screaming at him. It felt like my fault, anyway, not Brian's. If I hadn't yelled at Logan for drinking the Liquid Stupid, he'd still be alive. Maybe passed out or puking up his guts, but definitely not lying on the carpet upstairs surrounded by EMTs murmuring words like "synergy" and "ventricular fibrillation."

"Synergy," Megan scoffed as she rubbed my cold hands between hers. "I haven't heard that word since fifth grade. What's the point of teaching a bunch of ten-year-olds not to mix cocaine and alcohol? We forgot all about it by the time we turned eleven, much less seventeen."

"Oh God." My own heart felt like it would twitch and halt. "Logan died on his birthday."

"No, no, no." Her voice pitched up, like she was chiding a dog. "Look, it's already Saturday." She pointed at the grandfather clock in the corner.

One fifteen.

"Isn't there a song about one fifteen on a Saturday night?" Megan asked, obviously trying to distract me.

"Ten fifteen. By the Cure." My lungs seized in a sob. Even music would hurt now without Logan. Music, food, texting, shopping, the Inner Harbor, the Ocean City boardwalk. I wanted to move far away, take someone else's past and future. It would hurt too much to be me now.

Megan crammed another tissue into my hands just as Aunt Gina walked through the front door.

Gina looked up the stairs at the paramedics, police, and what used to be Logan. Her face remained still, like she had rehearsed this moment to stay calm. But the underside of her jaw twitched as she swallowed.

Gina turned to the living room. "Oh, sweetheart." She hurried over, and I realized she'd been waiting up for me. Her makeup was still on, and her short blond waves hadn't been combed out.

Somehow I managed to stand so she could hug me. "I'm so, so sorry," she whispered. "You have no idea."

She held me tight for several seconds, murmuring words I couldn't make out. I wanted to beg her to take me home, but she still had a job to do.

Gina kissed my cheek. "I'll be right back." She strode into the foyer and hustled up the stairs. As if from a distance, I heard her ask in her lawyer voice, "Who's the officer in charge?"

"No, it's not an emergency." Sitting in the corner armchair, Dylan spit his words into the phone receiver. "I'm calling at one a.m. because I have a tummyache and I want my mommy." He paused. "Well, you're, like, the fourth person I've talked to, and everyone asks the same thing, so obviously I do need to get sarcastic. Tell them to call home. Now." Dylan hung up. "It's such bullshit we can't get Mom and Dad."

"They don't have cell towers in the middle of the ocean," Megan pointed out.

"Call Aunt Jean," Siobhan said, sniffling. "Or Aunt Rosemary. They'll know what to do."

"No way." Dylan clasped the phone to his chest. "Mom and Dad should find out first. And the cops won't call anyone, since you and Mickey are eighteen. You're taking care of us." He flinched. "Of me, I mean."

Siobhan moaned, burying her face in Connor's chest. Dylan sank deeper in the chair and covered his face with the end of a Halloween throw blanket. Its black and orange tassels fluttered as he breathed out a heavy sigh.

"Does anyone want a drink?"

We all stared at Brian, who shoved his hands in his pockets.

"I don't mean—jeez, I meant like soda or something."

"I'll help you." Megan gave me a worried glance and followed Brian toward the kitchen.

I sat back on the sofa. My hand slid over something cold and wet. I lifted it to see a brown-yellow stain on the creamy beige cushion. Spilled Guinness, no doubt. My cheeks flamed at the memory of Logan's last several drinks.

I excused myself with a mumble, then slunk away to the downstairs bathroom.

Locking the door, I left the light off before remembering that, like all bathrooms, it would be BlackBoxed. That's why Logan wasn't in here. If he was a ghost, he'd come back to me, right?

I splashed cold water on my face until my contact lenses stung from the smeared eyeliner. I dried my face and hands, avoiding the mirror. One glimpse would start me sobbing again.

I opened the bathroom door and stepped into the foyer. From above my head came the noise of a heavy zipper.

I looked up the stairs, then wished I hadn't.

The paramedics had placed Logan's body onto a stretcher. One of them was sealing a long, greenish black bag.

I imagined the last glimpse of Logan, his bleached-blond hair, disappearing inside. My knees turned liquid, and I let out a little cry.

He can't breathe in there.

"Aura." My aunt waved her hand over the banister as if to shoo me. "Sweetie, you shouldn't see this. Go wait in one of the other rooms."

I wanted to launch myself up the stairs, rip open the bag, and cling to the only part of Logan I could still touch. I wanted to scream at the paramedics not to take him. Not yet.

Instead I ran into the den and slammed the door.

Light from the street filtered through the sheer curtains, glowing silver on the desk and bookshelves, and the globe that Mr. Keeley had insisted on buying, even though it was outdated by the time it arrived.

But it was dark enough for ghosts. "Logan," I whispered. "Don't let me remember that. I want to see you the way you are now. Please come back."

Nothing to hear but the pulse pounding in my temples. Nothing to see but ambulance headlights sweeping across the window.

Nothing to feel but alone.

Chapter Five

In my dream, Logan was red.

So red and so deep, I could see him in full sunshine. We lay on the beach, facing each other, with no towels between our bodies and the sand.

"You look like blood," I teased him.

He laughed, his mouth a dark chasm. "That's because I'm made of blood."

He stroked my face. His fingertips were warm and way too soft. He wasn't solid like a person, or air like a ghost. He was liquid—liquid that now dripped from my cheek and chin.

"Don't," I told him.

"What are you afraid of?" Logan drew his hand over the strap of my bikini and down my arm, leaving a glistening scarlet trail. "I won't hurt you. I just need to touch you again." His slippery-slick hand took mine. "Don't you want to touch me, Aura?"

I let out a whimper that verged on a moan. "You know I do." To prove it, I reached forward. My hand plunged into Logan's chest.

His limbs spasmed, and he threw back his head. "Not there!"

Something pulsed in my grip. It was like shoving my hand against a Jacuzzi nozzle. Then the current reversed, sucking me in.

"I can't let go!" My heels kicked at the sand, trying to gain traction. "Logan!"

His liquid fingers clutched my shoulders. My body slipped forward as if sliding down a steep hill.

Behind me, someone pulled. Someone as strong and solid as the earth itself.

But it wasn't enough. Caught in gravity's grasp, I crashed into Logan's body of blood.

My eyes opened. Flailing my arm, I rolled over, expecting to see Aunt Gina standing over my bed after shaking me awake.

"Sweetheart?"

Her voice came from the doorway, not my bedside.

"It's almost noon." Gina entered and sat next to me, then brushed the sweaty bangs off my forehead. "Can I get you some soup?"

Warm liquid. Entering my body. Through my mouth.

I lunged over Gina's lap and barfed into the trash can.

"I guess not," she murmured as she pulled back my hair.

When I stopped retching—which didn't take long, since there was nothing in my stomach—she handed me a tissue. I was already sick of tissues.

Gina picked up the pukey trash can. "I'll bring you some soda."

The house phone rang, and she hurried out before I could plead, "No liquids!"

A few minutes later the doorbell sounded. I had the urge to run, or at least hide, but my limbs felt like rubber.

Soon there was a soft knock on my bedroom door. Megan shambled in, carrying a plate of saltines and a fizzing glass of ginger ale.

"I thought about calling first," she said, "but I was afraid you'd tell me not to come. So I just came."

"Thanks." I sat up to take the crackers. The stoneware plate was cool and solid. "Put that drink where I can't see it, okay?"

Without questioning, Megan set the glass on my desk, then opened my calculus book and set it on its edge, as if the ginger ale were getting changed behind one of those old-fashioned dressing screens.

"How's Mickey?" I asked her.

"Horrible." She slouched over from the desk and sank onto the edge of the bed. "They finally got hold of Mr. and Mrs. Keeley on the cruise. They're flying back tonight when the ship stops in the Caymans." She rubbed her chapped nose. "A couple of aunts are already at the house, which pisses Mickey off. He says he can take care of the family until their folks come back, but of course he can't."

"Has Dylan seen—I mean, has Logan—"

"No one's seen Logan." She squeezed my knee through the red sheet. "I think he's really gone."

I slumped back on my pillow, knowing I should be relieved instead of crushed. "But it was so sudden. Most people like that stay ghosts for longer than ten minutes. No way was he already at peace."

I remembered Logan's face as his brother screamed at his dead body. Another tear dribbled out. "Maybe Logan's mad at us."

Megan groaned. "You too? Mickey blames himself. You blame yourself. None of what they say is true. You know better than anyone."

I shifted my head on the pillow. "What who says?"

Her mouth formed a tiny O. "Um, nothing. People online are, you know, bullshitting about last night."

I got so cold, it felt like my mattress had become a block of ice. "Where online?"

"Do not stress, okay? It's covered. I told them where they could stick their stupid rumors."

I sat up fast, my stomach somersaulting. "What rumors?"

"Aura . . ."

"If you don't show me, I'll look it up when you leave." I rolled off the other side of the bed.

"Okay, okay!" Megan followed me to my desk and stood behind me as I opened my laptop. "Start on Amy Koeller's profile."

"Amy?" Our class president, future Peace Corps volunteer, was gossiping about me? She was always so sweet to everyone. I brought up my friends list and clicked on her profile.

At the top of her page, her status read, *OMG Aura Salvatore's boyfriend Logan died of cardiac arrest last night. We should send flowers or something.*

"That's nice." I scrolled down to see a link that said, *View all 152 comments.* I clicked, then scrolled, and scrolled, and scrolled some more.

Megan tried to close the laptop screen. "Aura, one last time. Please don't read this."

I shoved her hand away and angled the screen so I could see. The first couple of dozen responses were sympathetic or shocked, lots of people remembering Logan from when he went to Ridgewood before his family moved out to the County. There were offers to pitch in five bucks for flowers, then an argument about whether they should donate the money to a charity in Logan's name instead.

Then Casey Crawford said, *You know it was drugs, right? Heard Aura gave them to him.*

"What?" I shouted.

Lauren Bankford: *No way. Aura pretends she's all badass, but she'd never have cocaine.*

Casey: *It's what I heard.*

Mike Brubaker: *I could totally see Logan OD'ing. I knew a guy who used to get high with him in eighth grade. Dude always had to take more hits off a joint than anyone else.*

Lauren: *You 'knew a guy,' huh, Mike? ;-)*

Amy: *People, can we get back to the charity topic? Maybe we should donate it to a drug awareness group.*

Mike: *You mean those retards who put on skits for assemblies? I'll feed the money to my dog instead—his turds are better quality than those plays.*

Lauren: *Shut up, Mike. I think it should go to the antidrug thing. When my granddad died, people gave money to cancer research.*

Amy: *Off to soup kitchen. Back later.*

Nate Hofstetler: *Maybe it should go to Viagra safety research.*

Mike: *ROFLMFAO @ Nate.*

Casey: *Wait. What's this about Viagra?*

Nate: *Logan had a heart attack. Viagra causes heart attacks.*

Lauren: *Does not.*

Nate: *See the commercials? They say it at the end.*

Lauren: *It's bc old guys use it and their hearts explode when they have sex, LOL.*

Sarah Greenwalt: *I don't think cardiac arrest is the same as a heart attack. I just looked it up.*

Nate: *Maybe it's not only old guys who use Viagra.*

Casey: *You are NOT saying what I think you're saying.*

Mike: *I'd need Viagra to get it up for Aura Salvatore.*

My stomach went cold, but I kept my face rigid so Megan wouldn't shut my laptop. I had to keep reading, find out who had started these rumors.

Casey: *No way, man, she's hot.*

Mike: *She's, like, three feet tall & she's a total ballbuster. Italians yell all the time.*

Casey: *Aura can yell in my ear all she wants while I'm doing her.*

Nate: *Yeah, she'd be yelling, "IS IT IN YET?"*

Mike: *Plus, you can tell she'll be fat in five years.*

Megan McConnell: *YOU GUYS ARE SUCH ASSHOLES. YOU WEREN'T EVEN THERE, SO YOU DON'T KNOW SHIT!! NONE OF YOU, SO STFU!!!*

Lauren: *Srsly, let's take this into chat. Amy'll zap this thread anyway when she gets home.*

Casey: *Bitches.*

My finger hovered over the refresh key.

"Don't do it," Megan said.

I hit F5 to reload the page. The thread disappeared.

"Thank God, Amy killed it." Megan reached for the laptop lid. "Don't worry about those idiots."

I grabbed the base of the computer. "No, I have to find out what they're saying now."

"What difference does it make?"

"What difference?" I shouted. "Logan's dead, and they're telling lies about him!"

"What are you gonna do, huh? Tell everyone the truth?" She tightened her hold on the laptop lid. "Gina will kill you if you talk about this online."

"I don't care!" I wrenched the computer to the left. Megan lost her balance and knocked over my propped-up calculus book.

The hidden glass of ginger ale flooded my keyboard. My laptop sizzled as the soda soaked into the frame.

"Oh my God!" Megan yanked a tissue out of the box, then flipped it over. "It's empty!"

I pulled the plug from the back of the laptop and held down the power button until the screen went black. Then I turned the computer upside down and propped it up like a tent so the liquid would drip out.

"Now what?" Megan dug her green fingernails into the tissue like it was the last one in the world.

"Nothing. It has to dry for at least a day."

"How did you know what to do?"

"Last year Logan spilled Coke on his laptop and totally fried it. So I looked up the procedure in case it ever happened to me."

"You're so sensible." She stroked my hair, picking out the gel-encrusted tangles. "And now you can't obsess over those lies."

I put my face in my soda-sticky hands. "They'll be talking about it at school Monday."

"I know, but you can't say anything, okay? Gina told me that the Keeleys called right before I got here. They might sue the guy who gave Logan the cocaine. They might even sue the record company."

"But without Logan, it's just the band's word against the company's, and Warrant will have a whole team of lawyers."

"You never know. Logan might still show up."

It was wrong to wish it, wrong to hope I'd ever see his smile again. I should've been praying for the passage of his soul, as Aunt Gina was probably doing downstairs, with a rosary and candles and an altar to Saint Peter.

But I couldn't help it. I wanted Logan back, even in violet.

Chapter Six

L ogan didn't return that night in any color, not even in my
dreams. Probably because I was sedated.

Gina thought Valium would help my "condition." I didn't
bother telling her that Logan was the only cure for my condition. I just
shut up and took the flat yellow pill. It helped, if only by getting her off
my case. Her eyes were full of grief, like *she'd* lost the love of her life.

I didn't wake up on Sunday until my cell phone rang. I picked it
up off my nightstand, dreading the gossip seekers.

The glowing screen said ZACHARY M. The name was vaguely
familiar, and connected with something important.

"Hello," came a deep lilting voice. "I never gave you my address."

"Ohhh, no." Friday seemed like it was three years ago. "I forgot
about going to College Park today. I should've canceled." We were
supposed to be there in an hour.

"Why?" he said. "What's wrong?"

This guy was outside my universe. He didn't know. "My boyfriend died." An imaginary knife twisted in my chest—a sign the sedatives were fading.

"Christ, I'm so sorry. What happened?"

"I don't want to talk about it."

"Okay." He waited a few seconds. "What's the name of the professor we're supposed to meet with?"

"Why?"

"I'll look up the number and ring them for you, to cancel."

My aunt opened the door a crack without knocking. "Who's on the phone, hon?"

"Someone from school." When she didn't retreat, I sent her a blank look. "This conversation is of an academic nature."

"No need to get snippy. I'm leaving." Except she didn't. "You sure I can't get you some soup? I made escarole. You love escarole."

I turned my head away from her scrunched-up Sympathy Face. "Yeah, I'll be down in a minute."

When Gina disappeared—leaving my door open, of course—I put the phone back to my ear. "What did you ask me?"

"The professor's name. Or number, if you have it. But I don't mind looking it up."

The thought of spending another day lying in bed crying, or taking phone calls, or reading rumors on the Internet (assuming my laptop hadn't suffered Death by Ginger Ale), made me shrivel up inside.

"Give me your address."

* * *

I picked Zachary up in front of his apartment building, on the other side of the Johns Hopkins University campus from my Charles Village neighborhood.

He set his book bag on the passenger's seat floor and slid inside. "Brilliant, right on time."

"I'm always on time."

"Me too. I hate when—" He stopped when he saw my face. "Bloody hell. You all right to drive?"

"Yep." I adjusted my glasses, the frames crooked from the time I'd sat on them. "The Valium's worn off." I pulled out into traffic, probably a little faster than I should have. "If we have to get together to work on this project, we could meet on campus halfway."

The car beside me honked, and Zachary grabbed the armrest as I swerved back to the center of my lane. Then he quickly let go and scratched his chin, as if to prove my driving didn't scare him.

"We're in a temporary let," he said, "while my dad gets settled at Hopkins. It's just one room, plus a wee kitchen."

"He's a guest lecturer?"

"Something like that."

"Which department?"

"Political science," Zachary said quickly, as if he'd been waiting for me to ask. "We're here for two semesters."

"Is that what you want to do too? Political science?"

He pressed his foot to the floor as we approached the stoplight, apparently too fast for his taste. "No, I could never do what he does."

"So three of you in a studio apartment? Or do you have siblings, too?" I didn't know why I cared. Trying to avoid silence, I guess.

"It's just me and him."

I stopped the car at the light and adjusted my passenger side mirror (I always forget that one). "Your mom's back in Scotland?"

"Er, maybe."

"Is it a secret? She's a spy or something?"

Zachary folded his arms and gave me a bitter look. "If it's a secret, I'm no' privy to it."

"Sorry." I probably should have revealed my own parental lack, so we could bond over the voids in our respective lives. But my nerves were too raw from losing Logan for me to talk about my mom and dad.

We both fell quiet until we got to the freeway and the sun came out.

"Don't laugh." I put on a pair of sunglasses in front of my regular glasses, officially becoming a gold-medal dork.

Zachary didn't laugh. "How do you see like that?"

"Better than squinting and getting a headache."

"Why not get prescription sunglasses?"

"They're expensive, and I never wear my glasses out of the house."

"Did you lose a contact lens, then?"

"No, they wouldn't fit." Maybe because my eyes were almost swollen shut from crying.

"Ah." Zachary shrugged out of his dark brown leather jacket, tugging it from under the seat belt's shoulder harness. I checked out his clothing in my peripheral vision. Just a few days ago, I would've envied his black shirt. Pre-Shifters had no idea what it was like to have to choose between wearing red or suffering major ghost harassment.

But I wasn't envious anymore. I twisted the hem of my raspberry-colored sweater and thought about its burgundy twin (or triplet, if you count the scarlet one too). Maybe some new clothes would bring Logan back.

My hands tightened on the steering wheel. *Get real, Aura. He's not coming back, not for clothes, not for anything.*

As we passed the Inner Harbor, Zachary craned his neck at the USS *Constellation* out the back window. "That ship's huge. Was it used for battles?"

"It's got cannons, so I guess so." Apparently, the testosterone-y obsession with weapons wasn't just for American guys.

"Have you been inside?"

"Ugh, not since I was a kid." I rubbed the bridge of my nose, already sore from the weight of two pairs of glasses. "It's terminally haunted."

"Oh, right. I guess they can't BlackBox it without tearing it apart."

I shrugged. "That, and it helps sell tickets."

On the interstate I changed the subject to our project. Zachary took notes on the research I'd done so far, which wasn't much. But I had set out the scope and direction, and I wasn't about to let him drag me off course.

I didn't tell Zachary how I'd found our adviser, Dr. Harris. That summer I'd discovered a locked box at the back of my aunt's closet. The key was in her bottom drawer with a bunch of other family keepsakes. When I unlocked the box, I found a journal and a pile of old photos from the Newgrange megalith in Ireland, including one of a girl my age—Eowyn Harris. All dated a year before my birth. All written in my mother's handwriting.

By this point, I had memorized Mom's journal entries.

Thursday, December 20

It's true what they say about Ireland—this place is magic. I never believed in any of that mystical crap before, not even Gina's supposed "ghost sight," but now I wonder. It feels like I was meant to come here, like my soul is home.

Nah, I'm probably just jet-lagged. Getting up early for the solstice sunrise tomorrow—woo-hoo!

Friday, December 21

There are no words to describe what happened this morning in Newgrange. But so, so, SO many questions.

Someone had torn out December 22's entry, but who? My mom? Aunt Gina?

Rather than making me feel gloomier, thinking about my mother and the stuff she left behind calmed the cyclone in my head. I was on my way to finish her quest.

Zachary and I arrived at the University of Maryland fifteen minutes early—good thing, because it took ten minutes of driving around the humongous College Park campus to find the right building.

I reached between the seats to get my book bag, then caught a glimpse of myself in the rearview mirror. Mistake.

"Gross, I'm so zombiefied." I pulled my matted hair forward to cover my puffy eyes. "Dr. Harris'll think I'm strung out or hungover. Great first impression."

"Amazing, though."

"What?"

Zachary started to answer, then brushed his lips with the side of his finger. "No, it's stupid."

I'd never seen someone use so much of their mouth for that word. "What's stupid, besides your mind games?"

"Okay, but if I start, you let me finish." He spoke to the radio instead of meeting my gaze. "The pieces of you are complete shite today, the bloated eyelids and splotchy skin and your hair all"—he waved his hand—"you know, and all together you should look pure hackit, but somehow you're more bonnie than ever."

I rewound his sentence in my head. Zachary's eyes flicked up to meet mine, and I must've seemed pissed, because he said, "Sorry," and reached for the car door handle.

"Wait. What's 'hackit'? What's that mean?"

"Ugly. But 'bonnie' means—"

"I know what 'bonnie' means."

Zachary held up a hand. "I'm no' flirting with you, not with your boyfriend just passing. I'm only making an observation."

I took off my sunglasses to see him better. He didn't look like he was trying to come on to me. He looked kind of pathetic, actually, for someone who was himself so, uh, bonnie.

"Thanks," I said, partly because I knew it would shock him if I didn't get offended. But mostly because his words made me feel better, seeing as I was, objectively speaking, pure hackit.

We stood in the doorway of Dr. Harris's vacant office. A midnight blue silk tapestry covered the ceiling, speckled with golden spots representing stars in their constellations. An MP3 docking station on the windowsill behind the desk played a hypnotic synthesizer tune.

Posters and paintings of ancient megaliths were stapled or nailed to the bookshelves, covering all but a few spaces, which held miniature replicas of standing-stone formations. The famous Stonehenge sat next to the grassy dome of Newgrange, which gave me a shiver of recognition.

Dozens of books were stacked on the floor next to the shelves. On the desk facing the door, more volumes stood in foot-high piles along the perimeter. It looked like someone had started to build a fort.

I clutched my book bag strap with sweaty palms. *I might actually get some answers today,* I thought. *I wish I still cared about the same questions.*

Zachary checked his watch. "We're on time," he whispered. "Where is she?"

"If by 'she,' you mean me"—a head popped up from behind the book fort—"I'm right here."

I almost jumped at the sight of the . . . professor? She looked only a little older than her teenage picture, and if she weren't slightly shorter than my five-foot-two, I would've believed she was a model. Her blond hair fell in waves to her waist. I'd never seen curly hair so long, and I wondered if it was a weave. But it moved like real hair, and she wore hardly any makeup—not that she needed it—so she seemed like a genuinely, obscenely, nature-is-so-unfair-ly gorgeous woman.

Beside me, Zachary stood with his mouth half-open. "Er . . . ah . . . ," he said, like he was having his tonsils checked.

I stepped forward. "I'm Aura. We talked on the phone? And this is my new partner, Zachary Moore. Mrs. Richards assigned him to help me."

"Lovely." Like her hair, Dr. Harris's voice reminded me of liquid gold, warm and soft and heavy. "Call me Eowyn." She held out her hands, one to each of us. I shook the right one, since it was closer to me.

Zachary awkwardly shook her left hand with his left. "Eowyn? Like the character from *Lord of the Rings*?"

Her head pitched back as she laughed. "My parents were huge Tolkien fans." She did look kind of like the lady from the movies. "It could've been worse," Eowyn said to me. "If I'd been a boy, they would've named me Gandalf."

I tried to return her smile, but apparently wasn't successful.

"Is something wrong?" she asked me, the corners of her deep blue eyes crinkling with concern.

I shook my head, then nodded. "Nothing to do with the project."

"But you *are* the project." Her smile widened. "By that I mean, you and your partner will pour yourselves into the work, and what comes out will reflect your personalities." She glanced between us, almost slyly. "Which I sense are very similar. Your stars may be closely aligned."

Please don't let her talk about astrology. This whole setup was weird enough without Zachary knowing we were born only a minute apart. And if he knew already, I didn't want him to know I knew he knew.

"How do we start, then?" Zachary asked.

"The way every fortunate endeavor begins." She unfurled her hand to gesture behind us. "With tea."

A small, low table was set up in the corner of her office. Two white mugs sat next to a teapot the blue of a twilit sky.

"Sit," she said. " I'll grab an extra mug from the cabinet here."

Zachary and I maneuvered around another stack of books, then stopped next to the two oblong cushions, placed on either side of the table.

"Go on," he said. "I'll take the floor."

"No, you won't." Eowyn glided over with the third mug. "You two will be putting your heads together a lot this year. It won't kill you to put your butts together now."

If I weren't so numb, I might've laughed, or at least blushed. But I just wanted to start this meeting so I could get some answers, then end it so I could be alone again. Faking okay-ness was exhausting me.

Zachary and I sat with a few inches between our bodies, on a sagging cushion that wanted to tumble us together. Eowyn lowered herself onto the cushion across from us, using a graceful, no-handed move that screamed of daily yoga practice. She placed the plain white mugs in a row on the table. "Choose one."

They all looked the same, but clearly this was some kind of test, judging by the gleam in her eye.

I chose the one on the left, in front of Zachary, and he chose the one that had been in the middle. For some reason it occurred to me that Logan would've reached for the one on the right, because it was the farthest away. I rubbed the achy spot on my chest.

Eowyn poured the tea, and I noticed she was wearing an obsidian ring in an oval setting. "Now watch."

Zachary returned my skeptical glance. Was she going to read our tea leaves? What did this have to do with ancient astronomy?

Slowly a picture began to appear on the side of each mug, broad red strokes on the white background.

"These are ogham letters, Irish runes. The designs are activated by the hot liquid," she said. "Ooh, I got *ur*, or heather, which signifies healing. Zachary, you have *duir*, the oak. That usually means strength. And Aura has *quert*."

I picked up my mug and examined the rune. It consisted of a straight vertical line and four short horizontal ones. It sort of looked like a toothbrush. "What's *quert*?"

"*Quert* is apple." Her eyes softened. "For love."

I froze. My hands tightened on the mug, though I wanted to hurl it against the wall and watch it shatter into a thousand pieces of deceitful white ceramic.

Zachary held up a finger. "Could I trouble you for some sugar?"

"Of course." Eowyn sprang to her feet. "Be right back." She slipped out of the office.

"Give me that," Zachary said in a low voice. He gently pried my fingers off the Love mug and took it from me. He replaced it with his Strength. "Just breathe."

I tried, but my lungs kept wanting to hitch into a sob. Desperate, I took a sip of the hot tea. It was bitter and sort of smoky. My next breath was almost normal.

"Here you go!" Eowyn swept back into the room, her blue gypsy skirt brushing her ankles. She tossed some sugar packets and a pair of plastic stirrers onto the shiny wooden table.

I unzipped my book bag. "I've made a lot of notes since the last time we e-mailed. I want to focus on—"

"Let's begin at the beginning." Eowyn sat down. "Crazy concept, huh? Tell me, have you always lived in the city?"

I nodded. "Why?"

"What about you?" she asked Zachary.

"I've lived all over." Covering the Love symbol on his mug, he stirred his tea, though he hadn't touched the sugar packets.

"So you're intimately acquainted with the night sky, and you can teach Aura. Not too much, though—she needs to learn on her own."

"Learn what?" I asked her.

Eowyn reached behind her and brought forward a large black vinyl portfolio, held shut with a red velvet tie. She undid the tie and unfolded the portfolio twice to make a three-by-three-foot square. Several gray sheets of paper were clipped to the inside.

"For your star maps." Her voice came from behind the portfolio. "Nine sheets. One per month between now and June. Ideally I'd like to see a full year, but this'll do."

I pointed to the ceiling, though Eowyn couldn't see me. "I already know the constellations."

"From real life or from books?"

I thought of my mother's photos. "What does this have to do with megaliths?"

"You need to understand." She folded the portfolio, then gave it to Zachary. "Think. How does a society organize itself, make decisions, have progress? By people getting together. How do they know when to get together? They use clocks and calendars. But what if there were no clocks and calendars? You'd have chaos."

She took a long sip of tea, holding the mug in both hands like a little kid. "The stars and moon and planets give us order. Except for comets and supernovae, we can count on the sky to look exactly the way we predict. Isn't that comforting?"

"Uh-huh." I didn't dare disagree with her sharp gaze. Surely this was leading somewhere.

She pointed to the Stonehenge poster tacked to her bookshelf. "The people who built the things you want to study? They were trying to make sense out of life and death."

I stared into my tea. *Yeah, good luck with that.*

Eowyn spoke softly. "I think that's what we're all looking for, isn't it?"

I nodded, but kept my head down, letting my hair droop forward in a veil.

"So." The professor's voice brightened. "To understand the ancient astronomers, you need to be in their place, at least one night a month."

"Where?" Zachary asked. "We can't see many stars from our neighborhood."

"Don't worry, I have a connection." She rose again and went to her desk. I pulled my sleeve down over my knuckles so I could wipe my eyes.

Eowyn continued. "A friend of mine has a farm up near the state line, where the sky is much darker." She brought me a white linen business card, which was one of hers but had another name and number scrawled on the back.

I pocketed the card. "Do you know if there are a lot of ghosts there?"

"Hmm." Eowyn fidgeted with her obsidian ring. "You can ask

Frank when you call. It's always been farmland, so probably not."

"I'll deal." I tried not to sound bitter. "I see them every night. Besides, who ever heard of an astronomer afraid of the dark?"

Eowyn raised her hand. "Me, for starters." She gave a nervous laugh. "So bring your first star chart when we meet again next month. It doesn't have to be perfect—in fact, if it's perfect, I'll know you copied it from a book. Just do your best."

I sat for a moment before realizing we'd been dismissed. "That's it? What about my research—I mean, our research?"

"We have all year for that." Eowyn squatted beside me like I was a kindergartner. "Here's something to remember. When you look at very faint stars, you'll notice that they often appear brighter from the corner of your eye. Averted vision, we call it."

"Okay," I said, for lack of a better response.

"Same with the answers you seek," she said. "You won't find them by staring until your eyes fall out. They'll come when you're looking at something else." She laid a soft hand upon my shoulder. "But they will come."

On the way home, Zachary and I didn't speak much. He used an app on his phone to check the weather forecast for the week, and we decided to head up to Farmer Frank's field on Thursday night, since it was predicted to be a clear night with a new moon.

I wasn't even sure I would survive that long. There was Logan's viewing tomorrow night, then the funeral two days later—not to mention school and the scrutiny that would come with it.

Instead of double-parking in front of his apartment building, I pulled into a metered spot on the street. A fat white Chihuahua in a jack-o'-lantern sweater barked at my car, prompting the owner to pick it up and tuck it under her arm.

"Thanks for the ride." Zachary wrapped the strap of his book bag around his hand but made no move to get out. "Are you all right?" He shook his head and looked away. "Stupid question."

I watched the woman set down the wiggly dog about twenty feet away. It trotted along the sidewalk, pulling on its leash, then stopped abruptly to sniff a parking meter.

"At school tomorrow," I said, "you're going to hear a lot of stuff about me. Most of it's bullshit."

"I won't believe a word. In fact, I'll just give them blank looks and say—" He uttered a series of guttural Gaelic syllables. All I could make out was something that sounded like *byorla*.

"What's that mean?"

"I don't speak bloody English."

I almost laughed, but it came out as a cough. Then I looked down at the gearshift in park, and realized I didn't want to go home and face Gina's pity.

"Do you want to know what really happened?" My voice squeaked at the end of the sentence. "It's kind of a long story."

Zachary reached over and turned off the ignition. "I've got time."

Chapter Seven

Monday morning I walked into a roomful of eyes.

Or at least it felt that way as I placed my late slip on the corner of Mrs. Wheeler's desk with a shaky hand. My peripheral vision was a big blur, but it looked like a wall of beetles, sitting in pairs.

"Thank you, Aura," my homeroom teacher said, whispering so as not to interrupt the sacred morning announcements on the PA. Maybe her eyes were kind, but I didn't look at her.

I'd worn my hair down, of course, the better to hide. Unfortunately, it also hid the end of Mrs. Wheeler's cane poking out from under her desk.

In my hurry to take a seat, I tripped over the cane and pitched forward. The floor rushed up, and only my flailing hands broke my fall. "Oufgh!"

Dead silence. I wished everyone would laugh, point, call me names. Anything but sit and stare, like I was the one who belonged in a graveyard.

"Aura, are you okay?" Mrs. Wheeler's panicky voice made it sound like I'd had a stroke, not a moment of klutziness.

"Fine." I adjusted my glasses, hoping they didn't look as crooked as they felt. "Can I have a bathroom pass?"

Before she could respond, the bell clanged, signaling the end of homeroom.

I was first to the door, smacking my book bag into the wall and knocking down a DMP recruitment poster taped there. Last week I would've been applauded for my accidental vandalism. Today there was silence.

Megan was at my locker, leaning against it with forced casualness. We'd both begged to stay home from school, but her parents and Aunt Gina had decreed that going would help us cope.

"Hey," Megan said as I approached, her eyes slightly dazed. "How's it going?" One side of her hair was yanked loose from her ponytail.

A fresh scratch marred her cheek. I reached up to touch it. "How'd you get that?"

"Huh?" She passed a hand over her face, then blanched at the thin streak of blood on her finger. "Oh! Um, my cat. Corrie's having a bitch-kitty day."

"And she messed up your hair?"

Just then a group of seniors passed by in a triangle spearheaded by the volleyball captain, Michele Lundquist, and her boyfriend, Steve Rayburn. The guys started meowing at Megan.

As they walked away, cackling and hissing, Megan's fair skin turned almost as red as her hair.

Then she looked past me and shook her head quickly.

I turned and saw Zachary halt a few feet away. "Oh. Hi." He scratched the left side of his face, where he had the beginnings of a bruise.

"Someone want to tell me what's going on?" I asked.

"Aura!"

Amy Koeller pushed past a group of cheerleaders, her long blond hair tangling with her backpack strap.

"I'm so sorry about Logan. That royally sucks." She hugged me, for the first time ever. "And, oh my God, if I knew those people online were going to be so mean, I never would've mentioned it. I am so incredibly sorry."

I gaped up at her. "How did you know I knew?"

She straightened her shoulders and lifted her chin, like she was on the witness stand. "Your friends had a little incident."

"Ha!" Megan exploded. "Nate and Lauren were talking shit about you, Aura, in the courtyard before school." She pointed behind her. "Then their douche bag friends joined in, so I told them to go screw themselves—"

"And then Lauren hit Megan." Amy's eyes got big. "I bet it was her class ring that made that cut."

"That's when he showed up." Megan raised her fist to Zachary. "Saved me from a serious ass-kicking."

He returned the brotherly gesture. "Actually, I think it was them I saved from you."

"Are you hurt?" I asked him.

"Had a lot worse rows in my life. At least none of the teachers saw."

"I gotta run to English." Amy squeezed my wrist. "Sorry again."

My battered friends flanked me as I opened my locker, snagging the sleeve of my ragged black hoodie on the latch.

"You guys didn't have to do that for me." I tugged out my American lit book. "If you'd gotten caught, you could've been suspended."

"But we didn't get caught," said Megan. "Hey, you know who was too chickenshit to stand up for you? Brian Knox. He was supposed to be Logan's friend, but he just stood there."

My memory flashed back to that odd almost-fight between Brian and Logan the night of the party.

Zachary checked his watch as the hallway started to empty, and I recalled his remark about hating being late. "Which one was Brian?" he asked Megan.

"About your height, sandy hair, always wears that stupid backward white baseball cap. Sorta beefy, like a wrestler, but that's mostly his beer gut." Megan lowered her voice. "He has a major problem. They all partied, but sometimes Brian would get wasted before a gig. Mickey and Logan were about to kick him out of the band."

"I didn't know that." I struggled to cram the book into my bag. "When did that happen?"

"Last week. But then those label guys called, and it was too late to get a new drummer."

"Logan didn't tell me." I guess we'd been too busy fighting about our own issues at the time. Regret stabbed at the tender place where my last ribs met, and it was all I could do to stand up straight.

"Hmm." Megan pinched her bottom lip as she thought. "I wonder if Brian was the one who started those rumors. None of the people talking online were actually at the party."

"I'll find out," Zachary said matter-of-factly, like it was already done.

"How?" I asked.

"Don't worry." His gaze flitted over the students as they hurried into the classrooms before the bell rang. "I have ways."

My aunt put her hand on mine as we pulled into a parking space at the McConnell Funeral Home Monday evening. "Ready?"

A blur of violet ghosts shifted and pulsed in front of the wide white building on North Avenue. At least it was totally Black-Boxed so these spirits couldn't follow us inside. They must have all mourned someone here while they were alive. As long as none of them were too "shady," I'd make it to the door without falling over or throwing up.

"Let's hurry," I said.

I kept my head down as we waded through the sea of ghosts. My path contorted to avoid each one, even though I couldn't physically bump into them. Aunt Gina didn't comment. She was used to it.

"Why won't they let me in?" an old man asked, keeping pace with my long strides. "They have my wife."

"They have my wife," shouted a young guy in a soldier's uniform. "I've waited for her all these years. Why hasn't she joined me?"

Apparently there was another viewing tonight besides Logan's.

I was glad the ghosts couldn't see and hear each other and start fighting over that poor dead (and apparently twice-widowed) lady inside.

A man I didn't recognize sat on a bench outside the front door, smoking a cigarette. He nodded in our direction, oblivious to the ghost weeping beside him.

Just a few more steps. I could see Megan through the glass doors in the lobby. It would be quiet in there.

"My poor, poor Logan."

The woman's voice froze my feet. Gina was holding the door open for me, but I had to turn around.

"Grandma Keeley?"

The man leaped up from the bench. "Shit." He coughed on his smoke. "There's one sitting next to me?"

The ghost ignored him and wiped her wispy violet eyes. "Hello, hon. I'm afraid I've forgotten your name."

"It's Aura. I remember you used to haunt Logan's old house on Calvert Street."

The man stubbed out his cigarette in the sandy ashtray. "I'll never get used to this." He strode through the door my aunt was still holding open.

"I can't get in," said Logan's ex-grandmother. "I can't go to my own grandson's viewing."

"But you can come to the funeral and burial on Wednesday," I said, trying to be helpful. I was pretty sure Logan's church wasn't BlackBoxed, though I'd heard they were taking up a collection.

"Pah." She waved her hand. "There'll be nothing to see but a casket. I want to see his beautiful face one more time."

"Me too," I whispered, and realized it was true. The dread I'd felt all day at the thought of viewing Logan's . . . corpse was suddenly swamped by the need to touch him, to drink in my last glimpse of him before he became nothing but a flat image in a hundred photographs.

The other ghosts began to gather around, lured by my presence.

"Sorry, I gotta go." I left Logan's ex-grandmother to cry alone in the dark.

Megan stood in the lobby, handing out programs and directing people like a playhouse usher. Working at her family's funeral home meant that since turning sixteen, she'd had an even creepier job than mine. For an extra charge, Mr. or Mrs. McConnell would bring her to a grieving family's home to see if the deceased's ghost appeared with any special requests, which were almost always weird.

Megan's hair was pulled back to cover the green streak, and her lipstick was a warm red shade instead of the usual near black.

She led an elderly couple toward the closest viewing room, which had a small sign outside: EDITH MASTERSON. The multiple-husband lady, no doubt.

Then Megan swept over and gave me a huge hug. "He looks as cute as ever," she whispered.

I guess that was supposed to comfort me.

"Logan's grandmom is outside," I told Megan.

"I know," she said as she hugged my aunt. "Dylan was talking to her for a long time. People walking by kept staring at him."

By "people," of course, she meant pre-Shifters.

A group of six guys wandered in, looking awkward in suits and ties. I'd seen them at the Keeley Brothers' gigs. My gut grew heavy as it hit me that there'd never be another show.

"Mickey's friends. I should say hi." Megan handed us a pair of green programs, then leaned over and kissed my cheek. "Be strong."

My legs felt numb carrying me down the corridor. When we turned into the viewing room, I clutched Gina's hand so tight I thought her bones would crumble. But she squeezed back just as hard. It was the only thing that kept me standing.

A sea of people filled the low-lit room, where a long line led between rows of chairs. Vaguely I recalled the viewings of my great-aunts and great-uncles in Philadelphia. We had filed past the family, hugged them (like at a wedding), kneeled in front of the open casket for an appropriate amount of time, then taken our seats. Zero drama.

Except for the hugging and kneeling, this was nothing like the old people's viewings. Sobs, sniffles, and a ragged chorus of "I can't believe it" drowned out the supposedly soothing organ music. Everyone leaned on one another like the pieces in a house of cards. I wanted to ask Gina if my mother's funeral had been this emotional.

I forced myself to breathe. *I can do this.*

Suddenly the line shifted as Siobhan and Mickey pushed past. Instinctively I put out my hands to them.

Siobhan lurched forward into my arms. "I can't take it anymore. Dylan's already lost it, he's holed up in the men's room."

Mickey had re-dyed his hair, replacing the blond-streaked jet-black with the natural Keeley nut brown. The same color as Logan's before he'd bleached it two years ago.

"Everyone's giving us looks." Mickey's upper lip curled to a near snarl. "Like we don't feel guilty enough."

"It's our fault," Siobhan cried. "We were supposed to take care of everything. We never should've had that party."

"Stop it, Siobhan." Mickey raked a hand through his hair, which now fell in short, soft waves instead of gelled-up spikes. "Let's get you some water and some air."

The line had moved on without me, and Gina gave me a small wave a few feet ahead. I joined her. The casket was visible now against the far wall. A light shone down from above, like a spotlight from heaven. But Logan's body was blocked by the people kneeling in front of the casket.

I can do this. I had to keep it together for Logan's parents.

"Oh, good Lord." Gina clicked her tongue. "That poor woman looks tranq'd to the gills. I don't blame her. I'd be comatose if anything ever happened to you."

In her black dress and hat, Mrs. Keeley stared past each greeter with distant, clouded eyes, nodding briefly at their words of comfort. She looked twice as stoned as I'd felt on Saturday after the Valium. Mr. Keeley seemed to be feeling the pain for both of them—his face was red, damp, and twisted with grief.

The line moved again, and there was Logan.

A chill spread up my body until I couldn't move or even blink.

His hair had been dyed back to brown. In his dark blue suit and red tie, he looked older and younger at the same time. Like a stockbroker or a kid playing dress-up.

This. Wasn't. Logan.

"No . . ." My eyes began to burn. "Why couldn't they—why did they have to—"

Through the flood of tears, I saw a blur of Gina's blond hair as she pulled me close, then pressed my face against her neck. Her perfume almost made me gag, but I didn't move away.

"Sweetie, I'm so, so sorry." Her own voice choked. "This should not happen. This should not ever happen."

Then she steered me away from the casket toward Logan's parents. Mrs. Keeley gazed past me and Gina as we greeted her, saying nothing but "Thank you so much for coming." I turned to Logan's father.

"Aura, hon." Mr. Keeley wrapped me up in a bear hug, so tight I couldn't breathe. "You poor girl. I can't even imagine . . ."

I grasped his back, scared he would collapse. He was the closest thing I'd ever had to a father. I couldn't lose him, too.

When Mr. Keeley finally let go, the funeral director touched his arm and whispered a question about the ceremony. Gina held on to Mrs. Keeley's hand, murmuring and shaking her head.

Leaving me alone with Logan.

As I approached his casket, the room behind me hushed. By now everyone knew I'd been the last to see him alive.

I dropped to my knees beside him. His skin had a rosy, unnaturally healthy hue. His lips were pink and full, like after we'd been making out for hours. I couldn't stop staring at them, remembering how they'd felt against mine.

But it was all so wrong. This wasn't Logan, and I don't mean because his spirit was in a better place. I mean it was *wrong*. Because those lips were just there, doing nothing. Not kissing, not singing, not smiling.

I lowered my chin to pray, sort of. *Sorry, God and the Pope, but this open casket thing is retarded.* I didn't want to remember Logan this way. I tried to recall my last image of him. His ghost had looked like he did when we were in bed together, his shirt open and his hair tousled by my hands.

I tried to go back to the full-color version, and found that the violet had blotted out my memory. But Logan the Ghost was a million times better than Logan the Corpse.

"Wherever you are," I whispered, "I hope you're smiling."

I felt my aunt kneel next to me, heard the rattle of her purse's zipper as she crossed herself. I knew she was praying silently, fervently, for Logan's soul to pass on and never come back.

I can't do this.

I ran.

It was a miracle I got out of the crowded room without stepping on anyone or breaking my leg. Megan called my name as I swept past her in the lobby, but I didn't slow down.

Grandma Keeley was waiting on the bench outside the front door. I sat beside her, and we cried together, while the ghosts of strangers held their own silent vigils.

Later that night the Keeleys had a gathering at their house, just for family and a hundred close friends. Brian Knox came but didn't speak to me, even when he literally bumped into me at the buffet table, spilling my punch all over my mini ham sandwich. He murmured an apology and left the room. It seemed Brian, Nadine, and Emily didn't stay long once they realized the adults were enforcing the drinking age.

Away from the somber funeral home, I held it together okay and managed to carry on a normal-ish conversation with Connor and a couple of Keeley cousins. But while part of my brain was listening (and even contributing a thought or two) to their discussion of the upcoming Ravens game, the rest of me was looking for a chance to run up to Logan's bedroom and crawl under his covers. I wondered if his pillowcase still smelled like his hair. If I folded it really tight, it would fit inside my jacket without leaving a bulge.

When the front foyer was empty, I moved toward the steps, pretending I was on my way to the bathroom.

A shriek came from the darkened upstairs. Children laughing. Not giggling or snickering. Howls of laughter.

I hurried up to find out what was going on. A little girl in a dark green velvet dress streaked down the dim hallway, her patent leather shoes slapping the carpet. Her laughter made her sway back and forth.

A boy her age poked his head out of the master bedroom and waved frantically. "He's in here now! Go back!"

The little girl slid to a stop, falling on her butt. The boy doubled over and pointed at her. A slightly older girl I recognized as Logan's cousin Elena appeared behind him.

"Danny, move! I almost got him." Elena pushed back a dark blond strand of hair that had fallen out of her butterfly barrette. "He's coming through the—"

"Ow!" came a voice from inside the wall.

My breath stopped.

Logan stepped into the hallway, rubbing his violet nose. "Man, I forgot the bathroom was BlackBoxed. You guys win this—"

He stopped short when he saw me. I uttered his name in the barest of whispers, afraid to wake myself from this new dream.

Logan broke into the widest smile ever. "Aura!" He streaked forward, and by reflex I raised my arms for him to hug me. Violet filled my vision, surrounding me, absorbing me.

But when I closed my eyes, I felt nothing.

Logan jumped back. "Sorry, I forgot. God, it's great to see you."

My heart crumpled at the sight of him like this, but I smiled so hard my chapped lips cracked. "Where have you been? I thought you'd moved on."

"No way," he said, like I'd suggested he spend the evening at the ballet. "Too much here for me." He took a step toward me, his gaze as intense as ever. "Especially you."

"But where have you *been*? Why didn't you, you know—"

"Haunt you?" Logan fidgeted with the tails of his open shirt, looking sheepish. "I knew you guys were mad at me."

"I'm not mad, I'm—" I curled my fingers near my face, as if I could sign-language the depth of my pain.

"Aura, please don't cry. I can't stand it, you know that."

I wiped my face. I hadn't even noticed the tears—these last few days, their presence seemed more normal than their absence. "So where were you?"

"Everywhere I've ever been. Dude, this is so amazing. Watch."

He disappeared. I grabbed the banister in my shock. The kids giggled.

"Logan?" I fought back panic.

He popped into view again. "Guess what? Just now I was back in Dublin." He spread his arms like a magician after a trick. "How cool is that?"

"Wow," I said, at a loss for other words.

"I missed you. A lot."

Logan was close enough for me to touch, to smell, to feel his breath on my forehead. Close enough to kiss. If only he were alive.

"I missed you, too." *I still miss you.* My legs felt watery as I backed away. How could it hurt so much to find him again? "It's been hell. Why didn't you come see me?"

"I'm sorry." He fisted his hands in his spiky blond hair. "Ugh, I was such an idiot. I'll make it up to you, I swear."

The kids were staring at us and fidgeting.

"Can we talk alone?" I whispered to Logan.

"Good idea." He brushed past me (minus the actual brushing) and moved toward his room. "See you guys later."

Elena twisted the lace on the front of her dress. "Promise you'll come back?"

"Of course I promise," Logan said with a wink. "You'll see me again."

She gave a quick knee-bend bounce. "Yay."

I moved past Logan toward his room, but just as I touched the doorknob, I heard the crash of shattered glass.

A voice behind us shouted, "Logan!"

We turned to see Dylan taking the stairs three at a time. In the foyer below, a broken glass lay next to a spreading puddle of soda.

Fear flitted across Logan's face, until he saw his brother was smiling.

"Where've you been?" Dylan exclaimed as he approached. "We all gave up on you."

"I'm sorry. I was giving you space."

"Fuck space." Dylan's grin looked like it would split his jaw. "I'd rather have my brother back."

But he's not really back, I thought. *Or is he?*

Below us, the foyer was filling with people, giving me a horrible feeling of déjà vu. The night he died, they'd all gathered and stared, just like now.

"Look!" some kid yelled. "He's here!"

I closed my eyes, wanting to run, wanting to hide. Wanting to be a ghost.

Feet of all sizes and weights stomped on the hardwood floor below. Voices cried out, some in joy, some in confusion.

And one in horror.

Mrs. Keeley's scream ricocheted off the high ceiling. It traveled down my spine, then back up.

When I opened my eyes, Logan was gone.

Chapter Eight

Megan was late to school the next day, so I didn't see her until lunch. But I knew from her midnight text message (THIS SUX) that things hadn't gone well at the Keeleys' house after Mrs. Keeley fainted. Everyone had left after that—everyone but the McConnells, that is, who needed to alter the funeral arrangements now that Logan's ghost was around to give his input.

"He wants to be cremated." Megan nudged a tomato off her salad with her fork. "Have his ashes scattered at the Hill of Tara in Ireland. There and Molly Malone's bar in L.A."

"Why there?"

"That's where Flogging Molly first played. But Catholics can't have their ashes scattered. Not everyone obeys that rule, but the Keeleys are hard-core."

"What did Logan say when they told him no?"

"He freaked." Megan set down her fork and shoved away her yellow plastic tray. "I swear, if he could've actually touched anything in that living room, the place would be a wreck. The more he tried to throw and kick stuff, the more pissed he got."

I sipped my iced tea through the straw, hoping it would settle my empty, aching stomach. "Did he get, you know ..." I almost didn't dare say the word. "Shady?"

"No way, nothing that bad."

"Really? You look kind of sick."

"Just tired." She took a swig from her water bottle. "Plus, I snuck a huge glass of wine while they were all arguing, so I'm a little hungover."

Zachary entered the cafeteria, flanked by two girls on each side. They watched him speak, their mouths open, tongues practically hanging out. That accent was deadly.

"How were Logan's parents?" I asked Megan.

"Mrs. Keeley couldn't stop sobbing. She kept begging Logan to go into the light. Between her crying and Mr. Keeley yelling, I couldn't get a word in for Logan." She slid her hands up into her sleeves and rubbed her knuckles together. "My dad was like, 'Can we please stay calm and make some decisions for your son's burial?' but they couldn't deal."

"The funeral Mass is tomorrow. They have to figure this stuff out."

"I know." She wiped her bleary, bloodshot eyes. "Oh, but they're letting Logan pick the music for the luncheon. He's pretty stoked about that."

"How did he seem to you?" I spoke softly because I was afraid of the answer.

"He seemed like Logan. You know, cute and charming until he doesn't get his way, and then a big-time brat." She rested her chin on her knuckles, shoulders sagging. "Funny, out of all of us in that room, he seemed the most normal. And he's the dead one."

That statement should've made me shiver. This was my boyfriend we were talking about, not some anonymous violet specter floating in the shadows of the food court.

But Logan didn't feel dead anymore. I'd never touch him again, but I'd see him and hear him. I was grateful that Megan also didn't refer to him as "ex-Logan." Maybe she was just being nice, or maybe he seemed too alive to be an "ex."

"I wish he'd come see me," I said.

"Yeah, he's been in your room a ton of times."

"In my bed, even. Once."

"I wonder why he hasn't visited you?"

"Aura."

Zachary's voice startled me. I turned to see him walking toward our table, accompanied by the quartet of smitten kittens.

"Hi." I looked up at the girls, all seniors, two of whom I'd considered my friends last week. This week everyone was avoiding me at school but Megan and Zachary. "Hey."

"Love your sweater, Aura." Becca Goldman (not a friend, former or otherwise) swept a mocking gaze over me. "Interesting color choice for someone your age."

"You look good in black," Zachary told me with a straight face.

"Thanks." Though black didn't do anything to deter ghosts, it was still the traditional color of mourning. Besides, it matched my mood.

"Feeling better today?" Zachary asked.

"A little." I rubbed one of my eyes, which were finally letting me wear contacts again.

Becca swished her hair conspicuously. "Zach, lunch'll be over in ten minutes."

"Can I sit down?" Zachary widened his eyes as if to plead with me to rescue him from the sea of shallowness. But I was too exhausted and confused to have a normal conversation.

"Sorry," I told him, "it's kind of a bad time."

He glanced at Megan, then back at me, looking slightly stunned. "I'll see you in history, then."

Zachary proceeded to the other end of the long, empty table. The girls followed like geese in formation. One of them, my neighbor and old friend Rachel Howard, gave me a quick look over her shoulder. Her forehead creased when our eyes met. I wondered if it was a frown of sympathy or disgust, then decided it would be easier not to care.

"Why didn't you want Zachary to sit here?" Megan said.

"What if they came with him? I don't have the energy to gush over Becca's new Coach bag or snark on last night's *Get a Life* loser." The reality show about families living with their loved ones' ghosts was now officially off my must-see list.

"If those bitch-faces had tried to sit here, I'd just show them this." She rummaged in her jacket pocket, then brought out her hand clad in a black glove with skeleton bones on it. In the design, all the finger bones folded into a fist except the middle one, which stuck straight up. It looked like a skeleton was flipping me off.

My eyes bugged out. "That is the coolest thing I've ever seen."

"Good. I got you a pair." She tossed them at me. "Found them at this shop in Hampden last week. I was going to save them for Halloween, but you clearly need them now."

I did. I needed them for every person who stared as I walked past, who whispered when they thought I was out of range, who acted like having a dead boyfriend was a contagious plague. I needed to give the finger to the whole world, minus three people (maybe four, including Gina).

Number One was sitting across from me. Number Two was at the other end of the table, glancing my way every minute or so. Number Three was—

I didn't know where Number Three was. Ireland? Disney World? The skate shop on Harford Road?

All I knew was that based on the look on Logan's face last night, he wasn't leaving this world any time soon. He'd been born into a new life, one of almost limitless adventure.

If only I knew which part of that adventure included me.

The funeral made no sense.

The priest did his best, remarking on the unbearable tragedy of losing such a young life and how it wasn't always easy to understand God's plan. But then he went on to say how Logan's spirit was now in "a better place."

Seriously.

Maybe the Keeleys hadn't told Father Carrick that Logan was a ghost, but you'd think he would've asked. He'd known Logan for more than a year, since they'd moved to Hunt Valley. Besides, priests always ask for details so they can make their remarks sound personalized.

As Father Carrick droned on, I looked over at Dylan, who sat on the end of the pew. He was leaning forward, elbows on his knees and his reddening face planted on his fists. The younger cousins stared up at the stained-glass windows, ignoring the priest. Megan sat with her mom several pews behind me, and I didn't dare turn toward her for fear of making an inappropriate face. I wished so bad I had those skeletal-middle-finger gloves.

So I just sat, eyes burning. Gina stuffed a tissue into my hand, but I didn't use it.

What would it take for the pre-Shifters to understand? Someday we'd figure out how to teach them, if they wanted to learn. Until then, all we had were people like Gina, people who squashed their own fear long enough to help us cope.

"Aura." Logan's disembodied whisper came from the aisle beside me.

My aunt must've thought my gasp was a stifled sob, because she dispensed another tissue.

"I thought of a place we can be alone," he said. "In the dark, so you can see me."

I glanced around, but all the people in the nearby pews were older. It was too bright for other post-Shifters to see Logan—he was hiding in the light.

"Go out to the vestibule," he said, "and take a left. Third booth."

I nodded, then coughed to hide the threat of a smile. As soon as everyone stood for the communion rite, I let go of Gina's hand.

"Stay here," I whispered to her. "I need a break."

She patted my cheek. I kept my face down as I walked past the jam-packed pews. His school must have declared his funeral an excusable absence. I wondered if they would've done that for a less popular student.

They were singing the slow and lilting Sanctus by the time the vestibule door swung shut behind me, muffling their voices. On the left sat a row of confessional booths. Dark confessional booths.

With a yip of anticipation, I dashed for the third one and opened the door. Logan was sitting on the gold velveteen cushion inside, looking pleased with himself. I slipped in and shut the door behind me.

"Finally," he said. "Being away from you was killing me." He frowned. "Sorry, bad choice of words."

I laughed for the first time since he'd died. In the dark booth, I could see every detail of his features—each hair on his head and even the touch of stubble that had appeared by Friday night. "You look great. For a ghost, I mean." I covered my mouth to stifle another burst of laughter.

He gestured to the cushion. "Sit down."

I squeezed in beside his violet form, noticing my strange aversion to touching him. When he was alive, I would've just sat on his lap.

"Have you been around?" I asked him. "Watching me when I can't see you?"

Logan shook his head. "That would be kinda stalker-ish, huh?"

"Not even a little?"

"I did come to your room once. I swear I was going to say something to wake you up, not just stand there staring."

"Why didn't you?"

"I had to leave. The red sheets made me dizzy, like my brain wanted to spin out of my ears."

I gasped. "I forgot about that. I'll buy new ones, swear."

"That'd be awesome." He shifted on the cushion to face me, brushing his knees through mine without touching. "I wanted to tell you about everything I've been through. It's amazing and horrible and bizarre and beautiful."

"What did it feel like to die?" I reached toward his chest, but not all the way. "Did it hurt?"

"No, it was so fast. I took the—the cocaine." He stumbled over the word. "I know, I'm an idiot. Anyway, I was getting ready to do another line, and then my heart started to flutter. It felt like my chest was full of wriggling worms."

"Ew."

"Then everything went dark. Next thing I know, I'm standing there looking down at my body. Because of the BlackBox, I couldn't get out of the bathroom until Mickey opened the door. I was stuck with myself."

Logan fell silent, staring at the floor, like he could see his corpse again. I waited for him to continue.

Finally he said, "I didn't feel dead. My mind was the same. I still had that song running through my head, the one on the stereo when I walked out the door." He touched his mouth and lifted his gaze to mine. "I thought I could still taste your skin."

My heart pounded at the thought of our last moments together. I'd called Logan *stupid*.

I swallowed, wanting to bury my darkest fear deep inside me instead of sharing it with the one it would hurt most. "I'm sorry I yelled at you. If I hadn't, you would've just passed out." The truth burned my tongue as I released it. "You'd still be alive."

"No!" His face twisted into a mass of violet. "Aura, don't you dare blame yourself. It was my choice. It was dumb, and it killed me, and I own it, okay?"

"Okay, okay."

He breathed hard, or at least made a sound like he did. "Please promise me you won't blame yourself."

I'd never lied to him. "I can't promise you."

"Spider-swear."

"Logan . . ."

"Do it." He held his hand out, four fingertips pointing at me. "Or I'll never haunt you again."

I hesitated. Spider-swear was sacred. "We're not six anymore. And besides, I can't—" A sob bubbled up inside my chest. "I can't touch you."

"It's okay." He glided his hand closer, like an airplane coming in for a landing. "Just pretend."

I remembered how cold his fingers had felt the last time he touched my face, before he walked down the hall to the end of his life.

Wait for me, he'd said.

Holding my breath, I spread my fingers, then slowly slid them between his, trying not to push through his ethereal flesh.

Our palms tilted down, so that if we were both solid, they would've pressed against each other. Our thumbs angled out to form the spider's antennas. Then we wiggled our eight fingers.

"Spider-swear," we said together, holding back our laughter long enough to get the words out.

"There, it's official," he said. "No more guilt."

"He says, sitting in a confession booth."

Logan laughed again. Our hands were still intertwined.

"Can you feel me?" I whispered.

He gazed down at me. "I'll always feel you, Aura."

I closed my eyes as Logan kissed me. This time, in my soul, I felt everything.

Chapter Nine

The next night I went to pick up Zachary at his apartment for our first star-mapping venture. When I arrived in front of his building, I put on my flashers so I wouldn't get a ticket, then fished in my bag for my phone.

Logan was sitting behind the passenger seat.

I yelped. "Don't scare me like that!"

"I'm a ghost. It's my job."

"No, it's not. Especially not me." I softened my voice. Just seeing Logan took away the heaviness in my heart. "But thanks for waiting until I put the car in park."

He leaned forward. "Did you get the sheets yet?"

"I'm getting them tonight. This was my first chance to use the car."

Logan peered out the window. "Why are you at the Broadview?"

"I have to pick up a classmate for a school project."

"Oh." He cleared his throat, though he certainly didn't need to. "What's her name?"

"His name is Zachary. It's for our history thesis." I finally found my phone. "We have to do star charts."

"Like astrology?"

"Like the constellations. We draw what we see."

"Wait, wait, wait." Logan put out his palms. "You have to sit in the dark under the stars with some random guy?"

"It's for school."

"Can I come?"

"I don't think you've been there. It's a farm up near Pennsylvania." I hit the number for Zachary's cell.

"You have him on speed-dial?" Logan said. "Who is this guy?"

"I told you, he's in my class." I thought of Monday morning, when Zachary and Megan had stood up for me in the courtyard. "And he's a friend. One of the few I have left."

Zachary picked up the phone. "I'm on my way down. Sorry I'm late."

"No, I'm early. See you in a minute." I hung up and looked at Logan. "I'll get some sheets tonight, and then you can come over." My hands trembled at the thought of him lying next to me in any form. "Wait until Gina goes to sleep, so she doesn't hear me talking to you."

"Uh-huh." He didn't move, just stared out the window and twitched his knee back and forth. "What store are you going to? Maybe I could help pick out the sheets."

"How rude would that be? Zachary's a pre-Shifter. He can't see or hear you. It'd be like when my aunts and uncles start speaking Italian around me."

"All right, I get it." He sat, twisting his lips. "Can I just see what he looks like?"

"Logan . . ."

"I'm going, I'm going."

But he didn't. He glued his gaze to the front door of Zachary's apartment building.

"I'll see you tonight," I told him. "Later."

Logan disappeared without saying good-bye or even acknowledging my words.

The passenger door opened, startling me. Zachary slid in, out of breath. He smelled of soap and shampoo.

"Sorry. Football match went into extra time."

"You play football?"

"Soccer. Nothing official, just mucking about with a group of Hopkins students from the building." He pushed a lock of damp, dark hair off his cheek. "They killed me. I'll never take the piss out of American players again." At my confused look, he said, "Make fun of them, I mean."

I took one last glance into the empty backseat, then put the car in drive. "I have to stop at the mall."

"Good, we can eat. I'm starving."

I frowned. It already sounded too much like a date.

We stopped at the department store first, so I could buy the sheets. It would be an excuse to make it clear that I was still Logan's girlfriend.

Then I saw the prices.

"I can't afford these." I went from one display to another, examining the few non-red sheet sets. None of them cost less than fifty-nine dollars. "I only get to keep half my paycheck. The rest goes for college."

Zachary surveyed the wall-size display of red sheets. "It looks like a bordello."

"Welcome to my life." *Hmm, that didn't come out right.*

"Why's it so important you can't wait for a sale?"

Here was my chance to explain. I'd tell him that Logan's death had not only *not* made me boyfriend-less, but it meant that said boyfriend would now be sleeping with me.

But all that came out was: "It's complicated."

"Sheets are complicated?"

"When they're not red."

Zachary looked at the soft white package in my hands. "Why would you want sheets that aren't red? Don't you want to keep the ghosts—oh." His quizzical expression flattened into embarrassment. "I heard your boyfriend came back. I didn't know you were . . ."

"Yeah." I ran my finger over the package's zipper. "Like I said, it's—"

"Complicated. Right." He shoved one hand into his pocket and pointed over my shoulder with the other. "Clearance."

"Huh?" It took a moment for my brain to translate his accent. "Oh. Thanks." I went to the discount bin and was dismayed to find a choice between blue and beige stripes and a skyscape of cloud-hugging teddy bears. Sadness.

"What about these?"

Zachary held up a dark indigo sheet set. They were almost black, speckled with tiny yellow and light blue spots, like paint-flecked stars on a night-sky canvas.

"Perfect!" I checked the price tag. "But thirty dollars too much. Figures."

He put the sheets in my arms. "I'll give you the money."

"No." I pushed them back. "I can't take it."

"I owe you. I haven't paid you for the petrol for all our trips."

"The what?"

"The gasoline."

"I haven't spent thirty dollars on gas."

"But you will."

"Zachary—"

"It's either this or I pay for the whole thing." He headed for the register, the sheet set tucked under his arm. "You can't stop me."

I trotted to keep up with his long, determined strides. "Yeah," I muttered. "I'm starting to figure that out."

To save time, Zachary and I grabbed takeout from the food court. At Farmer Frank's field, we set up a picnic next to our books, pencils, and giant pad.

"Who's going to draw this thing?" I asked him. "I suck at art."

"Me too." Zachary fished a pair of ice cubes out of his cup and tossed them into the grass—apparently they don't like super-cold soda in Europe. "It probably doesn't matter. We're just supposed to learn the process."

"I guess." I wrapped my hands around my coffee cup without sipping it. I'd bought it more for warmth than anything. "Eowyn said she wanted us to put ourselves into this project. Sucking at art is part of who we are."

"I'll drink to that." We tapped our cups together. "Do you see any ghosts?" Zachary asked.

"Not yet. Maybe no one ever visited here who died, or maybe it didn't mean enough to anyone to haunt. Or we got lucky and hit a quiet night."

"This'll help keep them away, aye?" He held up the flashlight. Its lens was painted over with red nail polish to protect our night vision. "They hate red?"

"Most of them." I remembered the crazy-mom ghost in the food court last week, then realized I hadn't seen her or any others when we were there tonight. Maybe the mall had finally sprung for BlackBoxing. But you'd think they would've advertised it.

"You're so lucky not to see them," I told Zachary.

"I dunno." He scooped out another ice cube. "I think it would be kind of interesting."

"Maybe, if it were just the ghosts. But then there's the DMP, ready to pounce on us the second we turn eighteen. I'm sick of their ads and letters and now these stupid assemblies."

"Won't they pay for your college?"

"That makes me even more suspicious. If it was such a great job, the government wouldn't have to bribe us."

"It's not bribery. It's paying for something they think is impor-tant. Like teachers in poor neighborhoods."

"I guess." I swished a French fry through a puddle of ketchup. "Megan's brother John made a deal where the government would pay off some of his med school loans if he'd be a doctor in Nowhere, North Dakota." Or maybe it was South Dakota. All I knew was that he said there was only one bar in the whole town, and in the winter some people left their cars running all night to keep the engines from freezing.

A cold breeze came up, as if I'd conjured it with my thoughts. I shivered so hard, the coffee splashed out of the little hole in the lid.

Zachary unzipped his dark brown leather jacket. "Here, take this."

"No, you'll freeze."

"Don't insult my rugged heritage." He shook out the coat and scooted over to me. "I'd be a real walloper if I let you shiver."

My eyebrows popped up. "A real what?"

"Never mind." He draped the coat over my shoulders. I trembled again from the sudden heat. "Put your arms in. Don't make me dress you like a wean."

I couldn't even ask what a "wean" was, because my brain was stuck on the scent of the warm leather. The jacket's collar came up around my chin. Was that how his neck smelled?

"Thanks." I cleared my throat. "I'll dress warmer next time."

"Me too." He tugged the cuff down over my wrist, his finger brushing the back of my hand. "Just in case."

I tried to focus on the star chart in front of me instead of the boy to my right. When Logan died, I'd stopped noticing Zachary's hotness, as if all my senses had switched off. Now that Logan was back (sort of), I'd become Little Miss Ho-Bag again.

"Um." I turned on the flashlight, casting a red glow over the book in my lap. "It says here to start by marking north, and not to cheat with a compass."

"Yeah, the way you do that is—"

"I know that much." I pointed to the Big Dipper and followed the last two stars to find the North Star, Polaris.

The pad was clipped to the board, which was good, because the wind was picking up. I suppressed another shiver—I did *not* want Zachary taking off any more clothes on my account.

We marked the other three directions, then found the celestial equator and the ecliptic, which laid out the approximate path of the zodiac, the sun, and the planets. Eowyn had given us lists of constellations to find and draw each month. After I did the first two, I let Zachary take over while I finished the gooey remains of my cheesesteak.

Over the next hour, we took turns eating and drinking and filling out the map. As our eyes grew adjusted to the dark, more stars became visible, which would've been annoying had it not been so utterly gorgeous. No garish sunset could compare to this pure, still brilliance.

"We don't have to put every star on the map," Zachary reminded me as he christened the grass with his soda's leftover ice. "Just the brightest ones."

"I know." I added another tiny point of light that didn't seem to belong to any constellation. "But I'm hoping if we make this insanely full of stars, we won't have to do it again."

"It's no' that bad, is it? Freezing our bums off to create something completely pointless?"

I laughed. It *wasn't* that bad to spend time with Zachary. The level of not-badness was almost scary.

"I'll survive. I hope Eowyn lets us move forward with our research next month."

"With *your* research, you mean." Zachary stuffed his empty cup in the fast-food bag. "Which you still haven't told me much about."

"I did tell you." I spoke forcefully to cover up my vagueness. "It's on megaliths."

"What about them?"

"I don't know yet. I have to read more before I can figure out the questions, much less the answers."

"Maybe I can help."

I straightened my posture and massaged my neck, which was stiff from looking at the sky. "I'll let you know."

"I'm your partner, remember. Not your bloody assistant." He took the pencil out of my hand. "And as your partner, I say we stop for the night, while you can still feel your fingers."

I put my nearly numb hands in my (his) jacket pockets before he could offer to warm them for me. "Fine. We can finish labeling the stars before our meeting next month."

As we packed up our stuff, Orion rose over the horizon, which meant it was getting really late.

"It's funny," I told Zachary. "I always heard that stars were different colors. That Betelgeuse was a red giant and Rigel was a blue giant. But I've never actually seen the colors before." I zipped up the bag of supplies and set it on the folded portfolio.

"You don't get out of the city much, do you?"

"Not at night." I hugged my knees to my chest to keep warm, not wanting to leave quite yet. "I don't usually like the dark."

"I can understand why."

We were whispering now, because even the crickets had gone to bed. "I haven't seen a single ghost all night." *Except Logan,* I added mentally.

"That's not true. Look at the Milky Way." Zachary leaned back on one hand and swept his other over his head. "Some of those stars are already dead. In the thousands of years it takes their light to reach us, they could've exploded or burned out."

I gazed up at the long, blurry stretch of silver that could've been mistaken for a high cloud. "So we're seeing them the way they were, not the way they are now."

We sat for a few more minutes in silence, and I began to understand why Eowyn was making us do this exercise. Three thousand years ago, people probably couldn't imagine the birth and death of stars. Those points of light were constant, dependable, eternal. Must have been comforting.

We packed up my car and drove home, under a sky full of ghosts.

Chapter Ten

Aunt Gina was already in bed when I got in at eleven o'clock. She'd left a note propped up against the coffee-maker.

Long day ahead tomorrow, so I turned in early.
Poke your head in my room when you get home, okay?
Love, Gina.

I tiptoed up the creaky wooden stairs, brushing my fingertips against the frames of my mother's photos—her first day of kinder-garten near the bottom step, her high school graduation in the middle; and the third one at the top, a month before she died, with me in her lap in front of the Christmas tree.

In every photo, her eyes glinted with good-natured defiance. Gina said that Mom had never let rules get in the way of having fun. Until now, I'd assumed this was a bad thing.

I snuck past Gina's room and into my bedroom before pulling the sheets from the bag.

The label on the package said, WASH PRIOR TO FIRST USE. I wondered why, until I unzipped it. The sheets were stiff and scratchy and smelled like the plastic casing. I calculated how long it would take to wash and dry them. Too long.

Stopping to think about it made me—well, stop to think.

How could I sleep on these sheets with Logan, when Zachary had not only picked them out, but helped pay for them? It felt almost like cheating. But on which guy?

A soft knock came at my door, and I shoved the sheets and bag under my bed. "Come in."

Gina cracked the door open. "Hi, hon, how was it?"

"Cold. But we got it done."

"It was chilly tonight." She leaned on the doorjamb, her green silk robe hanging loose around her fleece pajamas. "You should bring this boy by so I can meet him."

"It's not like that. Zachary's just a friend."

"A friend you're sitting alone with in a dark field. I need to meet him."

"He only serial-killed me a little bit, I swear."

She chuckled. "You seem better since the funeral yesterday."

"Yeah." I sat on the bed and took off my shoes. "Closure, you know." My voice sounded too casual—I suck at lying even worse than drawing.

"Aura." Gina's voice was the opposite of casual. "Have you seen Logan since the wake? Are you spending time with him?"

I pulled off my sock and examined it for holes. "I've run into him. But you know Logan, he never stays in one place for long."

Gina came to sit beside me. I held my breath as the heel of her embroidered slipper brushed the shopping bag handle under the bed.

"Sweetie," she said, which meant a lecture was coming. "I know it's hard. You thought you'd lost Logan forever, and then suddenly here he is again. It's confusing and agonizing and thrilling. It makes it very hard to accept reality."

"Uh-huh." I let my bracelet fall to the floor, pretending to accidentally drop it. When I bent to pick it up, I pushed the shopping bag with the sheets farther under the bed.

"But Aura, Logan is dead." She emphasized the last word. "He doesn't belong here."

Then I don't belong here, I thought, realizing how crazy that sounded, even in my head.

"You need to help him understand that," she continued, "so that he can move on."

"What if he doesn't want to?"

"He will." She smoothed down her springy blond bangs. "He doesn't know it yet, but he's very angry. At himself, but also at the people who enabled this."

I enabled this.

Aunt Gina dropped her hands in her lap, as if they were suddenly too heavy to hold up. "The Keeleys have asked me to file a wrongful death suit against Warrant Records."

I felt my guts shrivel. "Logan will have to testify." My head flashed hot as the worst part hit me. "About what happened right before he died!"

"Yes, and you'll need to be one of the witnesses."

"Are you kidding?" I sprang off the bed. "Do you have any clue what kind of story will come out? People are already gossiping about me and Logan."

"And this will give you a chance to set the record straight. To tell the truth."

"The truth is just as bad as the rumors." I clasped my hands together. "Please don't do this to us. I know you're worried you won't be able to afford my college, but—"

"You think this is about money?" She stood and wrapped her robe tight around herself. "This is about justice. That's more important than a few nasty rumors that everyone will forget the moment some celebrity gets a hangnail."

"Oh, so I'm *selfish* because I don't want our private life splashed all over the world?"

"If you're not thinking about the big picture, then yes, you are being selfish. You're forgetting what's at stake here."

"Yeah, millions of dollars."

"No. Logan's eternal soul."

I tried not to roll my eyes at her crusade. "He'll pass on when he's ready."

"What if he *can't*?" Gina shook a coral-painted fingertip at me. "What if he becomes a shade?"

"He wouldn't." My voice cracked with the desire to believe my own words. "Logan's a good guy."

"Plenty of good ghosts turn bad. They get bitter, watching the world go on without them. You know that better than I do."

I looked past her at my bed, remembering the day Logan lay there with me. The afternoon sun had slanted through the blinds, glowing golden against his bare skin. The light had seemed so much a part of him, I'd imagined it shining from within his body and streaming *out* the window instead of in.

No one was further from shade than Logan.

"I'm filing tomorrow," Gina said, "and we'll see when the courts can put it on the docket. It could be months." She came over and gripped my hand in her cool, soft one. "If we win, Logan will move on. He'll be at peace."

"And what if you lose?"

"Then it's up to him. But at least we'll have done everything we could." She let go of me and went to the door. "If you think about it, you'll realize what's right."

When she was gone, I changed my sheets at top speed. Wherever they came from, whoever had chosen them, their color was all that mattered. If Logan's time with me was limited, then I couldn't waste a single night without him by my side.

I picked out a deep purple button-down silk nightshirt that fell to the top of my thighs. It was something I usually wore in summer, not on a cold night like tonight. Logan's voice would keep me warm.

I went to the bathroom, where I washed my face, took out my contacts, and brushed my hair for several minutes. Logan couldn't touch it, but I wanted it to look soft. I even shaved my legs.

My footsteps slowed as I returned to my room. What if he forgot? What if the world had distracted him?

I stopped at the threshold, where my door stood slightly ajar. Holding my breath, I pushed it open.

Logan was sitting on the edge of my bed.

"Hi." He stood quickly as I moved inside the room. "Did you think I'd forget?"

I shut the door behind me. "Do I look worried?" I whispered.

"You look as nervous as I feel."

I went to the window, partly to hide my smile. If Logan could feel, he could live, sort of.

I lowered the blinds to block out the light from the street. In the total darkness, the details of Logan's features shone bright.

"I'm glad you came," I told him, hoping he grasped the force of my understatement.

"This is gonna be great." Logan reclined on the bed, though the mattress didn't compress with any weight. "Like when we were kids, remember? When we'd all camp out in our basement and pretend we were in the mountains?"

I hurried over to the other side of the bed, almost skipping in my giddiness. "Didn't we play 'doctor' for the first time on one of those camping trips?"

Logan laughed. "Yeah, that was before I found out about girl cooties."

I slipped under the covers next to him. He rolled onto his side to face me.

"Nice sheets," he said, and before he could see my guilt, his gaze traveled down the front of my shirt. "Nice outfit, too."

I felt suddenly shy. "Thanks."

"How was your sky gazing?"

"I wasn't sky gazing." I faked a playful punch. "I was working."

"Did he make you see stars?"

I suppressed a cackle. "Don't be a dick. And don't make me laugh, or Gina'll hear."

"Sorry." Logan bent his arm and rested his cheek on it. "I'll do the talking, so you don't get in trouble."

I nodded, swallowing a squeak of excitement. Logan was here. In my bed. He could talk the whole night about guitar strings and amp brands, for all I cared. I just wanted to hear his voice.

The lines of his face smoothed solemn. "I'm so sorry about Friday night. Not just for dying, but for getting so wasted we couldn't make love. It's like that Dead Kennedys song, 'Too Drunk to Fuck.' That's been running through my head all day."

"I'm glad you didn't ask for it to be played at the funeral luncheon."

He snorted. "What'd you think of my picks?"

"It was a kick-ass mix. Except for 'The Parting Glass.'"

"Hey, that's a traditional Irish funeral song."

"And drinking song," I snapped back. "Considering it was alcohol that killed you—"

"The cocaine killed me."

"It probably wouldn't have if you weren't so drunk. That's what the paramedics said. It was the interaction that made your heart go haywire."

"Oh. Wow."

I closed my eyes and held back a groan. Logan had made a mistake that had taken his life, and all he could say was "Wow"?

"Dylan told me Mom and Dad are suing the record company."

"I know." I kept my eyes shut, worried I would reveal my own hopes and fears.

"I can't get up on that stand and tell them everything. I don't care about my own reputation—I'm dead, after all—but you have to deal with the people who'll talk shit about you."

"My aunt said it would help you move on."

"*I'll* decide when I move on." Logan's voice snapped like a firecracker. "I don't have to listen to anyone now. I can do what I want."

As long as what he wanted didn't involve touching anything, or going anywhere he'd never been before.

"Hey, did you get to see my corpse?"

I opened my eyes. "I wish I hadn't."

"Was I still splotchy? I thought they could fix that."

"No, your color was fine."

"So how did I look?"

"You looked handsome."

His lip curled. "Handsome?"

"Yeah." I giggled. "Like a handsome shoe salesman."

"Aww, man." He rolled onto his back and covered his face. "They put me in that dark blue suit, didn't they?"

"That wasn't the worst part." I pushed out the words. "They dyed your hair."

Logan jerked to face me. "Like what Mickey did to his hair?"

"I don't know whose idea it was."

"I'll ask Dylan. If it was Mickey, I'll kill him."

"Just let it go. He's mad enough at himself as it is. So's Siobhan."

"No." Logan pounded a fist against the mattress and uttered a groan that wasn't quite human. "It's not their fault, and it's not your fault. I'll make it up to all of you. Somehow."

The words caught in my throat, the words I knew my aunt wanted me to speak. That the only way he could make things right was to move on, set his soul to rest.

But the thought of losing him again, this time forever, smothered all the words. I started to cry.

"Aura, please don't." Logan reached for my cheek. "Jeez, I can't even comfort you anymore. I'm so fucking helpless."

"No, you're not."

"Yes, I am." His whisper grew sharp and urgent. "I'm out there on the streets at night, and I see folks in some serious shit. Homeless people dying in alleys, hookers getting the crap beaten out of them, ten-year-olds dealing crack. And that's not even in the really bad neighborhoods, since I can't go into those." He swept his hand toward the window. "You see this on the news, and you forget about it, because really, what can any of us do, and we all have our own problems, right? But there was so much I could've done, compared to now. I could've made a difference."

I thought of how one day, when post-Shifters became cops, ghosts really could make a difference. They would be the ultimate Neighborhood Watch. I was about to point that out when Logan spoke again.

"Aura," he whispered, "I wish I could wipe away just one of your tears. Then I'd feel like a person again. Like I'm something more than a bunch of light."

"You can." I reached into the space between our bodies. "Just follow me."

He placed his left hand behind my right hand, creating a violet shadow. Together, slowly, we touched my face. The wetness soaked into the tip of my middle finger.

"I love you so much," he said. "I wish you never had to be sad."

The tear my finger had taken was replaced by another. "Let me cry, Logan. I need to."

He brought his face near mine, so bright I had to squint, and placed his head on my pillow, close enough that if he'd had breath, it would have caressed my eyelashes. "I'll stay until you sleep, and I'll come back tomorrow. If you want."

I nodded, then shut my eyes against his light.

Chapter Eleven

Logan spent every night with me for the next month. Not until morning, of course. He would leave after I dozed off, because to him, watching me sleep was (a) boring and (b) creepy.

If I called for him, he'd return, but I didn't unless I'd had a bad dream. It was enough to know he'd come again the following night.

Usually we listened to music together. Since Logan couldn't use earbuds anymore, I'd pull my MP3 docking station under the covers and play it at low volume. Or we'd read books or magazines by the light of his glow. If I had a test, he'd help me study, but since he couldn't turn the pages, this didn't always work.

When I got tired, Logan would sing me to sleep, sometimes a painfully appropriate song like Flogging Molly's "If I Ever Leave This World Alive" or Snow Patrol's "Chasing Cars." Sometimes he'd pick a lilting Irish lullaby, or even a song he'd written himself.

But never the song he'd meant to sing for me the night he died. Even Logan had his limits.

Mostly we talked. It felt like we were kids again, with a sleepover every night. When I laughed too much, Aunt Gina would knock on the door to see what was up, but I always told her I was watching a funny video. It wasn't like she could ever prove Logan was there.

Every Sunday morning before Gina did laundry, I changed my sheets back to red and hid the dark purple ones in a secret compartment under my bottom drawer. I spilled drops of soda and scattered cracker crumbs over the red sheets so they'd look used.

Even if she had suspected, how could she complain? I was happy. My boyfriend was dead, but in a way, he was with me more than ever.

During the day he haunted his younger brother Dylan, and some of our other friends, especially if they were having a party. But the nights were all ours, and Logan was all mine.

Zachary and I waited for Eowyn in her office before our second meeting. No tea was on the little table, so we sat in padded wooden chairs in front of the desk. The book fort was gone, replaced with uneven stacks of papers, a scattering of gnawed pencils, and a pair of laptop computers.

"Almost ten minutes late," Zachary said. His cell phone went off with a text message—I'd been around him enough to know his assigned ring tones—and his expression brightened. "Excuse me for a second?" He flipped open the phone and started texting. At least he was polite about it.

To occupy myself, I pulled my folders out of my book bag and started flipping through their contents. As always, I started with the purple folder, the one containing the journal and photos my mother had left.

Tuesday, December 25

Tried to call home to wish Mom and Gina a Merry Christmas (or "Happy Christmas," as they say here), but they barely spoke to me. Too pissed that I didn't come home for the holiday like I planned. Maybe now I'll never go back.

Nah, I'd miss the cheesesteaks.

Wednesday, December 26

Went to a St. Stephen's Day party at the local pub. I'm not the one in the family who sees ghosts (or even believes in them!), so maybe there was something in the whiskey (besides all that whiskey). But I swore I saw

The second page of that day's entry had been torn out midsentence. I ran my finger over the jagged edge left behind.

"Sorry I'm late!" Eowyn swept in, her shoes scuffing the carpet.

She had dark circles under her eyes, and her long blond curls were swept back in a glittery blue scarf. But her face looked bright, like it had just been splashed with cold water.

"Ooh, you brought me a present." She untied our portfolio, then opened our first star map and spread it on the desk before her. I placed my purple folder under the yellow one on my lap. My plan was to advance my research without telling anyone my exact theory. Not until I was sure I was right, and maybe even then it wouldn't be safe.

"Very nice work," Eowyn said. "But not so nice I'd think you were cheating. You've definitely nailed the fundamentals, and the level of detail is admirable." She sank into her chair. "Clearly you don't mind spending time together."

From the corner of my eye I saw Zachary mirror my squirming.

"If we got it right the first time," I said, "does that mean we can stop?"

"Is that what you were hoping?" Eowyn closed the portfolio. "The point is for you to see what changes over time and what stays the same." She folded her hands, shoulders sagging from what looked like exhaustion. "From year to year, the stars are the most constant thing we know. But within that time frame, they seem downright fickle. So yes, you still have to do this every month. Plan to dress warmly."

My face heated at the memory of Zachary's jacket around my shoulders, despite the casual turn our friendship had recently taken. Our conversations had grown less personal over the last few weeks. Sometimes he ate lunch with me and Megan and our friends who were starting to act like friends again, but it seemed like we were merely part of his social rotation. Zachary didn't hang out with anyone so much as he hung out with everyone.

"What's next?" he asked, and I realized he was speaking to me.

"I thought it would be cool to study ancient observatories that marked special times of the year, like equinoxes and solstices." I opened my yellow folder on the desk. "I figured we'd start with Stonehenge." I looked at Eowyn, then Zachary. "If that's okay with you."

The professor steepled her fingers under her chin. "What exactly did you want to study about Stonehenge?"

"How the ancient astronomers figured it all out. How they decided where to place the slabs of rock. It's so unique."

"Actually, there are many sites like it around the world," Eowyn told me. "Stonehenge is simply the most famous because its size is so impressive and its structure so distinctive."

I feigned surprise. "But it's the oldest, right?"

"The passage tomb Newgrange is older," Zachary said.

"Where's that?" I asked him, hoping my ignorance was convincing.

"In Ireland. It marks the winter solstice sunrise." He shifted to face me, his green eyes sparking with animation. "And up in the Orkney Islands in Scotland, Maeshowe marks the sunset on the same day. You should see it." He scratched his jaw, as if realizing he'd lost his sheen of guarded cool. "Because it's brilliant."

My pulse quickened from the way he'd looked at me, like he wanted to whisk me across the ocean. "How do they mark it?"

"I'll show you." Eowyn shoved some papers aside, then went to her bookshelf. She took down the model of Newgrange, a glistening white granite half-ring topped by a grassy dome, and laid it on her desk. I examined it as if I'd never seen it before—which I hadn't, in 3-D at least.

Back at the bookshelf, Eowyn flipped up one of the posters and pinned it to the frame of the shelf, which contained old, leather-bound, musty-looking books, the kind that make you want to roll around in them. (Well, that make *me* want to roll around in them. But I'm weird.)

She pulled out an armful of books and set them on a stool, letting out a whoosh of exertion. In the space left behind, I noticed an odd nick in the backing of the bookcase. It almost looked like a switch, the kind you press on to release a nearby panel. The Keeleys' old home in the city used to have hiding places like that—supposedly their house had been a speakeasy during Prohibition, and the secret compartments had held illegal liquor.

Eowyn unpinned the poster, and it fell back into place, hiding the shelf. When she saw me examining the spot, I looked away and pretended to adjust the zipper on my book bag.

She opened one of the books to a wrinkled, yellowed page filled with sepia-toned photographs.

"Here's what happens." She turned the domed model so that the door faced me, and pointed to a small rectangular window above the entrance. "On the morning of the winter solstice, the rising sun shines through this roof box into a chamber inside."

She opened the model's roof to reveal a narrow corridor with a round room at its end, then indicated the first photo. "Over the course of seventeen minutes, the light traces a pattern over the carved walls, through three recesses."

I studied the photograph. A man stood beside a spiral carved into the rock. I'd known about the solstice sunrise shining inside Newgrange, but I'd never heard of these recesses. They looked like rough versions of those cubbyholes that rich people use to display vases.

"What do they mean?" I asked her.

"Archaeologists believe that they signify mother, father, and child." She turned the page, revealing close-ups of the three ancient marks.

Zachary leaned over. "Can anyone go in there?"

"They give tours year-round," Eowyn said, "but to be there on a solstice you enter a lottery. Fifty names are drawn, and each person can bring a friend."

I scanned the images with greedy eyes. Was this where Mom had met my father? Was that why she hid the photos?

Turning the pages carefully, I said to Eowyn, "Have you been there?"

"Mm-hmm."

"When did you go?" Zachary asked her.

"Well." Eowyn spoke faster, drawing my attention back to her face. "I went several times for my work, but only once for the solstice. I can't remember which year." She shut the book, almost trapping my fingers. "There are also many other sites you could study. Zachary mentioned Maeshowe, and here in the States we have Chaco Canyon out in—"

"Can I borrow this?" I held on to the book's edge with fingers that felt like claws. "I know it's old, but I swear I'll take good care of it."

Eowyn hesitated, her eyes no longer sparkling. "Well, it does have a thorough bibliography. Primary sources, many of which we have here in the department." She tapped the cover in a quick staccato. "Things you'll never find on the Internet."

"Thank you." I slid the book toward my chest, resisting the urge to hug it.

"Let me get you a bag." She opened a drawer. "No offense, but I've seen inside teenagers' backpacks, and it's not exactly a sterile environment." She slipped a plastic bag over the heavy book and held it out for me.

In my eagerness to grab the book, I leaned forward and let go of the purple folder on my lap. It tipped, spilling my mother's photos on the floor. I let out a panicky gasp before realizing they'd fallen face-down. Whew.

"Here." Zachary slid out of his chair to help me.

"I've got it!" I scrambled to gather the pile of slick white squares.

"You missed a couple." He reached under the desk and extracted the runaway photos. As he pulled them out, he turned them over. One was of the bright white doorway of Newgrange; the other, of a young Eowyn Harris.

Zachary raised his gaze to meet mine. A flash of heat sparked between my shoulder blades.

Eowyn rounded the desk. "Everything okay?"

Zachary flipped the photos over and slid them into my folder. "We've got it." He winked at me, then said to Eowyn, "You were telling us about Chaco Canyon."

"Right!" Eowyn closed the Newgrange model and set it back on her shelf. "It's in New Mexico, and it marks the summer solstice...."

I tried to pay attention—or at least look like I was—as she described how the Anasazi people used the progress of a "sun dagger" across a spiral carving to know when to harvest. In the corner of my eye, the Newgrange model glowed white, the dark eye of its door beckoning my imagination.

At the end of our meeting, she told us to return the first week in January, after our next two star maps were finished and we had decided which megaliths we wanted to focus on. Maybe I was paranoid, but Eowyn seemed nervous as she showed us to the door, as though she were a mother sending kids off to army boot camp.

Zachary stayed quiet beside me as we exited the building and walked to the parking lot. The tension was killing me.

"Why don't you just ask?" I said as we approached my rain-soaked car. "You know you want to."

"Because I'm trying to decide if you'll really answer. Otherwise there's no point, aye?"

I gritted my teeth. "You're infuriatingly patient."

"You have no idea." Zachary smirked at me over the roof of the car. "Yet."

Chapter Twelve

Like most post-Shifters, Megan and I usually avoided the Free Spirit Café. The Charles Village coffee shop's ghost gimmick held no appeal for those of us who saw spirits on a regular basis. Most of its customers were twenty- and thirtysomething people who thought it would be cool to visit a "haunted" restaurant and have their kids waited on by friendly ghosts.

"I heard the service here sucks," Megan said as we squeezed into a tiny table by the window, which was painted over with swirling black strokes to keep the place dark. "I heard the ghosts pretend to take your order and then just disappear."

"At least they have an excuse. Some places, the living waiters do that."

A mural covered the wall above Megan's head. On a night-sky background, the violet ghosts of famous people floated together, dancing or talking. People who never could've hung out: Elvis and Socrates; Ben Franklin and Julius Caesar.

Like most pre-Shifters' ideas about ghosts, it was cute but inaccurate. First of all, they couldn't interact with each other, only with the living. Second, famous people usually got sick of afterlife on Earth pretty fast—after the funerals and TV retrospectives, the twenty-four-hour admiration stopped, so there wasn't much point in hanging around. Most of them moved on, but a few turned shade. Or so I'd heard, but I'm skeptical. Shades tend to be dark, seething, vaguely human-shaped masses, which wouldn't do much for a celebrity's image.

"Speaking of living, or not so much," Megan said, "how are you sleeping these days?"

"Fine." I stiffened my posture to simulate alertness.

"Really? Because I was thinking we wouldn't need to-go bags for our muffins. We can just use the ones under your eyes."

"I don't have muffins under my eyes."

"Dork." She shoved her sunglasses on top of her head. "If I bought you a new red top, would you wear it?"

"Sorry, got plenty of those." I picked at the gray fuzz balls on the sleeve of my cardigan.

"I never see you wear them anymore."

"I may have given them all to Goodwill."

"What about the ghosts?"

"They don't bug me as much as they used to." I held up my hands to cut her off. "Some of them really need help."

"If you want to take on charity cases, you could start with the living."

"Did you not just hear me say I donated a bunch of clothes to Goodwill?"

"Just because you're the girlfriend—or whatever you are—to a ghost doesn't mean you have to become a champion for them all." Megan jerked the zipper open on her purse. "You're turning into your aunt."

"Ouch. If I were dating a black guy, would you complain if I started having more black friends?"

"There's no comparison. Ghosts aren't people."

"Hello!" Next to our table appeared the ghost of a ponytailed woman in her early twenties. "I'm Stephanie. Is this your first time here?" When we nodded, she continued. "Okay, the way it works is I take your order back to Justin in the kitchen, and then he brings out your food and drinks." She beamed at me. "He's a liver."

"Liver?" I crinkled my forehead. "Oh. Live-r. I get it." I hadn't heard that term used to describe we who breathed. I didn't think it would catch on.

Ex-Stephanie gestured to the blackboard above the counter. "As you can see, our special dessert today is the white chocolate cheese-cake. I'm told it's to die for." She let out a string of giggles, and I joined in to be polite.

"Funny," Megan said through tight lips as she pulled out her wallet. "I think we'll just order at the counter."

I flapped my menu. "Oh, come on, this is cool." I turned to ex-Stephanie. "Do they pay you?"

"Under the table." She flipped the end of her ponytail. "My social security number expired when I did. The money goes to my kid."

I told Megan, "Make sure we leave a big tip."

She rolled her eyes and said to the ghost, "Two skinny mochas, extra whipped cream on mine."

"And the cheesecake," I added.

"Sounds great. Thank you!" Instead of walking away, ex-Stephanie vanished.

Megan dragged herself out of her chair. "I'll go see if she really put in our order."

My cell phone vibrated, still in silent mode from working that afternoon at the law office. I peeked at the caller ID and was surprised at the number.

"Hello?" I answered, half expecting to hear Logan's voice.

"Aura." Dylan spoke in a hushed tone. "Where are you?"

"I'm at Free Spirit with Megan. I just got off work, so I'm desperate for sugar."

"Have you seen Logan?"

"Last night. Why?"

"I figured I should tell you first—his headstone is almost ready. My mom said she was going to call your aunt so we could all go out together next week to see it."

My fingers turned cold at the thought, as if they were already caressing the hard granite proof of his death. "I don't want to see it," I said flatly.

"Me neither." There was a brushing noise, like he was shifting the phone to his other ear. "So when he comes over, what do you guys do? I mean, do you, you know . . ."

His implication made my face flush. "No. Mostly we just talk."

"About what?"

"Everything. Old times, I guess."

"Hey, you remember when we all went camping in Harpers Ferry, and my dad told ghost stories?"

I chuckled. "Yeah, I think I was what, seven? And you were six."

"I guess." His voice faded for a second, then brightened. "Anyway, then remember me and you pretended there were real ghosts at the campsite and freaked everyone out?"

"And they made us pack up all the tents and go to a motel? That was awesome. Except that there were actual ghosts in the motel."

"It was worth it, though, to see everyone get scared. I hated all the bugs outside, anyway."

A few silent moments passed. "Well, thanks for calling," I said. "I guess I'll see you at the cemetery."

Dylan paused, and I checked the phone to see if it had cut off. Finally he said, "I'm in the bathroom."

I scrunched up my face. "I didn't need to know that."

"I mean, I'm in the bathroom because I don't want Logan to hear."

The BlackBox, of course. "Wait, is it . . . that bathroom? In the upstairs hallway?"

"Yeah. Kinda funny, huh? A ghost who can't haunt the place he died? Everyone else is too creeped out to use it. Siobhan and Mickey started showering in Mom and Dad's bathroom. So it's pretty much all mine now. Which is cool. But I had to use the old land phone with the long cord to call you."

"What don't you want Logan to hear?"

"Oh." He continued in a near whisper, "Do you ever wish he would leave?"

A shiver ran up the arm that was holding the phone, as if his words carried an electrical shock. "You mean for good?"

"Yeah."

"No."

"Really?"

"Really."

"Swear?"

"Why, Dylan? Do you wish he would leave?"

"I don't know." He paused. "Sometimes. Maybe not for good, though. It's weird, seeing him like that. All purple and shit."

"I've gotten used to it."

"Me too. That's what scares me." He let out a hard breath. "What if he stays a really long time? He died when he was seventeen, right? What if one day seventeen years from now, he's still around? Then he would've been a ghost longer than he'd been a person."

"He's still a person."

"But did you ever think about that? What if one day we get married? I don't mean me and you," he rushed to add. "When we get married to other people, will Logan be at the wedding? Will he visit our kids? Will he sit in his old room every night, staring at that fucking guitar?"

A lump filled my throat at the image. "If your family wins the lawsuit in January, he'll pass on. That's a long time before either of us has kids." I twisted my tone. "Unless there's something you're not telling us."

"We might not win," said Dylan, ignoring my lame attempt at humor. "Dad says there's a fifty-fifty chance. Which means there's really a thirty-seventy chance. And then what if Logan—"

I waited a moment for him to finish his sentence, dreading its end. "What if Logan *what*?"

Dylan's voice dropped to the faintest whisper. "He could go shade."

"No!" I glanced at the older couple at the next table, who were giving me the evil eye for yelling, or maybe for existing. "Dylan, he would never."

He snorted. "Maybe Logan's all happy when he's with you, but I see him the way he really is. He's pissed as hell—about dying, about this stupid court case, about everything he can't do." The phone shifted again. "Sometimes he makes me so dizzy I think I'm gonna hurl."

My pulse surged, and I fought to keep my breath steady. "That never happens when he's with me."

"Well, that's just great. For you." Dylan's voice cracked. "Next thing we know, those Obsidian Corps people could be after him. They could lock him up forever."

"That won't happen." I clutched the phone, sweaty now against my cheek. "What do you want me to do, Dylan? Convince him to move on?"

"He'll listen to you."

"Not about this."

"Aura, just try, okay?" He let out a long, hissing sigh, like it was coming through his nose. "It was fun at first, having Logan back, me and him hanging out. It was like when we were kids and people used to call us 'the other twins,' before he got into music with Mickey and Siobhan. Now I just want to stay in the bathroom all the time."

I pictured Dylan huddled on top of the toilet seat, waiting for his brother to get bored and go away. I wondered what it would take to put me in that desperate, sick-of-Logan state.

It wasn't that Logan had never pissed me off. I'd suffered through his loudest prima donna fits, his heaviest drinking binges, his craziest thrill-seeking stunts.

But sitting in that café, surrounded by ordinary ghosts, I had a feeling that the world wasn't done with Logan.

And neither was I.

Chapter Thirteen

A new sky greeted Zachary and me the next time we went to Farmer Frank's field.

"I knew in my head that things would change." I craned my neck as Zachary laid the blanket down. "But somehow I'm still surprised." I gestured to Cygnus, the Swan, a large, pointy constellation that was diving headfirst beneath the western horizon. "A month ago, that would've just been starting to set."

"Eowyn would say, 'I told you so,' but I won't." Zachary smoothed out the blanket's corners. "How was your Thanksgiving?"

I let my shoulders relax a notch. I'd been waiting for him to ask me why I'd lied about my knowledge of Newgrange. But if we were small-talking about holidays, maybe he really was letting the subject go.

"It was busy." I settled on the blanket next to him. "We went to my grandmom's like always, in Philly. I have a million cousins up there that I only see a couple times a year. They hang out together all the time, so I feel kinda odd when I'm with them. I don't get their inside jokes, and they always—" I caught myself, remembering I was talking to a guy. "Never mind. It's stupid."

"Tell me anyway."

I studied my fingernails, where I'd picked off half of the black nail polish. "They look so perfect. Their hair is all sleek and shiny and cut in new styles, while mine is terminally frizzy. My cousin Gabi? She's twelve, and her makeup looks better than mine." I glanced over at him. "See, I told you it was stupid."

"I guess I'm the stupid one, since you don't seem to value my opinion."

"Opinion about what?"

He unzipped our packet of pencils. "Remember what I told you that first day we went to see Eowyn? What I said in the parking lot?"

My cheeks warmed along my hairline at the memory of his bonnier-than-ever declaration. "I thought you were trying to make me feel better."

"I was." Zachary focused on the drawing tools he was arranging between us. "Doesn't mean it's no' true."

I let the silence weigh heavy for a few moments, wondering how to respond. If we started flirting, it could be a long, unproductive evening. Not to mention frustrating, since I couldn't hook up with Zachary without contracting a major case of guilt. Logan and I were together, even though we couldn't *be* together.

"Most of your family lives in the same city?" Zachary asked.

I nodded, relieved to change the subject. "The same neighborhood, even. All but me and my aunt. Who wants to meet you, by the way. She's kind of overprotective."

"All right." He opened our constellation book and switched on the red-painted flashlight. "You never mention your parents."

"My mom died just after I turned three. Cancer. I don't know my dad." I kept my voice casual as I unfolded the portfolio. "I don't even know who he was. Or *is*, if he's still alive."

"No clue at all, then?"

"Just that he has brown eyes."

"How do you know that?"

"I have brown eyes and my mom had blue. Brown's dominant genetically, so if I have them, it means my father did. Does. Whatever." I replaced the top sheet in the portfolio—last month's star map—with a blank one. "Oh, and he might be Irish."

"Really?" Zachary said with a note of curiosity—or maybe disbelief.

"I think my mom was in Ireland when I was conceived." I gestured to my face. "I know, I don't look it, right? My grandmom always jokes that I look more Italian than the rest of my family put together. Her parents came from Tuscany, which is in northern Italy." I took a breath to pause the babble. "Which I'm sure you, uh, already know, being from Europe."

"What was your mum doing in Ireland?"

I'd said too much already. "Just travel. So what about you? I know you don't celebrate Thanksgiving, but did you do anything fun on your days off?"

Ugh. I sounded like the people at Gina's office, who would ask each other how their weekends were, without sounding like they cared about the answers. But I felt a great need for a subject change.

"My dad cooked a turkey. When in Rome, he says. It was bloody awful. I did like the pumpkin pie, though."

"That reminds me." I dug into my book bag and pulled out a white cardboard box tied with a string. "I brought these back for you."

He looked at the box, then at me, before slowly reaching out. "What are they?"

"Poisonous snakes. Open it."

Zachary untied the string. "They seem like very quiet snakes."

"They're stealthy. Or maybe dead."

He opened the box, and his face melted into a smile. "You brought me biscuits?"

"Italian cookies. My grandmom has a bakery that's kinda famous—in Philadelphia, at least."

He picked out a crescent-shaped cookie and bit into the end. Powdered sugar made a small blizzard on the front of his brown sweater. I had a sudden impulse to dust it off.

"Mm, almond," he said. "And—is it rum?"

"Yep, but don't worry. The alcohol bakes off. And besides, I'm your designated driver tonight."

"It's pure braw. Delicious, I mean." He set the box between us. "Thanks very much." His voice was muted and a little strained. He stared into the distant woods as he munched the other half of the cookie.

I wondered if I'd made some huge cross-cultural faux pas. "Are you okay?"

"Hmm? Yeah." Zachary rubbed his thumb and first two fingers together, as if to make the powdered sugar part of his skin. "My mum used to bake a lot."

Ah. I fidgeted with my pencil, deciding whether to leave the touchy subject alone or push forward. Either way, things would be tense.

I chose talking-tense instead of silent-tense. "You don't have any idea where she went?"

"All I know is that she left on purpose. My dad's job is—I can't tell you what it is exactly, and I sort of lied when I said he was a political science professor." Zachary looked at me out of the corner of his eye. "Sorry."

"That's okay. A lot of people around here have classified jobs."

"Anyway, it's the kind of career that takes over your life. Mum got tired of placing second to his work. She hated moving around all the time, and when Dad got assigned here in the States, I guess that was the last straw. She left."

"Why didn't she take you with her?" I winced as soon as the question left my mouth.

"I didn't want to go." Zachary creased the corner of the bakery box lid. "I thought if I went with her, she would never come back to him. So I said I wanted to stay with Dad."

"Was that true?"

"Not really. He's not bad or anything, just obsessed with his job. And they're still married, so maybe one day . . ." He folded his lips in, as if afraid to voice the hope.

"What happened when you told her you wanted to stay?"

Zachary didn't speak for several seconds. "She cried."

I had the worst desire to hug him. Even though I sometimes wondered if my father had left because of something I did, I knew it was crazy, since I hadn't been born at the time. But Zachary had to live with the fact that he'd made his mother leave him.

"You haven't talked to her since?"

"No' exactly." He scratched his ear. "I get e-mails sometimes, but they could be coming from anywhere."

"Why doesn't she want to be found?"

He leaned back on his hands and scanned the sky. "Bollocks. There's clouds moving in."

I looked to the east, where a single thin, stringy cirrus cloud stretched over Orion's Belt. That was all. It was Zachary's turn to change the subject.

Maybe his secrecy had to do with his dad's classified dealings. It seemed like half the people I knew had parents who worked at NSA or DMP or some other semicovert agency. Maybe Zachary's mom—whether she was an agent herself or not—would be in danger if anyone, even her son, knew where she was.

"We can work around the cloud," I told him. "Let's start before it gets worse."

Surprisingly, it wasn't as cold that night as it had been on our first sky-mapping trip in October. But it was just as hard not to shiver every time Zachary leaned in close to add another star. I tried not to notice the way his dark lashes flickered as his eyes searched the page, or the way he bit his lip as he figured out the perfect placement. I tried not to stare at the curve of his neck as he craned it to gaze at the sky, and wonder what it would feel like to kiss it, right at the hollow of his throat.

I failed.

Maybe it was the sugar rush of eating all those cookies, but my hands were trembling so hard I had to draw super slowly to keep the lines straight. It was taking forever to finish this stupid map.

"Wait a minute." I flipped the sheet to look at last month's chart of the southeastern sky. "That bright yellow one wasn't there before. Maybe it was too hazy that night?"

"Maybe. Let me see the other page."

I moved the flashlight closer and bent low over the chart. "It should have been here, in Taurus."

"Let me see."

"What star would be that bright? How could we have missed it last month?"

"Aura."

Out of the corner of my eye, I saw Zachary's hand near my face. Slowly he brushed back my hair, sliding it behind my shoulder. His fingertip grazed my bare neck right under my ear.

My entire body tensed. I held my breath to keep from gasping.

"Sorry." He quickly tucked the ends of my hair inside my hood. "It was in the way. I couldn't see."

I stared at the page in front of me. If I turned to look at him, it would be all over. I'd ask him to do it again. This time, put all ten fingers in my hair and on my neck and my shoulders and—

This was definitely not the sugar talking.

"What do you think it is?" I heard the huskiness of my voice.

"I know what it is," Zachary said softly. "But I think you should figure it out yourself."

I tried to force my mind back to the project instead of counting how many weeks it had been since anyone had touched me—*really* touched me, the way I wanted Zach to. I mean, the way I wanted Logan to.

Breathe. Blink. Focus.

Okay. A star where there hadn't been one before. A supernova? A comet?

I smacked my forehead. "Duh." I checked the steady yellow-white glow in the sky. "It's Jupiter."

"Is that your final answer?"

I finally dared to look at him. "It's my final answer."

In the faint red flashlight glow, his green eyes had turned almost black. "I think you're right."

"Good." I laughed a little, to relieve the tension.

"Yeah. Good." Zachary shifted, pulling one knee up and resting his elbow on it. I wondered if he knew this was one of his hottest poses.

"Your turn to draw." I tossed the pencil at his chest.

"At least my hair won't block your view."

"No, but your big head might." I crawled behind him so he could take my place in front of the chart.

"I'll have you know, my head is a perfectly average size." He spread his fingers. "My hands, though, are enormous, and you know what they say—"

"Shut up and draw, lad," I said in my best attempt at a Scottish accent.

"Ouch." Zachary covered his ears. "Don't try this at home, children."

"I thought it sounded good."

"In your head, maybe." He put down the pencil. "A few pointers on talking like a Scotsman. First, you don't trill your *r*'s, you gently roll them. Try it. Say 'no trill, just roll.'"

"No trill, just roll." I bit my lip. I had trilled. Possibly even spit on him.

"No, no, it's not Italian or Spanish. Don't bludgeon that poor *r* with your tongue."

"I can't help it." *Must change topic from what tongues should do.* "I took Spanish. And my family's Italian."

"They tell you to relax your mouth and let it go, right?" When I nodded, he replied, "That's the thing, then. Keep in mind, my people are extremely uptight. So to talk like a Scotsman, you've got to keep that mouth under control."

"That's no fun."

Zachary closed his lips. He blinked and looked to the right, then blinked again and looked back at me, as if preparing to share a secret. His voice came low and growly. "You'd be surprised how much fun it can be."

My heart slammed in my chest so hard, I thought it would pop open my ribs. "Surprise me."

Where had *that* come from?

Zachary hesitated, like he was waiting for me to take it back, then shifted so he was sitting in front of me. He took my face in his hands—which actually were pretty big—and placed his thumbs under my cheekbones, his little fingers under the curve of my jaw. "Now say it."

"Say what?"

"Anything," Zachary whispered.

My brain scrambled for a sentence that was suitably seductive, or at least funny. But at that moment of supreme panic, the only thing whirling around my mind was the Gettysburg Address.

"Four score and seven years ago, our fathers brought forth on this continent a new nation, conceived in liberty."

Zachary's grip kept my mouth from opening too far. The *r*'s rolled out softly, tapped by my tongue with a gentle restraint.

"And dedicated to the proposition that all men are created equal." I switched back to my regular accent. "I forget the rest."

"That was perfect." He stared into my eyes, breaking our gaze only to glance at my lips. His warm hands still held my face, and the energy from his touch sent shocks zinging down my spine and out into my limbs.

An extra-strong vibration came from my left side, near my heart. I closed my eyes and lifted my chin.

"Aura."

"Hmm?"

"Your, uh, your chest is humming." He let go of me.

"Huh?" I blinked at the sudden loss of his touch. "Oh, my phone!" I unzipped my jacket and fumbled in the inside pocket.

It was my dear aunt and her impeccable timing.

"What's wrong?" I answered.

"I'm just checking in," Gina said. "Making sure you haven't been eaten by wolves or hit by a stray bullet from a hunter."

"I'm on a farm, not in the Yukon."

"You know me. I have to be Turbo Godmother sometimes."

"It's fine. I'm fine."

"You sure? You sound out of breath."

"Yeah! I mean, we just moved our stuff because of the—uh, the smell. Of cows."

"Ew. Are you almost finished?"

Zachary was already bent over our map, adding stars with a new urgency.

"Yes," I told her through gritted teeth. "I'll be home soon."

When she said good-bye, I clicked off and put the phone back in my jacket.

"I also found Mars," Zachary said. "In Gemini." He pointed to the southeast without looking at me. "See the reddish orange one? It's barely risen."

"I see it." I flipped the page in our book to a new quadrant of the sky, my hands still shaking. I hadn't felt like this since the night Logan and I had first kissed, after his first concert a year ago.

A year ago tomorrow, I realized. I'd almost kissed another guy a few hours from our anniversary. Shame flushed my cheeks and forehead.

At least, I thought it was shame.

The moment I pulled away from Zachary's apartment building, I heard a voice beside me.

"Late for a school night, isn't it?"

My foot jammed the brake pedal in reflex. "Damn it, Logan! Not while I'm driving."

"Sorry." He laid his arm along the passenger-side window. "I got worried."

"You too? Gina thinks I'll be eaten by boll weevils or something."
I got the car moving again. "I'm probably a lot safer there than I am
on my own street."

"I bet it's nice out in the country."

"It's gorgeous. I can't get over how quiet it is."

He snorted. "Mr. Ed doesn't say much while you're making your
maps?"

I squinted at him, not getting the joke. "Mr. Ed?"

"I said, 'Mr. Red.' Your friend or whatever he is."

"Zachary? Why do you call him that?"

"I can't even look at him. Dude wears red shirts like they're going
out of style. Which unfortunately they never will," he grumbled.

"What are you talking about? Zach never wears red. He doesn't
have to, because he's a pre-Shifter. I told you that."

"So now he's 'Zach' to you? I never got a nickname."

I thought of several nicknames he wouldn't like. "Watch it, Logan.
The jealousy routine does not give me warm fuzzies."

"I don't know anything about this guy. Maybe if you filled me in,
I wouldn't be so—I don't know—"

"Threatened?"

"I'm *not* threatened." His voice rose, and the edges of his form
flickered and faded. The sight sent a chill ricocheting through me.

I had to calm him down. "There's not much to tell," I said as I turned
onto the parkway, which this late at night held none of its usual traffic.
"He's a junior, he's in my history class. Oh, and he's from Scotland."

"Did you know bagpipes were actually invented in Ireland?"

"No, I didn't."

Logan snickered. "Yeah, we gave them to Scotland as a practical joke. They still haven't figured it out."

I chuckled, if only to indulge him. I couldn't expect him not to be jealous—after all, Zachary could touch me, and Logan couldn't. All I had to do to get rid of Logan, even now, was take a turn down a new road. If I were standing in his shoes—his violet high-top Vans, to be exact—I'd be exploding with fear and frustration.

We reached a stoplight. "Logan, do you ever think about plans?"

"Plans for what?"

"For the future. Beyond next week or next month."

He didn't reply at first. The traffic light turned green before he spoke.

"I do have a plan," he said quietly, but didn't elaborate.

"Can you tell me?"

"I don't want to ruin the time we have together. Can we just enjoy this for now?"

My fingers grew cold on the steering wheel. "What are you planning? Are you going to—change?"

"Huh?" Logan sounded genuinely confused. "Change how?"

"I don't know." I turned onto my street a little too fast, and the tires made a tiny squeal. "Into a shade?"

"What?" Logan's shout echoed in the car. "Are you kidding? Aura, I would never in a million years. That's insane." He leaned toward me, his glow almost burning my eyes. "How can you even think it? Why would I want to be a"—his voice plummeted to a whisper—"shade?"

"Then you could go anywhere you wanted. You could hide in the dark."

"And lose any chance of going to heaven. I might not be in a hurry to leave this world, but when I do, I want to be at peace." He slumped back in his seat. "I must be acting like a total asshole for you to think I could shade out."

"Not with me." I bit my lip at my impending betrayal. "With your brother. He's worried."

"Shit." Logan rubbed his face hard with both hands, as if he was trying to wipe away his whole self. "I probably have been a jerk around him lately."

"He says you make him sick. Literally."

"Oh God," Logan whispered.

I focused on the road so I wouldn't see the fear on his face. The street sweepers were coming early the next morning, so I had to park around the block, near the Keeleys' old house.

"I didn't mean to," Logan said. "I swear."

His remorse dug claws into my heart. "Maybe you're not shading. Maybe Dylan felt sick and dizzy because he was upset. Maybe he needs some antianxiety medication."

"Great, I'm driving my little brother crazy. I am so going to hell."

"You are not. Only dictators and stuff go to hell."

"Dictators and shades. If being stuck here forever counts as eternal damnation."

A grunt was my only response as I concentrated on parallel parking. Logan's glow was destroying my night vision, so I had trouble seeing the exact position of the other cars, but I didn't want to ask him to get out, not in his current state of mind.

When we were parked, I turned off the car but didn't open the door.

Logan looked at me, his posture hunched. "You said I don't make you sick, right?"

"Right."

"So you still want me to come to bed with you?"

I looked at the dashboard clock. One hour and three minutes until our anniversary. "If I say yes, will you tell me your plan?"

"Not yet, but you'll be the first to know." He held out his hand, flat with fingers spread. "Spider-swear."

I slipped my solid fingers between his ethereal ones. My skin reflected his violet glow, which for tonight, at least, was strong and steady and seemed like it would never fade.

Chapter Fourteen

The heavy rain made the cemetery dark enough to see ghosts, and there were more than I'd expected. When Aunt Gina and I pulled up behind the Keeleys' SUV, half a dozen violet spirits lingered around the graves of their loved ones (or hated ones), but they didn't look at us, much less approach.

Most importantly, there was no Logan.

Before we got out of the car, Gina spoke to me in a gentle voice. "I think this'll be good for you, sweetie. Give you some closure, like you said."

When did I said that? I pulled up the hood of my windbreaker, grabbed the flower wreath between my knees, and opened the door.

Ahead of us, Mr. Keeley retrieved a giant blue golfing umbrella from the back of the SUV, then went to the passenger door and helped his wife step out onto the wet grass. She slipped a little in her high heels. My aunt hurried over to them, her own black umbrella wobbling on her shoulder.

This cemetery was smaller, with more trees, than the one my mother was buried in outside of Philadelphia. I always visited my mom when I went up there, and tried to go alone or with someone other than Gina, so that I could cry without making my aunt feel bad, as if she weren't a good enough substitute.

Like me, the remaining Keeley brothers and Siobhan had dressed for the weather, in jackets and rain shoes.

"I miss you." Siobhan hugged me hard. "The house feels so empty without you and Logan."

"I didn't know if I was welcome."

She kissed my temple. "Consider this an open invitation. And speaking of invitations." She fished in her purse and brought out a folded neon green paper. "Our next gig."

My stomach sank. How could the Keeley Brothers go on without Logan? I unfolded the flyer.

THE KEELEYS, it said, with a picture of Siobhan and Mickey. The venue was the Green Derby, a tiny Irish pub in Towson, and the date was mid-January. Right after the trial.

"We're doing acoustic sets now," Mickey added over her shoulder. "More traditional stuff."

"Nothing big," Siobhan said. "Just something to fill the time between now and college."

"No record companies." Mickey tugged his hood down over his face. "Never again."

Siobhan glanced at Aunt Gina, who was several feet away, talking to Mr. and Mrs. Keeley. "Can you make it? It's a bar, but you have a fake ID, right?"

I nodded. "I've been there before." So had Logan, which meant he'd probably show up if he hadn't passed on yet.

"We're dedicating our first show to him." The corners of her eyes drooped. "And probably our second show, and all the rest."

Mickey tapped her elbow. "They're ready."

They headed off for the grave, and I followed, falling into step beside Dylan.

"You must have talked to Logan," he said. "He's been less of a dick this week."

"Only less of one?"

"Okay, not at all. It's been cool."

"No more hot flashes or fainting spells?"

"Shut up," he snorted. "You make me sound like an old lady." He stopped and turned to me. "I'm telling you, that sick feeling was real. Logan was shading."

"And how many shades have you seen that you can be so sure?"

"Three. You don't forget the way they screw with your brain."

"I know." I'd only seen two in my life, and none until the past year. Sometimes I wondered if they'd always existed or if they'd evolved recently. In the month of November alone, four sixteen-year-olds had died in shade-related car accidents across the state.

"And then one time there was this really shady ghost," Dylan said, "at the GameStop in the Towson mall, before it was BlackBoxed? I think he was only a kid when he died. Anyway, he was almost totally black, hardly any violet left at all."

"What was the ghost doing?"

"That's the funny part. He was screaming about wanting the new Nintendo 64. My friend Kyle and I were like, dude, that came out a million years ago. Which just pissed him off. So then the Obsidians showed up and detained him."

"How did they do it?"

Dylan made an O with his hand. "They used this crystal disc thingie. I guess it was like bait."

"The summoner. We use them in court to get the ghosts to the witness stand. It lets them go places they never went during their lives."

He scoffed. "You mean places like a little black box?"

"Is that where they put that kid's ghost?"

"Yeah. It was about the size of a remote control." Dylan fidgeted with the Velcro pocket of his windbreaker, ripping it open and smoothing it closed. "He was still screaming when they locked it."

"Whoa."

"It was pretty close." Rip. Smooth. "I think he was about to shade all the way, and then they never could've caught him." Rip. Smooth. "Afterward the Obsidian guys talked to us and let us play with some of their equipment. It was cool."

"Cool?" I rolled my eyes. "It's called recruitment. And I bet one day the dumpers won't bother anymore. They'll make us work for them whether we want to or not. Like a draft."

"So maybe it's better to volunteer. At least that way we get free college. And probably sweeter assignments." Dylan wiped a rivulet of rain off the bridge of his nose. "In this Vietnam game I played once, all the draftees—that was the lowest level—got deployed to these hard-ass jungles really far from the towns where they could get hookers and stuff. But when you had enough points to re-enlist, you got more weapons and better armor." He shoved his hands into the front pouch of his windbreaker, pulling the hood low over his forehead. "So maybe if the DMP drafts you, you end up at some crap-basket in the Middle East where you can't have alcohol, but if you sign up, maybe you get to work where it's air-conditioned."

I didn't even try to follow his pinball imagination. "Just be careful, Dylan."

"You coming?" Mickey called to us, bellowing over the roar of rain on hundreds of granite slabs.

We waved at him. "At least Logan remembered my birthday today," Dylan said.

"Oh! Happy birth—" I cut myself off as I realized it was anything but happy. "I'm sorry. And it's your sixteenth, too. Have you gotten any presents?"

"Shyeah, right. No one's even said anything." He shrugged and turned away. "Come on."

Grass hadn't grown on Logan's grave yet, so it still looked fresh, except for divots where puddles had formed over the last few rainy weeks.

The Keeleys stepped aside so I could place my heart-shaped wreath of red and white roses next to the bigger one they had just laid at his grave. The soft, spongy earth gave way easily as I pushed the thin stakes into the ground.

"I love you, Logan," I whispered, below the rush of rain. A lock of my hair fell out from underneath my hood and was instantly soaked.

Logan's headstone was the standard gray granite. Under his name and dates of birth and death, it simply read, FOR WHAT IS SEEN IS TEMPORARY, BUT WHAT IS UNSEEN IS ETERNAL. I remembered that same Bible verse from his funeral Mass. It made me shiver, thinking of shades.

I took a step back, into a puddle in the waterlogged grass. Cold rain seeped over the top of my right shoe.

"What does he say to you?"

I realized Mrs. Keeley was speaking to me.

I cleared my throat. "When?"

"Whenever. Dylan won't tell us anymore." She clasped Mr. Keeley's arm beside her. "We think he's holding back."

Dylan scuffed his feet against the grass. "Mom . . ."

"The house is so quiet." Mrs. Keeley shifted her black leather gloves from hand to hand. "I never realized how much Logan talked until he was gone. His grandmother always called him her little chatter-bug." She glanced at each of her other children. "He never hid anything from us."

"Except that tattoo," Mr. Keeley added. He showed a hint of a smile, as if he admired Logan's little rebellion.

"Yes, there was that." Mrs. Keeley narrowed her eyes at him, and when she looked back at me, some of that hostility remained. "Can you tell us anything? How does he spend his time? Where does he go? Is he—" She dropped one of her gloves. "Oh."

Mr. Keeley grunted as he tried to bend over to get the glove without smacking her with the umbrella.

"I got it." Mickey stepped around the end of the grave and picked up the glove.

Instead of taking it from him, Mrs. Keeley grasped Mickey's arm and tucked him close to her side. He winced at the grip on his biceps.

"This one's muter than a mime," she said with a nervous laugh. "I expect he'll be joining a monastery soon and make his vow of silence official."

Mickey's mouth drew into a tight straight line, as if to prove her point.

"Aura," she said, "is Logan searching for peace?"

"Um . . . I don't know," was my brilliant response.

"How can we help him find it? Besides the trial, I mean. It rips us apart to think of Logan in this purgatory."

I wanted to scream at Mr. and Mrs. Keeley to drop the case, but at the same time I was relieved they were speaking to me again. "I'm sure he doesn't want to upset you."

"He never wanted to upset anyone," Siobhan murmured. "That's why he always upset everyone."

Dylan snorted again, louder.

"What?" his sister snapped at him. "You think I'm full of it?"

"No, I just hate when you talk about him like he's gone."

"He *is* gone!" Siobhan said with a snarl. "To us he's gone. He's dead, Dylan. Logan's dead." She spat out the last word, then covered her mouth. "Damn it."

Mrs. Keeley moaned as she pressed her face against her husband's shoulder. I felt Gina's hand on my back and leaned against it to steady myself.

Dylan kicked a clump of grass into the side of the headstone. "This rain bites. I'm going back to the car." He stalked off.

Released from his mother's hold, Mickey sank to a crouch. He picked up a clod of mud from the gravesite and crumbled it in his fingers, muttering words I couldn't hear. Siobhan stifled her sobs with her cashmere scarf.

I looked across the soggy cemetery for Logan's light. I waited to hear his voice, complaining about the inscription or claiming he'd wanted black marble, or a carved granite guitar.

But he wasn't here. Maybe he was starting to understand that these things weren't for him. The funeral and the headstone were for those he'd left behind—his parents and Mickey and Siobhan.

Dylan and I were somewhere in the middle, alive but connected to the dead, left behind but not abandoned. These things did nothing but mock our memories of Logan.

Because we didn't just remember him in living color. We remembered him last night, and the night before that, in violet.

Chapter Fifteen

I feel like a chauffeur." Megan glared in the rearview mirror at me and Logan.

"Would you rather we all sit up front?" he asked. "Then I could just hover between you guys on top of the gear shift. Or sit on your lap."

She stomped the brake pedal. "Asshole." I hoped she was referring to the tourist who'd just staggered across the street from one Fells Point waterfront bar to another. "Next time, Aura, you drive."

"My aunt always needs the car at night now."

"Working late on my case, remember?" Logan began to imitate the VH1 *Behind the Music* announcer. "Was it the tragic end to a sky-rocketing career—or was it just the beginning?"

"Stay tuned," I added, fluttering my fingers to signal the commercial break.

"Speaking of tragedy, I can't wait to see Dork Squad again, now that the bassist is out of a coma." He slapped the seat in a flourish that made no sound. "Remember the first time we saw them? Well, not really saw, because that shithole in Dundalk was too small and we had to stand on the sidewalk."

"I remember." It had been so humid that night, we could barely breathe. But we'd made out hard in the alleyway near the back door, our shirts shoved up to feel each other's skin. Tiny bits of dirt had stuck to my back, adhered with sweat, and fallen out on my floor that night when I undressed for bed. If the show had lasted two more songs, we would've done it right there, right then.

I looked out the window at the Fells Point crowds, remembering all the times Logan and I had nearly had sex. There was always something that kept any given opportunity from being just right—too cramped, too rushed, too lacking in condoms. And then when we finally had a comfortable place with plenty of time—my bed, two months ago—I'd chickened out. I'd let a little pain convince me something was wrong.

Because if we were really in love, I'd thought, shouldn't our first time be perfect? Planets aligning? Clouds sparkling? Comets exploding?

I'd been such an idiot. And Logan had died a virgin. For all I knew, so would I, because I couldn't imagine being with anyone else.

Okay, I could imagine it, and did, every time Zachary spoke my name. I imagined that tongue of his curling around more than a pair of syllables.

But I could also imagine the fallout, Logan's anger and sadness and jealousy, and knew it wouldn't be worth it. Not for a long time.

"Nelson's isn't a shithole," Megan told Logan. "Just because they sell Guinness in bottles instead of on tap."

"It's a shithole by default, for being in Dundalk."

She smacked the steering wheel. "God, Logan, you are such a princess. Ever since you guys moved out to the County, suddenly you're all picky about where we hang out."

I bent over to retie my shoelaces, hiding my smile. They used to have this same argument when Logan was alive. Hearing it again, hearing her speak of him in the present tense, made things feel normal.

"I'm just saying," Logan went on, "when you're a public figure, you gotta be careful where you're seen."

We both laughed at that. "Who's a public figure?" Megan asked. "You?"

"Yeah, me," he said. "Because of the band, and now because of this stupid lawsuit. Other people are constantly measuring our coolness. If you think that's bullshit, you're living in a dreamworld."

I have a boyfriend who's a ghost, I thought. *Of course I'm living in a dreamworld.*

"But if you're cool enough," I pointed out, "anywhere you go is automatically cool."

Logan considered this for a moment. "I don't think any of us are that cool. Yet." He looked out the front window, then leaned forward and pointed across Megan's face. "There's a spot. Pull in there."

"Fine. Stop shining on me." She put on her turn signal, but as she approached the street where he was pointing, she flicked it off and gunned the engine.

"What are you doing?" Logan said. "That was a perfect parking spot. Half a block from Faces."

"We're not going to Faces."

"But Dork Squad is playing."

"And you can go see them yourself. Cool part is, I don't even have to slow down for you to get out of the car."

I pushed on the back of the driver's seat. "Megan, come on."

"Aura, we're going to a new place in Canton. Jenna said it was totally beyond."

I couldn't remember ever going to that part of Baltimore with Logan. It was just a few blocks east, but until recently, it hadn't had any clubs we would've liked.

"I've never been there," Logan growled. "I've never even been past Chester Street."

She paused. "I know."

My throat tightened. "Megan, don't do this to me."

"I'm doing this *for* you." Just as we approached the intersection of Aliceanna and Chester, the light turned green. "Sorry, Logan."

"No!" he and I shouted.

The car sped forward, and he disappeared.

"Turn around!" Through the back windshield I saw Logan standing in the middle of the road, waving his arms. A white SUV bore down on him, not even slowing. "Stop!"

Before I could cover my eyes, the SUV zoomed through Logan's body.

"He didn't feel it." Megan's voice had softened. "He's fine."

"He's not fine!" I gripped her seat. "He's all alone."

"Please. Logan's never alone for long. He'll find a party if it—" She cut herself off. "Sorry."

"If it what?" I snapped. "If it kills him?"

"I said I'm sorry."

"This isn't funny."

"Do you see me laughing?" Megan accelerated, tossing me back against the seat.

"Pull over."

"No."

"I want to move to the front seat. I feel stupid sitting here by myself."

"Now you know how I feel." She turned onto a side street and eased the car to the curb next to a fire hydrant before putting on the flashers.

I unbuckled my seat belt and yanked the door handle, but it wouldn't go. "Unlock it."

"Just climb between the seats."

"Unlock the door, Megan! I'm not a little kid."

"Really?"

We sat there for a minute, maybe more. Megan retrieved an emery board from the storage space between the seats and started filing her nails. I stared at the house across the street, counting the fake bricks on its Formstone facade.

Finally Megan's stubbornness overcame mine. I squeezed between the two front seats and plopped into the passenger side. Then I snapped on my seat belt with an angry click. "You. Suck."

* * *

Friday was apparently Underage Night at the Black Weeds club, so I showed my real ID for a green hand stamp, which got me unlimited non-alcoholic drinks for a five-dollar cover charge. Megan had a flask of rum in her purse if the scene turned out to be tragic. The line outside was a promising length, though, and I didn't see anyone leaving as we entered.

We walked down a green-carpeted hallway illuminated by blinking teal, turquoise, and lavender ceiling lights. It looked like the Easter Bunny had projectile-vomited a Christmas tree.

"This place better not be glam," I said to Megan.

"Jenna said they were remodeling. Besides, Siobhan said Connor's the new bassist for this band Something Wicked."

I stopped. "Is that the real reason we're here?" I couldn't face seeing parts of the Keeley Brothers scattered all over the city.

"Not the only reason. But Siobhan has to get up early for the SATs tomorrow, so she wanted me to see if they're any good." Megan tugged on my arm. "Come on, let's give it a chance."

We went through the wide wooden door into the club, and I knew I was the one with no chance.

It was like any other indie/emo/punk club, trying too hard with the starkness. The walls were dull brown wood paneling, splashed with paper flowers straight out of a first-grade art class (but too perfect to have been made by real children). They might as well have been captioned, "Check out our irony!"

Logan would have loved it. I would have loved it, if he'd been here. If he'd been here, the thump of bass guitar and the crash of drums would have filled me with something other than knee-weakening, soul-ripping anguish.

Megan saw the look on my face and seized my hand. "Bar."

I followed, willing my feet not to stumble over what suddenly seemed like a very lumpy carpet.

"Two Cokes!" Megan shouted at the bartender, holding up our green-stamped hands. Then she plucked two red straws from the dispenser and bent one in half. "Short straw equals designated driver." She put them behind her back for a moment, then held them up in one fist.

I saw the long one sticking out from under her thumb. I pulled on the short one.

She didn't let go. "No, you need to drink more than I do tonight."

"The rum'll just make me cry."

Megan's face crumpled. "Aura, I'm so sorry. I thought coming here would get your mind off Logan."

"I don't want to get my mind off Logan."

"But you have to move on." She nodded to the bartender as he slid our sodas across the bar. I held her glass under the closest table while she unscrewed her flask and dumped the contents into the Coke. "You sure you don't want a sip?"

"It's no fun drinking without him. It's no fun listening to music without him."

"But when he was alive, we did those things on our own, and you had fun."

"You're not getting it." The song ended, and I paused while Megan briefly clapped and cheered. "How would you feel if Mickey became a ghost?" I asked her.

She gave a bitter laugh. "Like he's not already? I've seen him, seriously, six times since Logan died, including the viewing and the funeral. He's always got an excuse."

"He's in mourning."

"And I could comfort him. But he won't let me." She set down her drink. "Here's what he does. You're me, and I'm him, okay?"

"Huh?"

"Pretend! It's a dramatization." She pointed to her chest. "Try to hug and kiss me. Don't let go until I make you. Just be me."

I wrapped my arms around her neck, moving my mouth toward hers. She angled her face away so that my lips landed on the corner of her jaw. Her arms stayed limp at her side. I hugged harder. Megan finally gave me a quick, impatient back pat.

"Oh God." I let go of her quickly and stepped away. "A back pat?"

"That's when I get close enough to hug him in the first place." She picked up her drink. "Usually he shifts out of the way too fast."

I was speechless. What cave had I been living in, not to realize how much Logan's death had screwed up everyone else?

Megan took a short sip. "We haven't even had a real kiss since Logan died. With tongue, I mean."

The band had paused while the lead singer told a story about the girl he'd written the next song for, so I kept my voice low and private.

"I'm sorry," I said to Megan. "Why didn't you tell me you guys were having problems?"

"It seemed mean to complain about Mickey to you. At least he's still alive."

"Yeah, but—" I stopped myself from pointing out that at the moment, Logan and I were a happier couple than Megan and Mickey.

"That guy behind you is checking us out."

A tall, skinny boy with swooping black hair was standing next to a pillar, about twenty feet from us. When he saw us noticing him, he stepped back as if to hide behind the pillar.

"He's totally your type," I told Megan. "Go talk to him."

"I can't."

I poked her arm. "You don't have to spawn his children. Just talk. Or don't talk. Dance."

"What about you?"

"I don't feel like dancing."

Megan fidgeted with the ragged side seam of her black cami. "Then what are you going to do?"

I saw a side room with a small arcade. "Play games."

"Okay." Taking a deep breath, she handed me her drink. "Here, I'll drive home. I always puke when I drink and dance, anyway."

I watched her approach the boy, who turned out to be really cute when he smiled. He must have given her a good opening line, because she laughed and put a hand to her cheek like she did when she blushed. It was good to see her really smile again.

The band started a new song, and Megan led the guy to the floor near the stage. I turned away, since I didn't want to see Connor playing for some other singer not nearly as talented as Logan. Instead I carried both glasses to the darkened back corner of the bar area. A couple wearing Johns Hopkins lacrosse shirts popped up from a small table and went off to dance.

Score. I sat at their empty table and placed one of the glasses in front of the other chair to purposely make it look like I was waiting for someone to return any second. That way no one would talk to me.

"Hi."

I sighed. No one *alive* would talk to me.

A violet boy stood next to my table. He was maybe two years younger than me and wore a vintage Cure T-shirt, the *Disintegration* one that a lot of emo boys like.

"Hi," I said.

"Cool." He gave a giant ghostly grin. "Most girls pretend they can't see me."

I tried not to grimace. I had a feeling girls had blown him off when he was alive, too.

"Can I sit down?" he asked.

"Without a real ass? Probably not, but go for it."

He laughed as he sank into the chair, which wasn't even pulled out. "You're Aura, right?"

I froze in the middle of a sip. "How do you know my name?" It wasn't like he could've heard it—or heard anything—from another ghost.

"I was reading about you online before I died. You help people pass on, right?"

I relaxed a little, glad he wasn't referring to my alleged role in Logan's death. "Not directly. I just translate for ghosts at my job." I switched my phone to the calendar function. "If you need help, we could make an appointment." Whatever it took for him to go away before people saw me talking to a dead freshman.

The ghost's eyes bugged out. "That'd be awesome!"

"Let's figure out where we can meet closer to my aunt's office so she can hear your story. Have you ever been to—"

"Wait." He looked confused. "Can't it just be you?"

"Huh?" I put down my phone.

"Okay." The boy placed his hands on the table. "The thing is . . . I died before I got to see real live tits. Not just on the Internet." He hurried to add, "I wouldn't touch you or nothing. Obviously. But even if I could, I wouldn't do that to you." He looked at his hands as he dropped them into his lap. "I just want to see."

My mouth had frozen in an O. I couldn't throw my drink in his face, or slap him, or knee him in the nuts. I couldn't lose him without running to the bathroom, and I was not about to leave this choice table and spend the rest of the evening leaning against the wall.

"You want me to flash you," I said.

He nodded vigorously, like I'd asked if he wanted fries with that.

"And then you'll pass on."

"That's all I want. So, yeah."

I could almost believe that a fourteen-year-old boy could find deep spiritual peace from a pair of real boobs.

"What's your name?" I asked him.

"Jake. Sorry, I should've said that before."

"How did you die?"

He frowned. "What's that got to do with it?"

"Just tell me."

"My stepfather ran over me with his car."

I gaped at him. "You're kidding."

"I was standing in the garage when he pulled in. He told my mom he meant to hit the brake."

"Do you think that's the truth?"

"I don't know. He didn't look real surprised at the time."

"Maybe that's why you're a ghost. You need justice."

Ex-Jake seemed to ponder this for several seconds, then shook his head. "Nah. I really just want to see some tits."

I groaned and put my face in my hands. "Go. Away."

When I peeked through my fingers, the boy had disappeared. But what I did see was even worse.

Three tables over, Zachary was sliding into a large, semicircular booth with Becca Goldman. She crowded close to him, first flipping her dark brown hair over her shoulder, then twirling a strand around her finger.

I was now willing to give up my table. I grabbed my glass and stood up, turning to flee before he saw me. Unfortunately, I crashed into someone solid.

"Oh!"

My lifelong neighbor and former friend Rachel Howard stood with her arms out, her (thankfully) brown Wilco T-shirt soaked in rum and Coke.

"Sorry," was all I could say. "I gotta go."

"No." She touched my arm. "*I'm* sorry. That's what I came over to tell you." Rachel let go of my sleeve and sat down, her eyes pleading with me.

I took my seat again. "Sorry for what?"

"I was such a crappy so-called friend after Logan died. I didn't know what to say, so I didn't say anything." Rachel hunched her shoulders. "My sister, she works at the hospice over at Sinai. She said that when someone's grieving, saying nothing is even worse than saying the wrong thing." She clutched her hands together on the table. "Can you forgive me?"

"Of course." I sopped up the puddle of condensation with the sleeve of my hoodie. "The whole thing is too bizarre for anyone to deal with."

"That's no excuse."

"Forget it."

"Thank you." She lifted the wet part of her shirt to her nose. "You have rum?"

"Megan has it. She's dancing." I folded the paper coaster into a half circle. "Are you here with Becca and Zachary?"

"Yeah, and Jenna and Christopher." She leaned in. "It's not what Becca's making it look like. We're here as a group. No one's hooking up."

I shrugged. "I don't care. We're just friends."

"Riiight." Rachel slurped the last of her soda, then wiped her dark, sweat-damp bangs out of her eyes. "If you wanted Zach, all you'd have to do is this." She curled her index finger. "No wait, this." She did the same gesture with her pinky. "And it's not like he'll be here forever. He's going back to Hotland in June."

"It's complicated. Logan's still around."

"I know. My little brother's seen him in the neighborhood, near his old house." She picked up her empty glass as she stood. "I'm going back over there so Zach can come talk to you without leaving Becca alone. He's so polite. Must be a British thing."

"Don't let him hear you call him British," I called after her.

Rachel slid into their booth, and Zachary waved at me. But when Becca's hand went under the table into his lap, I cut short my answering wave. Far be it from me to keep my "friend" from getting some tonight.

Just then Megan stomped up, tears streaming down her face. "You're right. I suck!"

"What happened?"

She dropped into the chair. "He kissed me."

"Who?"

"Eric, that guy I was dancing with. We were slamming, totally in sync, and it just happened."

"What'd you do?"

"I kissed him back. A lot. I can't believe I did that." She slumped to rest her chin on her fist. "I know Mickey needs me, even though he doesn't show it. But I wanted to feel alive. Everywhere else, I'm surrounded by dead people, or living people obsessed with dead people." She put a hand over her mouth. "Sorry, I don't mean you."

"Yes, you do, but don't be sorry. And don't worry, I won't tell Mickey about Eric."

"Thanks, but we were right in front of Connor. He'll tell Siobhan and then she'll tell Mickey." Megan sniffled as she pulled out her phone. "I better tell him myself. His friends could be here, texting him right this second." Her thumb hovered over the keypad. "What should I say?"

"How about, 'I just kissed a guy at Black Weeds because you've been ignoring me. P.S. I love you.'"

While she texted rapidly, I wondered what Logan would do in Mickey's place. As a ghost he would probably freak, seeing it as a sign I was moving on without him. When he was alive . . . well, I couldn't imagine, because Logan never would have shut me out in the first place. He wasn't the broody type.

Megan laid the phone on the table. "One way or another, things'll change now."

I rattled the ice in the bottom of my empty glass. "So this guy was a good kisser?"

"Beyond good. Especially for a first time."

I tried to remember my first kiss with Logan. But my memory could only conjure up that last cold, numb kiss at his bedroom doorway.

I forced myself back to the present. "Something Wicked sounds awesome," I told Megan. "The drummer is amazing."

"You know who it is, right?"

"No, I can't see the stage from here."

"It's Brian. Eric said the band needed a sub, and I guess Connor got Brian in."

Great, I thought. *Someone else who's moved on.*

The song ended. Becca stood on the seat of their booth, the hem of her black spandex microskirt above Zachary's eye line. She cheered and whistled as she hopped up and down.

Then Becca "accidentally" slipped, falling against Zachary's shoulder so he had to catch her. Laughing, she slid down against his body, ending up in his lap, in a graceful move that would've looked goofy if anyone else had tried it.

Megan jabbed her thumb over her shoulder. "Aura, you have got to do something there. How long do you expect Zachary to ignore the 'Screw Me' sign on Becca's forehead?"

"As long as he wants."

She picked up her phone and stared at the empty screen. "You should ask him to dance."

The thought made me queasy. "If he said no, I'd look like a loser. If he said yes, Becca would look like a loser, and Monday morning I'd get a world-record-size bitch-slap."

"Whatever." Megan's phone buzzed in her hand. "Mickey!" She tapped the screen, then squeaked. She turned the phone so I could see: COME OVER HERE. PS I LOVE YOU MORE.

"Doesn't he have the SATs tomorrow too?"

"Yeah, and he's probably really stressed." She gave me a wicked grin. "I can help with that."

Relieved to have an excuse to leave, I asked, "Drop me off at home on your way?"

"We can stay until the set's over. I don't want to ruin your night."

I made for the door before she could stop me. "Too late."

Logan was sitting on my bed when I got home.

I shut the door softly and went to him, brushing my hand through his in our new routine greeting. "I'm so sorry for leaving you."

"It wasn't your fault. And Dork Squad was better than ever. Lionel kicked ass."

So I'd spent all night feeling guilty for nothing. "Who?"

"The bass player, the one who was in that motorcycle accident? He had this one solo where he was just wailing." Logan held his hands in a perfect mime, his fingers slapping the thick strings of an invisible bass. "*Bow-didda-bow-didda-bow-bow.* But he had to be kinda propped against the speaker for the last couple songs, and they cut the set short." He shifted to "his" side of the bed and stretched out his legs. "Where'd you go?"

"Black Weeds. You would've liked it." I decided not to mention that two-fifths of the Keeley Brothers were in the band. "It wasn't the same without you."

Logan was quiet for several seconds. "I'm ready to tell you my plan now."

My heartbeat stumbled. I slipped off my shoes, then scooted up the bed to sit beside him.

He stared at his hand lying next to mine. "Promise you won't cry?"

"I promise I *will* cry."

His smile was sad, crinkling the corner of just one eye. "You know I love you."

I nodded, not trusting myself to speak.

"And that's why I have to leave," he said.

"No." I still couldn't imagine a world without him.

"I can't get on that stand and tell everyone what happened the night I died. I can't put you through that." Logan bowed his head. "So I'm going to pass on."

I gulped a rising clump of tears so I could push out one word. "When?"

"Before the trial. I'd lie on the stand if I could, to protect you. I'd tell them I took the cocaine for the thrill of it. God knows I've done enough stupid things for that reason. Remember when I broke my arm skateboarding, trying to ollie that double set of stairs by the library?" He rubbed the spot below his elbow where the bone had pierced the skin. "But I can't lie. And I can't run away. They've already tagged me with that subpoena thing, so if I don't show up, the DMP will track me down."

I hated the thought of Logan being "tagged" like a dog. On a judge's orders, the unique "vibration signature" of each ghost could be used to summon them, but only for specific times and places. The DMP didn't track Logan's every move—that would be illegal and expensive—but if they thought he wouldn't show up in court, they'd detain him until after the trial.

My chest grew tight, trapping the urge to utter his only alternative: turning shade. It would change his signature and free him from the reach of the DMP, but he would be forever lost to me in the worst way.

"I'm not ashamed to testify," I told him. "I don't care what people think."

"That's bullshit, and you know it."

"Don't you dare do this just for me."

"I'm not. Mostly for you, but—" He formed a fist as his voice roughened. "I wanted so much in life. I wanted to play music, connect with people. Now I can't hold a guitar, and most people can't even see me, much less hear me."

"You can still sing. And as time goes on, more people will be able to see and hear you. The A and R reps at your show were what, twenty-two, twenty-three? In six or seven years, post-Shifters will have those jobs."

What was I saying? Did I really want Logan to stick around that long?

"I can't wait six years," Logan said. "I can't wait six weeks." He curved his hand over mine in our facsimile of touch. "I have to let you go, so that one of us can live."

"I feel alive with you."

"It's not fair. You're living like a nun. I can't kiss you. I can't touch" you." His whisper filled with pain. "God, I want to touch you so bad. Everywhere, like before. I want to make you feel like I used to."

I fingered the zipper of my hoodie. "Maybe you still can." My pulse pounded in my ears. "Tell me what you'd do."

He sucked in a breath, which sounded real enough to make me ache. Logan reached out, and his hand guided mine to draw down the zipper, revealing the black crop top I once loved to dance in. The cool night air made goose bumps on the bare skin of my belly, illuminated by his violet glow.

"Take these off." His palm moved to the top of my jeans. "I want to see all of you."

I followed his lead, until my clothes were in a pile on the floor, and I lay naked on top of the covers. I wasn't cold anymore.

Logan placed his hand over mine again. "Shut your eyes."

He spoke to me, low and breathless, describing how he would touch me. With my eyes closed and my memories open, I could almost feel his hands and mouth on my skin.

It was only my own fingers circling, stroking, exploring. We didn't move together in a quickening rhythm. He couldn't feel my rising tension or its explosive release.

But with Logan's voice in my ear, we could pretend.

Chapter Sixteen

Despite an ever-deepening state of sleep deprivation, I managed to make it through the next three weeks without failing tests or forgetting to buy Christmas presents. As if watching an actor onstage, I witnessed myself go through the motions and marveled at my ability to maintain absolute normalcy.

But it turned out, I was only fooling myself.

On the last day of school before winter break, I sat in world history class, staring through the Spread of the Black Plague map at the front of the room, when Brian came in just as the bell rang. He hurried for his desk, walking with his head down and his jacket collar turned up.

As he passed me, Logan's former friend and drummer angled his face away, but not before I saw the bruise forming under his left eye.

Near the window, Zachary was watching the season's first snow flurry. He tapped his pen against his textbook in an absentminded rhythm, which drew my attention to his bandaged right hand.

As I gathered up my books after class, Zachary slid behind the desk next to me. "I have a request you can't refuse."

I frowned, wondering if it was supposed to be a *Godfather* reference. "You mean an *offer* I can't refuse?"

"I promised no Italian jokes, remember? Tomorrow's my birthday, and I want to go downtown."

"Why do you need me for that?"

"I don't need you. I want you." After a blink, he added, "To take me to the Inner Harbor. You promised."

"No, I didn't."

"Well, not out loud. Look, I'll pay for everything, in exchange for a tour."

I tried to think of an excuse other than the truth—I wanted to spend my birthday with my dead boyfriend. "My aunt's taking me out to dinner tomorrow night."

"Special occasion?"

I still hadn't told him that we shared a birthday, and nothing in his eyes said he knew. "Early Christmas."

"We'll go during the day, then."

"We will, huh?" I slapped down my pen. "Maybe I don't want to be told how I'm spending my first day of break. Maybe I don't want to be pushed."

"Aura." He leaned in close, his face serious now. "You need pushing, and it looks like most everyone else has given up." He touched my elbow. "You're turning into a ghost."

I jerked away, my face burning. "I don't need your pity." I pointed to his bandaged hand. "Or your protection."

"Fine." Zachary snatched up his bag. "Forget it. Happy Christmas." He worked his way between the seats toward the classroom door.

His holiday greeting reminded me of my mother's Ireland journal—and her seize-the-day attitude. If she were here, would she let me turn down a real live hot guy who actually seemed to care about me?

"Wait."

I'd spoken softly, but Zachary stopped and turned.

"I never said no."

December 21 was not kidding about being the first day of winter. I bundled up like a kid on a snow day, my hat and hood flattening my hair in a necessary sacrifice to stay warm. It was only twenty degrees in the sun—not that Baltimore has much sun in December.

Zachary was his usual flirty self, though a little distracted. When our light-rail train stopped at each station, he'd get quiet, examining every person entering and leaving. When we had lunch, he chose the chair with his back to the wall, without even asking which seat I wanted. When we went up to the Trade Center observation deck, his eyes scanned the sidewalks below us instead of looking out into the bay or across the city.

I wondered if he was worried we'd run into Becca Goldman. They'd been eating lunch together every Friday (not that I noticed—much), and Megan had heard that last week he'd gone to one of Becca's exclusive parties. If my aunt ever heard the stories that came out of those parties, she'd order me a custom-built chastity belt, on the microscopically slim chance I was ever invited.

Or maybe Zachary was trying reverse psychology—drawing me out by being erratically aloof. Like most reverse psychology, it worked.

"Let's go see Santa," I told him as we passed Kris Kringle's pavilion draped in white lights and fake holly. "It'll be warm in there. And you can vouch for me."

"Huh?" he asked, dragging his attention from the crowd near the waterfront.

"You can tell him if I've been naughty or nice."

This got a smile. "A wee bit of both, I think."

"Which one more?" Hands in my pockets, I bumped him with my shoulder.

Zachary threaded his arm through mine and leaned close. "I think it would be nice if you'd let yourself be naughty."

I shivered, and not from the cold. He'd spoken like we weren't in the middle of a crowd. He'd spoken like we were alone, and definitely not wearing four layers of clothing.

Once I found my breath, I said, "Now I know which list you're on."

"No, you don't know." He stopped. "You don't know me at all."

His expression was so serious and intense, I thought for sure he was going to kiss me. I stepped back as I realized Logan had been to the Inner Harbor a hundred times—he could be watching us right now, hidden by sunlight.

"But I'm going to change that," Zachary said. "Right now."

I followed his gaze across the wide brick sidewalk, to the little hut on the waterfront.

"Perfect," he whispered.

"Paddleboats? Paddleboats are perfect?"

"They are." He headed down the ramp toward the tiny vessels— few of which, not surprisingly, were deployed.

"Are you crazy?" I ran to catch up. "It's freezing. It'll be even colder out there." I pointed to the harbor's murky water, which the wind was rippling into choppy gray waves.

"But it's my birthday," he said as he kept walking.

I'd had enough. We'd eaten crabs (I hate seafood), gone up in the Trade Center (I hate heights), and visited the National Aquarium (did I mention I hate seafood?)—all because Zachary kept playing the birthday card.

"Damn it," I yelled after him. "It's my birthday too!"

"I know."

I stopped short. I swear the sky darkened at that exact moment. A cloud passed over the low-hanging sun, blotting out the weak light.

Zachary approached the small white shed where an old man huddled behind a smudged window.

The man slid up the window's bottom section. "Nice day for paddlin'," he said with an ironic grin. "What'll it be?"

Zachary read the sign as he drew out his wallet. "What's a Chessie?"

"That's Chessie the sea monster. Named after the Chesapeake Bay."

Zachary examined the group of boats shaped like purple and green dragons. "We'll take a regular, without the monster. Please." He held out a ten-dollar bill.

The man squinted at him and shook his head. "Too tall. You'll need a Chessie."

"What?" Zachary looked scandalized.

"With the regular paddleboats, your knees'll be at your ears the whole time."

"I'm no' driving a grotesque purple rip-off of the Loch Ness—"

"And when you get out, it'll feel like someone walked a mile wearing your balls for sandals."

Zachary stared at him. "Aye. Chessie it is, then." He crammed an extra five bucks into the man's palm, then made what he must have thought was a subtle adjustment of his own jeans.

We put on incredibly attractive orange lifejackets and paddled away from the dock. There was no steering wheel—turning the boat required paddling faster on one side than the other. Zachary was overly eager, so we went in a circle until he slowed down to my speed.

The exertion warmed me, and by the time we were out in the harbor, I was sweating inside my wool coat.

"That's far enough," he said.

I collapsed in my seat, panting. The garish purple head of the dragon—or sea monster, or whatever—smirked down at me. "Far enough for what?"

"For them not to hear." Zachary reached under his life vest and unzipped his jacket.

"Who?"

"The DMP. They're watching us. They've been watching you for a long time."

My sweat turned cold. "Why? And wait—how do you know?"

"My dad's in the MI-X, the DMP's UK counterpart. That's why we're here in the States."

"To find me?"

"No. Yes. Uh, partly." Zachary shook his head. "I'll start from the beginning, but in case they're watching us, we can't look like we're arguing." He took my hand, and I could feel his warmth through my glove. "Just stay calm. I swear I'll tell you everything I know."

I breathed deeply, unsure of which was making my head spin more, his touch or his words.

No. Definitely his words.

"I told you when we met," he said, "that I was born a minute before the Shift, seventeen years ago this morning. And you probably know you were born a minute after. But what you don't know is that we were the only ones."

"The only ones what?"

"Every minute that goes by on this planet, an average of four hundred babies are born. During my minute, and yours? Only one. Us."

The chill of dread chased away the warmth of his touch. "What happened to the other babies? Did they die?"

"There weren't any. I think they just—" He waved his hand. "Waited. Or hurried. In any case, they weren't born when we were."

"Why not?"

"I don't know. But it can't be a coincidence."

I put a hand to my tightening throat. I was the First. I always knew it was possible. No—with all the mystery surrounding my birth, it was more than possible. Did that mean I'd made it happen?

"How do you know for sure?" I asked Zachary. "Your dad told you?"

"Right."

I wondered who was watching us from the crowded shoreline. I had a mad desire to paddle as far as this sea monster would take us. "Who else knows?"

"Anyone who needs to. People high up in the agencies."

"How high is your dad?"

"It's classified."

I looked away, at the pale amber sunlight reflected in the glass facade of the aquarium.

Okay. Collecting thoughts. I'm the First, Zach's the Last, his dad is a secret agent, and my own government has been watching me since, well, forever.

I rewound my thoughts past the holy-crap-world-shattering implications, back to the part about Spy Dad. My stomach began a slow, heavy sink.

All this time, Zachary's interest in me could have been totally fake. My mind skimmed through all of our "moments"—him declaring me bonnie when I looked like ass, the mug exchange at our first meeting with Eowyn, the near kiss after our impromptu Scottish lesson. Were *any* of them real?

I pulled my hand out of his. "Did your father make you hang out with me? Is this"—I gestured to the space between us—"some kind of spy mission?"

His eyes widened in horror. "No! No. Aura, listen to me."

I really didn't want to. If it had been warmer, I'd have swum for shore. But I was trapped.

"To be honest, it started out that way," he said. "My dad asked me to keep an eye on you at school, but he didn't tell me to join your research project. That was my idea." Zachary lifted his hands as if to reach for me, then let them drop onto the knees of his blue jeans. "So was falling for you. My idea," he added quietly.

My mouth opened, instantly drying from the bitter wind and my rush of emotion. "Falling for me?"

"Come on, you're not blind." He tugged on the collars of his sweater and shirt as if suddenly warm. "As I was saying, my dad wanted me to tell him if the DMP approached you at school. He's spent the last two months negotiating with them."

"For what? My freedom? My life?" I was still reeling from the confession of his feelings. Discovering I was the subject of an international dialogue was putting me over the edge.

"For a lot of things. Let me explain." Zachary's breath made a cloud as he spoke into the frigid air. "The group that's now the MI-X used to be this paranormal brotherhood that went back centuries. They know how to handle ghosts without hurting them."

"Can they teach the DMP those tricks?"

"They're trying. But the DMP was started by some of the most paranoid people in U.S. military and intelligence. They think that everything different is dangerous."

I massaged my temples, fending off a headache. "How can I even trust what you say? You know so much about me, but I don't know anything about you."

"That's no' true." He leaned forward, his green eyes reflecting the gray water behind me. "I just told you my second-deepest secret, that I'm the absolutely last person born pre-Shift. No one else knows that, except my parents."

"And probably half of MI-X, and the DMP, too. Big deal."

He made a frustrated noise and turned to face the front of the paddleboat. "I don't blame you for not trusting me. I've kept so many secrets for so long, it's a habit." His face finally dropped the mask of confidence. "But the way I feel about you, I'd put it all in your hands."

"All what?"

"All my secrets, even the one my dad doesn't know."

"You can tell me." I hooked my finger inside his elbow. "You can trust me."

"If I told you, you wouldn't believe." Zachary lifted his head to look across the harbor, and suddenly his gaze sharpened. "But I could show you."

Chapter Seventeen

As we walked up the gangplank of the USS *Constellation*, I kept a close eye on the descending sun. Historical landmarks like this nineteenth-century battleship were always haunted by the oldest, craziest ghosts.

But Zachary had insisted, and my curiosity ordered me to follow him.

Once onboard, though, he turned into a complete guy, distracted by the sails and the cannons and the pole thingies. While he examined every gadget and read every plaque, I stood at the chest-high railing of the wooden deck and kept vigil over the Inner Harbor.

The Christmas crowds now looked sinister. How many of the shoppers were secret DMP agents? Did my aunt know they'd been watching me? Did it have something to do with my mom and dad? How could it not, if it was about my birth?

As always, it was easy to pick out the post-Shifters by the colors they wore. I thought about the future, when almost everyone would wear red. The color of life would become the color of sameness, of disconnection. I looked down at my black coat and sapphire blue sweater and wondered how long I could hold out.

Zachary called my name from the top of the staircase leading down into the ship.

I thought of all the ghosts I'd seen belowdecks during our elementary school field trip. "You go ahead. I'll wait up here."

"It'll be okay, I promise."

I followed him reluctantly down the short, steep stairway.

The first level was a large open space with cannons lining the outer edge, each pointing out a large square porthole. Light shone through these openings, but the room was dark enough that I would've seen any ghosts. During my last visit, this room had been full of them, wandering among the cannons, most dressed in their navy uniforms.

I tried to remember if Logan had gone on that field trip, and wondered why he hadn't spoken to me once today. My phone was full of voice mail and text messages from Megan and my other friends wishing me a happy birthday, but no word from my supposed boyfriend? I didn't know whether to feel hurt or worried, so I chose both, imagining him having fun without me in one of the Keeleys' vacation spots, or chased by the Obsidians after deciding that shading was the new extreme sport.

"Look." Zachary pointed to the low ceiling, where long poles were suspended on racks above each cannon. "They used those to load the gunpowder."

"Uh-huh." A sign near the staircase said the barracks were on the level below. That seemed slightly more interesting than a bunch of old guns. Plus, the wide-open windows here made it almost as cold as outside.

"I'm going down," I told Zachary.

"I'll be along." He kept reading the wood-framed plaque on the wall.

I gripped the railing to descend, wondering when Zachary would reveal his secret. His obsession with facts and details came in handy for our research project, but not so much on a date (if that's what this was).

The level below was warmer, tighter, and darker. Immediately a violet man appeared beside me, dressed in a captain's uniform, spine straight as if awaiting inspection by the admiral.

"Excuse me, miss," the ghost said, "I seem to have misplaced my pipe."

I pivoted and headed for the more brightly lit bow (or maybe it was the stern), trying not to look like I was running away.

The ex-captain followed. "Just one smoke and I'll move on. I've made that vow and I intend to keep it."

Tugging off my hat and gloves, I entered a room at the end of the ship, lined with sleeping berths that opened onto a common area. The white doors listed the ranks of the sailors.

A middle-aged couple stood at the far end, twenty feet away. The woman held up an unfolded brochure so the man with her could read the map over her shoulder.

"This was where the officers slept," she said. "The enlisted used those hammocks in that other room."

Her companion scoffed. "Some things never change. When I was on that carrier, the officers had their own dining room, too."

"Please help," the captain's ghost said behind me. "Perhaps you could write a letter on my behalf."

I bit back a rude response. He could follow me anywhere. This was his ship. He'd probably been over every inch of it a thousand times during his life.

The lanterns were brighter here, but I could still see a long violet form on a bed in the third lieutenant's berth.

The couple passed through the ex-captain on their way out.

"I don't wish to frighten you." The ghost's pale beard bobbed as he spoke to me. "But you remind me of my daughter."

I'd heard that line a thousand times.

"I don't have a pipe," I told him, "and even if I did, you couldn't hold it. You're wasting your time wishing for something you can't have."

"But is that not human nature?"

The man in the third lieutenant's berth sat up. God, not two at once. My fists balled in anger at Zachary. I didn't want to come aboard this stupid ship in the first place.

The ex-lieutenant charged out of his chamber. "She sent me a letter! We were supposed to be married, but she found someone else. Tell her I forgive her."

"She's dead by now," I told him. "You have to move on."

"They never paid my family," came a deep voice from my left, another ghost.

I backed up against the far wall. "Please stop."

A chorus grew around me—five, six, seven men yanked from their lives, spewing their grudges. Though they couldn't hear each other, they seemed to be shouting to be heard over the cacophony.

"Leave me alone," I whispered, squeezing my eyes shut.

"Just one pipe, that's all I ask."

"That three hundred dollars would have paid the rent for a year."

"Why couldn't she wait for me?"

"Stop it." I covered my ears, but the voices grew louder.

"No one understands."

"No one listens."

"No one cares."

"YOU TASTE WRONG!!"

My eyes slammed open at the new sound. "No . . . ," I whimpered.

The shade shot toward me, streaking through the other ghosts in a quaking, purple-black haze.

"GET OFF OUR WORLD!" Its voice crackled and screeched like a smashed-up electric guitar. "YOU DON'T BELONG HERE!"

My stomach pitched as if the boat had capsized. My head pounded so hard, I couldn't even scream. I sank against the wall, arms over my face. The shade hovered above me, its shrieks piercing like giant claws.

"I SEE WHAT YOU ARE!"

I collapsed onto my stomach and tried to crawl away across the worn wooden floor. In the background, the ghosts still shouted their pleas.

Then, silence.

I waited for a long moment, shoulders braced against another attack. When I heard footsteps, I opened my eyes but kept my face to the floor. No human outside of the Obsidian Corps could save me from this torment.

"Aura."

I turned to see Zachary standing alone in the cabin's dark doorway. The ghosts had disappeared. The shade was gone.

In a near whisper, he said, "Now you know."

My mind flashed back to Logan's sudden fade the day I'd picked up Zachary for our first star-mapping mission, and how that night I hadn't seen any ghosts in the food court.

I couldn't remember when I'd ever seen a ghost in the presence of Zachary. Logan's *Mr. Red*.

"You did this."

"I think so." Zachary hurried to kneel beside me. "But I don't know how."

"And you've never told anyone?"

"Of course not." He steadied me as I sat up.

I pressed my hands against my temples, reminding my brain which way was up. "If you can't see ghosts, how do you know you can get rid of them?"

"One of my—someone I knew back home. Younger than I am, obviously. They figured it out, and we tested it."

"How could no one else know?"

"I try to stay out of dark places unless they're crowded, or wide open like our field. Or I avoid younger people." Zachary looked over his shoulder at the doorway. "No one can ever know."

"Not even your dad?"

"Especially not him. Can you imagine, the last person born

pre-Shift turns out to be a walking BlackBox? I'd spend the rest of my life in a laboratory."

Even now my mind was denying it—he had the one power I'd always longed for (before Logan died, at least). I broke away from him. "Stay in this room until I call you."

I hurried out of the officers' quarters and into the enlisted men's barracks, a wide, dark space empty of tourists. Hammocks hung from the ceiling, resembling empty body bags. The only light came from a few dim yellow bulbs, and from small portholes spaced along the outer wall.

And from the ghosts themselves. Dozens converged on me, blurring in one giant violet mass. From a distance, the shade began to scream.

I turned and called Zachary's name. The moment he ducked through the door of the officers' quarters, the ghosts vanished and the shade was silenced.

"Whoa," I breathed.

"It worked again, then?"

"It worked. Oh my God, that's amazing!" I bounced over to where he stood near the stairway, feeling light for the first time in months. "How do you do that? Can you teach me?"

"I don't do anything." He spread his arms. "I just am."

"Since when?" My mind raced with the implications.

"Forever, I think."

"Why?"

"I dunno," he said with a touch of amusement.

"What's your range? How close do you have to be to scare the ghosts?"

"Close enough for them to see me, I think. What are you doing?"

I froze, my hands against his stomach. What *was* I doing? I was patting him down like a rookie cop making her first arrest.

"Looking for obsidian?" The last word squeaked, but I didn't let go.

"No ghostproof vest, if that's what you mean." Zachary's voice lowered. "I've got nought on under here."

My fingers quivered against the wool of his dark green sweater. "Maybe it's part of you."

"The obsidian? That'd make me a bit inflexible."

One corner of his mouth twitched, and I stared at it, thinking about flexibility.

I inched my hands over his rib cage toward his sides, pinching a little to test that it was truly his flesh under the sweater. "To me you seem pretty, um, solid."

His eyelashes flickered in the low light, then he took my elbows and eased me away from him. "Don't you be playing with me, now. Not on my birthday."

"I'm not playing." I cut the distance between us back to zero. "And it's my birthday too."

The humor in Zachary's eyes faded, and he seemed to come to a decision, one that I had apparently already made.

He cupped my chin and whispered, "Then happy birthday to us."

I closed my eyes as Zachary leaned in to kiss me.

"Howard, it's almost dinnertime!"

The scolding female voice from above was followed by the thump of a man's dress shoes on the stairs beside us. I gave a silent curse as I pulled away from Zachary.

"Margie," the man said, "I paid my ten dollars, I want to see the whole ship. Now get down here."

"Be careful," said the woman, standing on the level above us. "Go very slow."

I looked up at Zachary, stifling a laugh. "Good advice."

"Bollocks." He took my hand, without gloves now, and led me over to one of the small portholes.

Margie came down the stairs, huffing her exasperation. Her shoe-laces carried jingle bells, which made me want to giggle. Or maybe my giddiness came from the feel of Zachary's body close behind me as I stood before the porthole. My hand tingled, enveloped in his, my skin sensitive from touching nothing but nothing for so many weeks.

The couple wandered around the large open area, examining the hammocks. Despite their bickering, they were holding hands too.

"They're so cute," I whispered.

"Mm." Zachary's thumb traced a circle in my palm. "They'd be even cuter if they buggered off right about now."

I laughed, tilting back against his chest. He took my other hand and slid both arms around me from behind. I rested there, savoring his sturdiness.

"Aura," he whispered into my hair. "You don't know how long I've wanted to do this."

I didn't want to guess. I only wanted to feel his solid body press against mine and hear him speak my name. "Can I ask you something important?"

"Anything."

"What's your favorite song?"

He hesitated. "Anything but that. Not now."

"You can tell me your deepest secret, but not your favorite song?"

"I can tell you my favorite song, just not now. Ask me something else."

I thought of another tactic. "Do you want to kiss me?"

"Easy one. Yes."

"Then tell me your favorite song."

He laughed softly in my ear. "That's your price, aye?"

"Aye."

"Hmm." His voice made his chest vibrate gently against my back. "Is that just the price to kiss your lips? What about other places?"

I turned my head to press my cheek against him, unable to speak, since that would've required breathing.

As the couple moved on, Zachary swept my hair over my left shoulder, baring my neck. His lips brushed the corner of my jaw, just below my ear. My knees turned to honey.

Zachary's arms suddenly tightened around me. "Uh-oh."

I opened my eyes. He pointed straight out the brass-rimmed porthole.

Beyond the smudgy glass, three DMP agents stood on the docks, their white uniforms gleaming in what was left of the afternoon sun. Weapons were holstered in wide black straps over their shoulders.

"What are they doing?" I whispered.

"Looking for someone." As the dumpers rushed up the *Constellation*'s gangplank, Zachary dragged me toward the stairs. "Looking for us."

"How do you know? Maybe they're looking for that shade."

"Regular dumpers don't handle shades, and those guns have real bullets. Come on, we can't get past them." He gestured for me to go down first. "We'll have to hide."

We climbed down to the lowest level, but the wide-open engine room offered no safe places. Our last option was the kitchen, off-limits for restoration.

Zachary stepped over the yellow KEEP OUT tape. "Perfect."

I followed him. A large wooden box stood at the far corner of the kitchen.

"Potato bin." He lifted the handle and leaned the open lid against the white wall. I placed my hands on his shoulders so he could lift me into the bin with minimal noise. Once inside, I scrunched my body over to make room. At its highest angle, the top of the bin barely cleared my skull.

Zachary joined me, then lowered the lid. We sat with our shoulders crammed together. The compartment smelled of dust and mildew.

Soon I heard the rap of hard-soled shoes above the kitchen's ceiling. The thought of facing real DMP agents made my knees shake. Gina had told me nightmare tales of people getting "dumped," detained for questioning. I didn't want to share one iota of what I knew—about myself, about my mom, about Zachary.

Then the floor vibrated from the impact of heavy feet. The dumpers had entered the kitchen. I suddenly had to pee really bad.

"Check every inch."

I almost jumped out of my skin when the deep voice barked the order.

"This is the last room," the man said.

I held back a shudder. There was no way we could've gotten out without passing them, and they knew it.

The agents split off, opening and closing squeaky compartment doors.

"Watch it!" the lead agent said. "If we break a piece of a historic landmark, I'll be up to my ass in paperwork."

The agents came closer. Zachary tensed beside me. Did he plan to fight his way out of this one?

Radio static squawked, and the lead agent cursed under his breath. "Reynolds." He paused. "You're kidding. Which way? . . . But we had reports that—yes, sir. We'll be right there." The radio chirped, then he shouted, "Move out! Now!"

A compartment slammed shut. One of the agents asked the leader, "What happened?"

"Command has confirmed that the subjects left the ship at sixteen-thirty. They've been spotted at the Hard Rock Cafe in the Power Plant building."

"But how did—"

"What's it matter? Just go!"

"Yes, sir."

In the distance the stairway creaked with the weight of the agents, and then all sound ceased but our breath.

We stayed frozen—literally. The ship wasn't heated, and we were sitting near the outer wall. A biting wind seeped through the hull and the tiny cracks of the bin.

Zachary's teeth chattered. So much for his rugged heritage.

When I couldn't feel my butt anymore, I squirmed and whispered,

"I think they're gone, but there could still be agents outside the ship."

Zachary grunted as he moved his legs. "Too bad I didn't find us better accommodation."

I rotated my ankles to wake my sleeping feet. Pins and needles pricked my calves.

"I figured they were watching us," he whispered, "but that was bleeding insane. They were armed."

"The DMP doesn't mess around. But what did we do to deserve that? You think they knew what you did upstairs, saving me from that shade? Maybe another post-Shifter was watching."

"There was no one else near our age on the whole level. But maybe the DMP has ways of detecting these things." Zachary shifted again, his leather jacket rustling. "If anyone ever finds out, my life as I know it is over."

"I promise I'll never tell."

"Don't promise that," he said in an ultraserious voice. "If they try to hurt you and the only way to protect yourself is to tell them what you know about me, then you tell them. Straight off, okay?"

"No."

"Promise me."

"No!"

"I will possess your heart."

Heat flared along the back of my neck. "What did you say?"

"My favorite song. 'I Will Possess Your Heart.'"

"By Death Cab for Cutie?"

He snorted. "No, the little-known T.I. hip-hop remix. Yes, Death Cab for Cutie."

I smiled at the cute way he said "cutie." "Really?"

"Why? What's wrong with it?"

"Nothing, but it doesn't seem to fit you. It's kind of a sad song."

"No, it's pure confident. It's not 'I want' or 'I need,' none of that crap." He slipped his hand over mine. "It's 'I will.'"

A nervous laugh bubbled up. "You will, huh?"

His fingers brushed my cheek, then slid into my hair. "I will."

Somehow, in the darkness, his lips found mine.

I should've been ready. We'd been dancing around each other for months, and we were, after all, in a situation of forced snuggling.

But my inexplicable surprise kinda made me blow into his mouth.

"Oh my God." I turned my face away in embarrassment. "I can't believe I just did that."

He laughed. "American girls are so kinky. And overrated."

"Hey." I grabbed his head with both hands and pulled him back to kiss me.

This time it worked. Holy Father with a flamethrower, did it ever work. We fit together like we'd been kissing for years in some parallel universe that had suddenly intersected with the one we were living in now.

After the exploding-comet impact, Zachary kissed me carefully, like every millimeter of my mouth deserved its own exploration. Like the bottom lip would've been jealous if the top lip had gotten more attention. And the tongue that had given me a thousand subliminal licks at the sound of his voice? It was mine now.

He cupped my shoulder blade and pulled me closer. I slid my hands to the back of his neck.

Wow. I'd forgotten how soft a guy's hair could be. Logan's usually had some kind of gel to make it spiky.

But remembering Logan made my gut clench in sudden longing. For weeks I'd wanted to kiss and touch him again, almost more than I'd wanted my next breath. And now, the memory of Logan and the reality of Zachary were tearing my heart in two.

My grip tightened with the force of my grief, pulling Zachary into a deeper kiss. A little noise came from the back of his throat, making his lips tremble against mine.

I let myself fall into the abyss of the kiss, let it swallow all thoughts of the past and future. I heard nothing but the rush of blood in my ears, felt nothing but the warmth of Zachary's mouth, and in the total darkness I saw nothing but the images in my mind. Images of touching, pressing, lying down.

Which explains why neither of us heard the footsteps.

The lid of the bin popped open. I jumped away from Zachary and shielded my eyes from the light. Fear jolted through me at the sight of the strange man in a dark suit and tie looming over us. I waited for him to pull out a weapon and point it at our heads.

Then Zachary let out a heavy sigh. "Hi, Dad."

Chapter Eighteen

Well." The man straightened up and crossed his arms. "Good to see you're maintaining absolute vigilance."

Zachary extracted his arm from behind my back. "Aura, this is my father, Ian Moore. Dad, this is—"

"I know who she is, son."

"I know you know who she is," Zachary said with a slight edge. "I'm just being thorough."

I smoothed my disheveled hair. "Nice to meet you." I didn't know what else to say after being caught making out by an international man of mystery.

"Likewise." He arched a gray and black eyebrow. "Perhaps you'd like to be gettin' out of there now."

"It's safe, then?" Zachary helped me to my feet.

"I took care of it at the directorate level." Ian offered an arm to steady me as I climbed out of the potato bin. "Spent a lifetime's worth of political capital on this one."

"Thanks." I brushed a cobweb off my sleeve, then checked my butt for dampness. "Does that mean we can leave?"

"It means we *must* leave. And then go somewhere private where no one will hear the screams when I kill you both." Ian strode toward the kitchen door.

"He's kidding." Zachary gestured for me to precede him. "I think."

We followed Ian up three levels, all of which were void of the living and dead, until we reached the *Constellation*'s top deck. It was also completely abandoned. Even the uniformed tour guides were gone.

They'd evacuated the entire ship on our account. Oops.

But what was the big deal? What could Zachary and I have done this afternoon to piss off such powerful people?

I had to trot down the gangplank to keep up with Ian's pace. We passed through the empty gift shop on our way out, and Ian glared when Zachary slowed down next to a display of pirate hats.

Outside, half a dozen police officers waited, holding back the ogling crowd. The officers nodded to Ian as he passed, as did another man, whose dark glasses and coat screamed federal agent. Sunglass Man pulled out a walkie-talkie, then hurried past Santa's pavilion toward the busy traffic of Pratt Street. We followed him.

As we approached the road, a black car with tinted windows pulled up to the curb. The car blocked the right lane's traffic, so a police officer stepped out and directed the angry drivers around it.

The unnamed agent opened both passenger-side doors. Ian stood at the front. "Get in."

I hesitated, reluctant to enter a car with strangers, even if they all had badges. Especially if they all had badges.

"It's safe." Zachary's voice held a touch of pleading as he put his hand on the back door. "Trust me."

"You first."

I followed Zachary into the car and sat behind his father. The sedan's black leather seats were seductively soft, like they wanted me to sink into them, close my eyes, and forget all my very sensible fears.

"Seat belts," Ian said crisply, then told the man behind the wheel, "Just drive, please."

"Where are we going?" I asked him.

"Nowhere." He rotated in his seat to face Zachary. "Now what the bloody hell were you thinking?"

Zachary looked sullen. "When?"

"Today! You know what's at stake here."

"No, I don't. You won't tell me." His voice was steady and cool, the opposite of his father's.

"I looked all over the city for you—"

"I left you a note—"

"—and then the DMP rings me, saying you're with her, of all people."

"Hey," I said. "What's wrong with—"

"Why didn't you answer my calls?" Ian asked Zachary.

"I didn't want to lie to you about who I was with." He lifted his chin. "*I* prefer honesty."

Ian's nostrils flared. "Son, hiding the truth is just the coward's way to lie."

Zachary's face twisted. He spat out something in Gaelic—at least, I thought it was Gaelic. Ian responded, and then they were off, yelling a barrage of indecipherable words that made my ears ring. To increase my disorientation, the car was speeding, bumping over potholes and forcing me to grab the door handle around turns.

It took me almost half a minute to realize that Ian and Zachary were speaking some form of English. Only then did I appreciate how much Zachary toned down his native Glasgow accent at school. Watching them go at it, I noticed they had the same strong, stubborn jaw and animated green eyes that darkened to a formidable glower in the heat of anger.

I tried to pick up any recognizable phrase so I could insert myself into the conversation.

Ian said something-something-something ". . . the two of you in public?"

I interrupted with, "Why can't we go out in public?"

"Because this is what happens." Ian jabbed his finger at the looming Power Plant entertainment complex, where a DMP van was parked outside. "The dumpers get suspicious."

"Suspicious of what?"

"I don't know," he blurted, his voice pitching higher. "I don't know what they think a couple of kids are capable of. But they see the First and the Last together—" He waved a hand beside his head. "The agents' wee minds start churning out conspiracy theories. It's no wonder, when you chose today of all days."

"It's our birthday," Zachary said.

"It's also the buggering solstice!" Ian coughed as he ran a hand through his thick salt-and-pepper hair. Then he faced forward and thumped his head on the headrest in frustration. "What am I going to do with you?"

I spoke up again. "You could start by telling us what's going on."

"What's going on is that I've spent months trying to convince the DMP that you're of no interest. That the fact that you're the First is an insignificant accident. Someone had to be first. Why no' you?"

I wondered if Ian believed that, if he thought he was pushing the truth or a lie. I wanted to believe it was a coincidence—it seemed self-centered to think my birth could have caused something as colossal as the Shift. But between my mystery dad and Mom's cryptic notes—not to mention Zachary's strange power—there were too many questions and not enough answers.

"And then you two go and call attention to yourselves like this," Ian continued. "Holding hands in a pedalo, for Christ's sake. They must have been frothing at the mouth at the thought of you two reproducing, wondering if you'd give birth to some kind of metaphysically enhanced creature or a bottomless black hole."

I gaped at him. *Reproducing? Giving birth?*

"Dad . . ." Zachary leaned his elbow on the window and covered his eyes. "Can you stop now, please?"

Yeesh. And I thought my aunt was embarrassing.

Thinking of Gina made me channel her suspicious nature. "Mr. Moore, why do you care what the DMP thinks of me? Why do I matter so much to you?"

"It's my job," he said, too quickly, still facing front. "And I want to keep the DMP as far from my son as possible."

I thought of everything Zachary and I had in common, the weirdness of our shared birthday—shared birth *hour*—and suddenly my fingers turned to ice. My mind spiraled out of control, all the missing pieces fitting together in one terrible possibility.

"Mr. Moore, is Zach my twin brother?"

"What?!" Zachary sputtered. "Good God, why would you think that?"

I counted off the reasons on my fingers. "My father's missing. So's your mother. We were born a minute apart. Now your dad is freaking out over us going on a date."

Zachary put a hand to his chest. "Dad, tell her it's no' true. It can't be, right? Right?" His voice was so tight it almost squeaked.

Ian faced the backseat again. "Of course I'm not her father." It was his turn to be the calm one. "I never even met her mother."

"So? They have ways—"

"Zach, it's okay." I touched his arm, wishing I hadn't said anything. "I just realized he can't be my father. He doesn't have brown eyes."

"Oh." Zachary slumped back in his seat. "Right. That's a relief."

Understatement of a lifetime.

So that eliminated one candidate, which wasn't very helpful. But Ian probably knew more about me than he was letting on. If I was the First, then MI-X and DMP must have considered the possibility that my birth—and therefore my heritage—was connected to the Shift.

"Do you know who my father is?" I asked Ian, though I doubted I'd get a straight answer.

He quirked his chin, not quite a nod or a head shake. "We have our theories. Some are outrageous, to say the least."

"Like what?"

"Even if I were allowed to tell you, you wouldn't believe them. And until we know for sure, we can't have you going off on a wild-goose chase." He adjusted his dark blue tie. "It could lead to questions that are too big for amateurs to answer."

I frowned at his warning. I wanted to be the first to know who I was, not the last. I was determined to find out, even if I had to unravel the mystery of the Shift in the process.

From the corner of my eye, I saw Zachary's hand rest on the seat between us, two of the knuckles still bandaged. I reached out to take it. Maybe I didn't have to be alone in my quest.

As my hand moved, I caught sight of my watch. "I'm supposed to have dinner with my aunt soon."

"Where?" Ian asked.

"In Little Italy." We had just driven onto President Street, verging on the freeway. "Turn right here."

The driver didn't turn right. In fact, he didn't turn at all.

My pulse quickened, thumping in my throat. "Where are we going?"

Ian pulled out his phone. "Someplace quieter."

"You have got to be kidding me."

I gaped up at the front windows of the redbrick row home on Amity Street. The dark green shutters were locked tight.

Beside me, Zachary let out a low whistle. "I told you MI-X has been around a long time."

"Don't worry, Aura." Ian knocked on the white wooden front door. "I've been assured it's no longer haunted."

"The ghosts are probably too scared to come here," I muttered. I couldn't reveal, of course, that no ghosts would come near Zachary anyway.

The front door opened, and an old man appeared. To the surprise of my runaway imagination, he wasn't hunched over, wheezing, and carrying a lantern. He wore a flannel shirt, khaki pants, and a Ravens cap.

"Come on in." The man grinned as he backed up so we could climb the porch stairs and enter. "Ever been to the Poe House before?"

I shook my head. My life was creepy enough without spending any of it in the home of America's Bizarrest Dead Writer.

"Dining room's in the back." He led the way through the dim, narrow living room, which was filled with exhibits like china, crystal, and artwork—and a lock of Edgar Allan Poe's hair. Ick.

As we passed the fireplace, Zachary stopped in front of a portrait of a young woman.

"She was beautiful," he whispered, and I got a little chill at the way his mouth released that word.

"She was his cousin," I told him, "and only thirteen when they got married."

"Her death at age twenty-five affected him profoundly," the old man said. "Many of Poe's later works feature the demise of beautiful young women."

Young, I thought. At least she made it to her twenties. Logan only got seventeen years and a few hours. I massaged the sudden sore spot on my chest, the one that hadn't ached for weeks. This place was already glooming me out.

"Pizza should be here soon." The museum guy showed us into a small, dark dining room, where an antique table was set, oddly enough, with paper plates and napkins. Its surface had been covered in protective plastic, like the kind that was on my grandmother's sofa.

Pizza at Poe's house. Just when I thought my life couldn't get weirder.

I sat at the table, facing a narrow, twisted staircase. Despite the house's spookiness, I was dying to explore.

"Feel free to look around," the old man said to me. "It's all public except for the basement." He pointed to a door with a red NO ENTRY sign, then winked at Zachary. "That's where we keep the bodies."

He disappeared into the living room, shutting the door behind him.

Zachary sat beside me. "Well, Dad, I can't wait to hear how you pulled this one off."

Ian gave a self-satisfied smile that reminded me of his son. "Back in the nineteen thirties, the city wanted to tear this house down for public housing projects. It was haunted at the time, so we and a few other paranormal organizations intervened and saved it on behalf of the Poe Society." He spoke directly to me. "Our philosophy dictates that if ghosts can't or won't pass on, they should at least be placated. A contented ghost is a harmless ghost. That's one reason why BlackBoxing is less common in the UK."

Zachary shifted his feet under the table. No wonder he didn't want his father to know he had such an obsidian-like vibe. It didn't exactly fit with MI-X's ghost-friendly mission.

"Anyway," Ian continued, "in return for our past assistance, the Poe Society lets us use this place during the off-season as a short-term safe house. Mr. Pomeroy here has been a good friend to the agency."

A muffled knock came from what sounded like the front door, and I heard Gina's voice in the living room.

"Aura, thank God you're okay!" she said as she swept into the dining room.

"I told you I was fine on the phone."

She gave me a too-tight hug. "For all I knew, your kidnappers were making you say that."

Ian came around the table to greet her. I made quick introductions.

She shook Zachary's hand first. "It's about time, young man. I've been nagging Aura to bring you by the house."

Ian shook her hand and gave a warm nod. "A pleasure to meet you. We have a wonderful thing in common, so we do."

"Oh." She smiled like he'd just told her she won a prize. No one was immune to that accent. "And what's that?"

He pulled out her chair. "Seventeen years ago today, a bonnie child entered each of our lives."

Gina's mouth dropped open, and she hit the chair harder than she should have. "It's your birthday too, Zachary?"

"It is."

"And you're turning seventeen. Small world." Her voice twisted the last sentence.

"It gets smaller," Ian said. "My son is a minute older than your niece."

Aunt Gina stared at Ian, as if she would nab me and make a run for it.

"Zach was the last one born before the Shift," I told her, "and I was the first one after."

"Wait—what do you mean?" she stammered. "The *very* first? And how do you know for sure?"

A knock came from the front door.

"Thank God," Zachary said. "I'm starving."

He and his dad helped Mr. Pomeroy bring to the table three large white pizza boxes, a bottle of red wine, and a pair of soda cans.

Ian handed one of the boxes to our host. "Be sure the agent in the car outside gets some, and you as well." He placed a hundred-dollar bill in Mr. Pomeroy's palm. "Some utensils for the boy and me would be brilliant."

I hid my smirk, having seen Zachary in the school cafeteria eating pizza the British way, with a knife and fork.

When we were settled with our dinner, Gina turned to Ian, looking flustered but determined. "So Mr. Moore, how do you—"

"Please, call me Ian."

She didn't. "How do you know so much about us?"

"I'm a special agent with MI-X. That's the UK—"

"I know what MI-X is. What's it got to do with Aura?" Her voice was strained, as if she already knew his horrible answers.

"Aura is of special interest to all of us." He pointed his fork at his son and chewed as he spoke. "As is Zachary, to a lesser extent."

Zachary narrowed his eyes, then set aside his utensils with a clatter and picked up the slice of pizza with his hands.

"I've done my best," Ian continued, "to deflect the DMP's attention from Aura. It's one of the reasons I've been assigned here in the States."

"Forgive my cynicism," Gina said, "but why do you care?"

Ian drained his glass of wine. He coughed as he refilled it. "Before Aura was born, I was with her mother, Maria."

My spine went cold. "What? You told me you never met my mom!"

"That was the truth." Ian rotated his glass on the table. "We were once in the same place together. The circumstances of our children's births, I believe, are connected by an event that happened to us—an event I cannot, for security reasons, elaborate upon. Much to my regret." Avoiding our eyes, he lifted the glass to take a sip.

I spoke before I could lose my nerve. "You were at Newgrange."

Ian froze with his glass to his lips. He and Gina stared at me.

"Something happened there," I rushed to tell them, "a year before I was born. Mom kept pictures and a journal, but most of the pages are missing." I looked at Gina, my throat lumping. "Did you tear them out?"

"No, hon," she said quietly, "your mother tore them out."

"Where are they?"

"I think she destroyed them. Those memories brought her a lot of pain, so I assume the pages had something to do with your father."

I twisted the napkin in my lap, trying to hide my raging disappointment over the missing journal pages, apparently gone forever. "Why wouldn't she want me to know who he was?"

"Aura . . . whoever your father was, he certainly wasn't *around*. Not when you were born, and not when your mother got sick."

"If she was mad at him, then why didn't she destroy the whole journal? She left me pieces, and she made it sound so mysterious."

"Of course she did," Gina snapped. "She wanted him to be an enigma, not a deadbeat. Please don't fall into that same trap. And please stay out of my closet."

"I'm not giving up on this puzzle." I looked at Zachary, who was valiantly battling the oozing cheese on his pizza. "We're not giving up. Neither is Eowyn Harris."

Ian stared at me in disbelief. "You know *Eowyn Harris?*"

"I got her name from Mom's box of photos. I think my mother contacted her once a long time ago." The temperature in the room seemed to drop. "Is she important?"

"'Is she important?'" he murmured to himself. Ian picked up his utensils, then set them down, as if too overcome by shock to eat. "I can't believe you know her."

Zachary raised his hand. "I know her too, if it matters."

So Zachary had kept our project a secret from his father. I wondered where he'd told Ian he was going on those nights.

"Eowyn's our adviser for our history thesis," I told Ian. "It's not specifically on Newgrange. I sort of broadened the topic so no one would know exactly what I was looking for." I threw Zachary a sheepish glance. "Not even you. Sorry."

He gave me a smile that warmed my toes. "I'd started to guess."

"What have you found out?" Ian's voice held a hint of thunder.

My gut churned, and I knew I had to answer carefully. "Just that Newgrange marks the winter solstice sunrise, and that it was an ancient burial tomb. I'm trying to decipher the markings on the walls of the solstice chamber."

"Why?" he demanded. "Surely it's more than general curiosity."

I smoothed my hair back from my eyes, trying not to squirm. "That place and time seemed so important to my mom. She blew off a semester of college to stay there for three months after winter break. And the fact that she was at Newgrange on the solstice, exactly a year before I was born, seemed like too much of a coincidence to be . . . well, a coincidence."

"And what about Eowyn Harris?" Zachary asked his dad. "How is she involved?"

Ian picked up the wine bottle and filled Gina's glass, though it wasn't empty yet. "Eowyn Harris was at Newgrange with your mum and I," he told me, "the year before you were born. Along with ninety-seven other randomly chosen people from around the world."

I said, "Do you have all their names memorized like you do Eowyn's?"

"Aye, I do." He picked up his knife and fork. "And that, my friends, must end this conversation, or I will get sacked."

After an uncomfortable moment, Aunt Gina cleared her throat. "So how about this weather? So bitter cold the last few days."

I looked at Zachary, and his eyes reflected my frustration with the aborted discussion.

Gina opened the pizza box for another slice. "At least tonight I know I'll be going home to some warm flannel sheets."

I started at her last words, especially the way she emphasized them. "Flannel sheets already?" I asked, hoping my eyes didn't look as wide as they felt.

"It's almost Christmas," she said. "I usually put them on our beds around Thanksgiving, but this year it's been so warm." She raised her eyebrows at me and took a sip of wine. "Now we'll both be cozy and ready for winter."

My pulse racing, I dropped my gaze to my half-eaten pizza slice and picked at the crust.

She knew. She'd seen my non-red sheets. By now they were probably in a Dumpster, or given to Goodwill. My nights with Logan—the few we had left before he passed on—were done. On my birthday, of all days.

Beside me, Zachary shifted in his chair. My coconspirator in sheet buying. If I looked too upset, he'd take it personally. But did he expect me to break up with Logan now that he and I had kissed? Was it even possible to break up with a dead person?

Zachary leaned over and said, "Did you want to see the rest of the house?"

I nodded at him in gratitude—and with admiration for distracting me from thoughts of Logan. He wasn't backing down.

"Go on," Ian said. "It's fascinating."

Zachary and I climbed the narrow stairs, stepping carefully as they curved to the left. He put his hand on my back as he followed—to steady me, no doubt, but it had the opposite effect.

On the second floor, two small bedrooms were decorated in lace and feminine colors. In one of them, an even narrower staircase led up to the attic. I climbed it, though the light was so dim I could barely see my feet.

The tiny room at the top of the house was empty except for a low bed and a desk by the window. Beside the desk hung an electric lantern, one that simulated a weak flame. It cast shifting shadows on the bare, off-white walls.

"Ow."

Zachary held his head, which he'd hit on the sloped ceiling. He moved to stand in the center, though his hair still grazed the surface.

Even I had to duck on my way to the attic window, the only one in the house not shuttered. In the vacant lot across the street, the ghost of a man in a raincoat wandered, examining the mud using his own violet light. I wondered if he'd lived in a house torn down long ago, like this one almost was.

"I don't suppose we're allowed to sit on the bed," Zachary said.

"It doesn't look much softer than the floor, anyway."

We sat cross-legged facing each other on the thin area rug. "Thank you for getting me away from them," I said.

"I'm sorry your birthday has been such crap."

"Not totally." I slid my finger along the grain of the ebony floorboard, picturing a telltale heart lying underneath. "And it's not over yet. It could become more crap."

"My dad can be a real bastard sometimes. Always about the mission, nothing else matters."

"Can't be fun for you, either." I worked up the nerve to take his hand. "Is it true what you told me about your mom leaving?"

"Partly." The wall lantern cast shadows where his eyelashes brushed his cheeks. "She wasn't happy, but that wasn't why she left. My dad sent her away somewhere for her own protection when things started to get dodgy."

"But not you?"

"I chose to stay. I wanted to find out who I was—*why* I was—and I couldn't do that from a safe house in some godforsaken English village." He ran his thumb over my knuckles. "When I met you, I knew I'd made the right choice."

"What about Becca Goldman?" I asked, only half teasing. "Hasn't she been a good ambassador?"

"Becca." Zachary rubbed his reddening face. "I should explain about that."

"Did you hang out with her because she's older and wouldn't see you scare off ghosts?" I cursed the pathetic hopefulness in my voice.

"That's part of it. But the main reason was for reconnaissance."

"Huh?"

"You wanted to know who started those rumors about you."

"It was Becca?" Rage surged up my throat, almost making me hiccup.

"No. But by joining that group, I heard all the gossip and eventually figured out the truth. It was Brian, just like Megan suspected."

"Why would he do that? Does he hate me?"

"No, but he did it for someone who does hate you. Nadine, a girl from Logan's school who liked him. Liked Logan, that is. Brian wanted to shag Nadine like mad." Zachary spit out the words with a grimace, like they tasted awful. "Making you miserable was their little project. Something they could bond over. That's what Brian was hoping."

I brushed my fingers over the bandages on his knuckles. "When did you find out for sure?"

"At Becca's party last week."

"So it's true, you went. How was it?"

"It was brilliant. The Goldmans have the most blinding collection of single-malt scotches. And a hot tub."

My pulse sped up at the thought of him and Becca wet and nearly naked.

"Nothing happened beyond a bit of soaking." He tilted his head. "Well, no' between us. Some of the others, I could tell you stories."

"Stories about who?"

"Ah no, you won't get that for free. You have to be nice to me for two minutes straight."

"I am nice to you."

"I mean, really nice." He nudged my knee with his foot. "Father Christmas might call it naughty, but he's a filthy old bugger."

My insides quivered. I wanted to be very, very nice to Zachary, for longer than two minutes. But first I had to clear up a few things.

"Why wouldn't you tell me your favorite song when we were standing at the porthole? Why did you wait until we were in the dark?"

"With you being so serious about music, I was intimidated." He traced the lines of my palm with his fingertips. "I thought maybe it wouldn't be cool enough."

His touch was lighting up my whole arm. I had to concentrate to keep my words in the right order. "'I Will Possess Your Heart' is definitely cool enough," I told him.

"See? You judged. What if I'd named something less cool?" At the corner of his jaw, a tiny muscle twitched. "In the dark at least I wouldn't have had to see you laugh."

I wanted to laugh right then, to keep calm—and keep from throwing myself at him. "I think it's cute that you were trying to impress me."

"I wasn't. If I were, I'd have just named a song I knew you liked.

One where you couldn't analyze every line and wonder if it was about us."

I locked my gaze on his green eyes. "Is it?"

"Not the stalker part." He lifted my hand toward his lips. "Just the part where he gets the girl."

I closed my eyes as he kissed the pulse at my wrist, wondering if I should point out that in the song, the guy doesn't get the girl. But surely Zachary knew that, and it wasn't the point. The point was the wanting and the waiting.

The point was the "Will."

Chapter Nineteen

Aunt Gina and I didn't speak much on the short drive home. I was still kind of pissed from our argument, and besides, I was too busy thinking to talk. My mind sorted through the day's events, trying to sift them into categories: the good (kissing Zachary), the bad (chased by dumpers), and the ugly (shade attack).

But each of the good parts had some bad and ugly mixed in, and vice versa. I wasn't sure how I felt about any of it. I only knew I felt roughly ten thousand miles from sleep.

When we entered the house, Gina took my arm with a gentle tug. "I'm sorry if I upset you with what I said about your father. I just want you to be happy."

"I know. It's been a crazy day," I added, to dismiss the subject.

"Speaking of the day." Gina led me into the dining room, where a small box sat wrapped in metallic blue paper with a purple bow (she knew I hated getting birthday presents in Christmas wrapping). "I wanted to give this to you alone. I hope you didn't think I forgot."

"Of course not." I gave her a quick hug, then opened the card and scanned the affectionate message, waiting a polite amount of time before I could dig into the gift. "Thank you, that's really sweet." I picked up the wrapped box and shook it. "Ooh, jewelry?"

"I'm sorry there's only one gift. I was surprised how much these things cost, but you said last year your heart was set on having one."

I gave her an eager glance, clueless as to what I had wanted for my sixteenth birthday. That felt like a century ago.

I unveiled a white box from my favorite local jeweler—they did super-funky, one-of-a-kind items—and bounced on my toes, savoring the last few moments of anticipation.

I opened the box and swept off the layer of cotton protecting the . . . *oh God*. My stomach sank slowly, lying down in surrender.

"Do you like it?" Gina asked. "We can exchange it if you want a different length."

I lifted the necklace from the box. The eighteen-karat gold chain and setting gleamed in the chandelier's glow. But the teardrop-shaped stone reflected no light at all.

Obsidian.

"When did you buy this?" I whispered.

"I ordered it last month," she said in a quiet but firm voice. "Right before Thanksgiving."

Last month. After Logan's death.

I laid the stone in the center of my palm. It was solid black, but if I stared hard enough, I could see red flecks deep within.

Every muscle in my face went rigid. I had to say something, *any-thing* nice to keep from screaming. "It's beautiful." Not a lie. But tornados were beautiful too.

"Sweetie, you probably feel like you don't want that right now. But please keep it. You'll want it soon enough."

I wanted to hurl it across the room. But instead I handed it to Gina, then turned my back and lifted my hair so she could put it on me. The sooner it was on, the sooner I could take it off.

"The clasp is stubborn." She gave a little grunt. "We might have to ask them to loosen it." She looped it around my neck, where the stone thudded against my chest. A click came from behind my head. "There. Let's see how it looks."

We went to the mirror. The fake Christmas pine boughs draped over it made a frame for our faces. I smiled to please Gina, but my eyes fixed on the dead cold black of the obsidian.

Aunt Gina hugged me. "Happy birthday."

"You too," I said absently, then realized what she'd said. "I mean, thanks." I kissed her cheek and tucked the pendant inside my sweater. "I'm gonna go to bed early, okay?"

"Wait." She blinked rapidly. "There's something you should know." *You changed my sheets.*

"Mr. Keeley called today," Gina said. "Apparently Logan plans to leave this world before the trial." She paused, as if waiting for me to confirm the information. "But the Keeleys want to push forward with the lawsuit, even in his absence."

"Are you kidding?" I steadied myself with the table edge. "I thought the whole point was to get Logan to move on, to save his soul. If he finds peace, why not drop the case?"

"It's become their crusade." She swiped a tired hand across her forehead. "I've seen this happen with other clients. They lose a loved one, and the only way they can find meaning in that death is to prevent others like it."

"How does suing the record company keep other musicians from snorting coke?"

"If it makes these men think twice before luring ambitious kids with free drugs, it'll be a moral victory. Even if we lose."

"Without Logan, you *will* lose. The whole case depends on proving he didn't know what he was doing when he took the drugs."

"We'll still have your testimony as to his state of mind. We'll also have Logan's deposition, which the jury can read. It's not as effective as hearing his testimony, so to speak, but it's better than nothing." She clenched her fists. "If only the state had passed that drug dealer liability law, Warrant would've settled out of court weeks ago."

I turned away from her, my mind spinning. If it was already too late to avoid the shame of the trial, Logan might as well stay indefinitely. But did I want him to? The choice was ours again.

I pressed the heels of my hands to my cheekbones. "I don't know what to do."

Gina pulled out two of the dining room chairs. "Aura, I'm about to tell you something I've never told anyone but Father Rotella."

I dropped my hands. I was right when I'd told Zachary my birthday could become more crap.

When we sat down, Gina smoothed the crease in the green-and-gold tablecloth. "You know that before the Shift, I was able to see ghosts. But what you don't know is that I was once in love with a man who—" She pursed her glossy pink lips. "He died and became a ghost. Just like Logan."

I sucked in a sharp breath. "Why didn't you ever tell me?" My voice pitched an octave higher than usual.

"Because I was married at the time, but not to him. We had an affair." Gina rotated one of the brass candlestick holders flanking the centerpiece, avoiding my gaze. "To make matters worse, your mother had a mad crush on him. Then again, your mother had a mad crush on just about every man she ever saw," she added with a tender smile. "But I knew it would hurt her if she found out." She rubbed her thumb against a spot of wax on the candlestick holder, smudging it. "Then he died in an accident and came back to haunt me. I was so distraught, I left my husband. I never told him why, just that I didn't love him anymore."

I thought of my reaction to Zachary's kiss, how it had made me miss Logan more than ever.

The candle toppled out of the holder. Gina set it aside. "It was probably true in that moment," she said, "but leaving him was the stupidest thing I ever did. By the time I realized my mistake, he'd gotten over me, found someone else."

"That's horrible." I'd known Gina had been married before I was born, but the family never discussed her ex-husband. "What about the ghost? Did he pass on?"

"I think so. He said good-bye, and I never saw him again." She swept her blond bangs off her forehead as if the room had turned hot. "After you were born, I never saw any ghosts again."

"So you get it," I said gently. "You know what I'm going through."

"More than anyone." She lifted her heavy gaze to mine. "I also know how futile it is to chase a ghost, how they can break your heart." Gina placed a cool hand against my cheek. "Zachary seems like a good guy."

I fought the urge to pull away. "I'm sorry about—about that man." She hadn't mentioned his name, maybe because it would make her cry. I couldn't bear to see that, so I didn't ask. "And your husband, too."

"Thank you." Gina sat back with a sigh. "Ah, well, maybe it was all for the best. Being single freed me up to move here to take care of you and your mother when she got sick."

She looked at the photo on the wall next to the mirror, of her and Mom on the Philadelphia waterfront, mugging for the camera with their arms around each other. Gina was seventeen, sleek and blond; my mother was still a tomboy at twelve, her frizzy dark hair coming loose from her ponytail.

Gina laid her hand on mine. "It will always be the most important thing I've ever done." Her eyes went round and wet. "Whatever you decide—about Logan, about your future—I want you to know that I'm very proud of you. Your mother would have been proud too, to see what you've become."

My eyes heated. *I don't know what I've become.*

"Thank you." I fidgeted with the obsidian pendant through my sweater. I suddenly remembered why I'd wanted one for my sixteenth birthday—I'd just had my first encounter with a shade, at the Arundel Mills Mall before a movie. They'd had to shut down the theater for the night, so many customers were sick. I'd heard that one kid had passed out and fallen down the escalator.

"Back when you could see ghosts," I asked Gina, "were any of them shades?"

She shook her head emphatically, swinging her dangly gold earrings. "It's all different now. Ghosts were in full color, as you know, not in violet, and they just looked like wispy versions of live persons. Some of them were angry, but they never looked like dark shadows or made me feel sick and dizzy."

"I wonder why no one ever saw any shades until the last couple of years."

"My theory? It's that BlackBox technology. When the ghosts can't haunt the places and people they love, they get bitter." She held up a finger. "Mark my words, one day studies will show it twists them into shades, and by then it'll be too late. Everything'll be BlackBoxed."

I touched the chain around my neck. "If you think that stuff is so bad, why did you give me this?"

"Because I'm a hypocrite, and I love you." She touched my wrist. "I want you to be safe, Aura."

"I love you, too." I smiled at her, but my gaze tripped past her to the stairs.

"Well, I have some work to do, and I know you're tired, so . . ." Gina stood and drew my head to her chest so she could kiss the top of it. "Happy birthday, sweetie," she whispered. Her hand tightened on my shoulder, enough to make me wince.

"Good night." I dragged myself to my feet, then trudged upstairs, feeling incredibly old. The obsidian around my neck seemed to weigh twenty pounds.

I opened my bedroom door. No Logan.

I tiptoed inside and softly dropped my purse on the floor, as if trying not to wake someone, then switched on the nightstand lamp.

Red sheets.

The soft fleece felt warm against my palm as I stroked my pillow. I reached across the bed and touched Logan's pillow, the place where he'd laid his head, once for real and many times unreal.

The pillow was cold. Instinctively I drew it into my lap. I clutched it against my chest and rubbed my chin over the seam of the flannel case.

His name caught in my throat. If I called to Logan and he came, the red would hurt him. I'd be nothing but bait for a trap of pain.

But maybe I already was. Logan could see and hear me, but never touch me. How long could we pretend? How long could we forget the world?

My fingers dug into the soft material, sinking and stroking the way they could never do with his skin again.

Then I noticed that my laundry hamper's lid was slightly askew, as if the bin were overstuffed. I slid off the edge of the bed and crept over to it, still clutching the pillow.

I lifted the lid. Purple-black sheets. Aunt Gina had left them here on purpose, letting me choose.

I pulled out the fitted sheet. It would've taken only two or three minutes to switch the sheets back and make the bedroom a safe, happy place for Logan on my birthday.

But I used that much time, maybe twice as much, to stand there thinking.

Thinking how Logan's fingers clenched when he talked about his guitar. Thinking how Mrs. Keeley's back had stooped when she stood by Logan's grave—a grave that might as well be empty.

Thinking how Zachary's lips had felt on mine.

Thinking. Deciding. Choosing.

I stuffed the sheet back into the hamper and tamped it down so that the lid would close.

"I'm sorry," I whispered, my face already damp. I was tired of tears, tired of the constant heat behind my eyes, tired of my cheeks feeling stretched and dry.

I set the pillow carefully on the bed, then changed into a mismatched pair of flannel pajamas. I just wanted to be warm.

The sheets pressed heavy against my skin when I slid between them, my back to the window. I shivered as my own heat wrapped around me like a cocoon in the dark. Like the arms of a real live boy.

The tears came harder, but for the first time, they felt something less than endless.

"Aura." Logan's voice was strained.

I rolled on my back. He stood by the window, shimmering.

"Aunt Gina knows," I told him. "She changed the sheets."

"Can you change them back?" he asked quickly.

"Um . . ." I fumbled for an answer. "The thing is—"

"Happy birthday," he said. "I'm sorry I don't have a gift or a card or anything."

"You have a good excuse."

He gave a labored laugh. "True. I guess you heard about the trial. There's no way we can stop it now. Everyone will know what happened." He staggered forward, his mouth twisting like he was walking on hot coals. "I hate my parents."

His pain and rage made my heart fold inward. "You can still leave. Save yourself."

"No! I won't let you go through it alone." Logan's outline flickered again. "We'll do this together. We'll have each other's backs, like always. I may be dead, but I'm still your boyfriend." He took another heavy step. "Right?"

Every word I needed to say jumbled up inside my head. Words like "breakup" and "over" and "good-bye." But how could I hurt him when he was such a wreck?

I sat up and reached for him. "Listen—"

He ducked, as if from a punch. "Shit, the red is so much worse than before. Feels like I'm disintegrating." He tried to straighten up again and failed. "We need to talk. Come outside."

Logan disappeared. I threw back the covers. Outside, where he wasn't in pain, I could tell him it was over, that he had to move on without me, for both of us. But the thought of breaking up with Logan made my insides twist and tangle like a set of earbud wires.

I put on a cardigan and sneakers, then opened my bedroom door. Down the hall, Aunt Gina's door was ajar. The sounds of shuffling papers and tapping laptop keys came from her room. Who else would be working at eleven o'clock on a Saturday night?

I closed the door, then opened my window. Logan was pacing in front of the house, his form slightly faded in the glow from the streetlights.

"Hey." I spoke quietly. "She's still up, so I can't come out through the door." I hoisted myself through the window and set my foot on the gentle slope of the porch roof we shared with our next-door neighbor.

"Be careful," Logan said.

"I've done this a hundred times, remember?"

"I know, but I can't catch you anymore."

I peered over. It was too far down to jump, and even if I could, I'd be locked out of the house. So I swung my legs over to sit on the edge of the roof above the front walkway.

"How was your birthday?" Logan shifted his nonexistent weight from one foot to the other. "Did you guys have dinner?"

"We did." My fingers tightened on the shingles as I realized he could have shown up at the restaurant tonight. He'd taken me there before the homecoming dance, so it would be part of his ghostly habitat. "But not at Chiapparelli's."

"I know. I looked for you. Where did you go?"

"To someone's house."

"I went everywhere I could think of." Logan flailed his arms. "The whole day, I looked all the places you could've gone, but whenever I tried to get to you, something freaky would happen."

My pulse skipped. "Really?"

"Yeah, really." He swaggered up to the edge of the grass. "It's that guy, isn't it?"

"I don't—"

"What is his *deal*?" Logan's voice crackled. "Why is he so fucking bright I can't look at him?"

I shook my head, but the motion made me so dizzy, I had to blink hard to clear my vision.

"Is that why you like him, Aura? He's all red and shiny?" The edges of Logan's image fizzled black, like he was being swarmed by a thousand gnats. "Or is it the accent? I mean, what's he got that I don't—no, don't answer that. Duh. A body."

"Logan, please calm down."

"Are you going to change the sheets or not?" He looked at the front door, then up at me. "Do you want me to come back?"

I stared into his eyes for a long moment. I could almost imagine them blue as a September sky.

"Aura." His whisper seemed to be right at my ear. "Do you still love me?"

It was the wrong question, because boy or ghost or shade, there would always be only one answer.

"Yes."

Logan's dark outline brightened to pure violet again, and I let myself breathe.

"I love you, too." He bounced on his toes. "So we're cool, then? I'll come over tomorrow after you put the other sheets on. You leave for your grandmom's on Monday, right?"

"I do, but—I don't think you should come here . . . tomorrow night." I cursed myself for wussing out at the end of the sentence. I'd never broken up with anyone before Logan. I'd never loved anyone before Logan.

"When are you getting back from Philly?" he asked me. "I'll stop by then."

"I—no. I don't want you to come here." I shuddered at the sound of my words. "I can't see you anymore."

Logan went very still, as if caught in a freeze-frame. "You said you love me."

"I do love you."

"But you're leaving me."

"It's the only way to—"

"I've lost you." He stepped back and looked up and down the sidewalk. "Because I died, I've lost you."

"Logan, don't—"

"God, this isn't happening. It was one thing to lose my life, but this." He dragged his hands up his face, into his hair. "What can I do, Aura? Tell me what to do."

"There's nothing you can do."

"No!" He lunged through the iron gate into the yard, then stopped with a hiss, like something had pushed him back. "There's got to be something. Got to be!"

Black lightning shot through his body, ripping him apart.

"Logan?" I reached for him. "Logan, don't!"

Something slithered over the back of my neck as I moved. The chain of the obsidian pendant. I wrenched my body to keep the stone inside my shirt, but it swung out, dangling in the air before him.

Logan hurled a gurgling, staticky shriek. "THERE MUST BE SOMETHING!"

My brain tilted. I grabbed for the edge of the roof, but my hands went in the wrong direction. Up was down and down was up.

As the world dropped away, I saw Logan's shadowy figure streak toward me.

"AURA!"

Then I was twisting, slipping, scrambling.

And finally, falling.

In the long, gray moments that followed, I heard Logan calling for help. He screamed my aunt's name, but of course she couldn't hear him. I lay on the cold concrete walkway, trying not to let the desperation in his voice make my own lungs seize. It hurt to breathe.

"Aura." Logan knelt beside me, sobbing. His voice had lost its crackle. "I'm gonna get Megan. I'll be right back. Don't move, okay?" When I didn't respond, he shouted into my ear. "Aura! Can you hear me?"

"Yes," I whispered. "Go."

His violet hands reached for me, but then he snatched them back as if I'd burned them. "Don't move. And don't fall asleep. Think of a song."

"A song?"

"Something fast. Think of 'Devil's Dance Floor.' Remember?"

He blurted out the first line to jog my memory, then disappeared. A moment later I heard his voice from two blocks over, shouting Megan's name again and again.

I tried to turn my mind to the song, remembering how he would lock his gaze with mine on the first verse, how he would pull each musician into the interlude like a wizard coaxing the four elements, how he stoked the crowd through the frenzied finale, urging them to swing a little more on the devil's dance floor.

The song ended and he finally quieted, in both imagination and reality. I closed my eyes and let the gray turn to black.

Chapter Twenty

W ake up, dork."

I opened my eyes reluctantly to see the pock-marked tiles of the hospital room ceiling.

"It's been two hours already?" I asked Megan.

"Yep. The nurse is on her way to check on you again. Figured you'd rather wake up to my pretty face than hers."

I tried to roll over in bed, but the sharp ache in my side stopped me. "Ow!"

"More painkillers you need," Megan said, using the new Yoda puppet she'd bought for my birthday.

"Where's Gina?"

"In the lounge she is, her messages, she is checking." Megan coughed and lowered the puppet. "It hurts to do that voice. How do you feel?"

Once again my mind was slammed by the events of the previous night. Logan shimmering in pain. Logan raging over our breakup. Logan turning shade.

"I just want to sleep."

Megan's eyes widened. "Uh-oh."

"No." I gritted my teeth as I used my one good hand to help myself sit up. "I'm sleepy because I fell off my roof and got poked at by doctors until five a.m. I'm not sleepy because my brain is sloshed."

"Are you sure? I can ring the bell and have the nurse come quicker."

"I don't feel sick. I'm actually kinda hungry."

"That's supposed to be a good sign." Megan straightened the thin knit blanket over the sheets. "You could totally use this head injury thing when school starts again. If you flunk a test, just say you had memory loss from your concussion."

Ha. If only the injury could clear the memories I dreaded most. But I knew I'd never get that lucky.

The nurse came in then, and I understood Megan's point about not wanting to wake up to that face. "Agatha" (according to her name tag) scowled at me as she took my blood pressure and checked my chart. She asked me several questions and seemed disappointed with my unremarkable answers.

"The neurologist will be in shortly to examine you. Until then, don't move." Agatha shook her finger at Megan on her way out, like my friend might challenge me to a game of one-on-one.

"Do you want me to call Zach for you?" Megan said. "You can't use cell phones in hospital rooms."

"No. Give me the regular phone." I picked up the receiver from the clunky contraption on my nightstand.

She pressed on the hook to keep me from dialing. "What are you going to tell him?" she asked in a serious tone.

"The truth." One version of it, at least. "Why?"

"Maybe you should leave out some of the details."

"Which details?"

"The ones with Logan in them." She placed the phone in my lap so I could dial, then slipped the puppet back on her hand. "Leave you alone I will. An idiot do not be."

When Zachary picked up, his voice was cautious, no doubt unfamiliar with the number on his caller ID. "Hello?"

"It's Aura."

"Good morning." His warm tone gave me a shivery reminder of our time alone together. Then he said, "Wait, where are you?"

"In the hospital. I kind of had an accident."

He drew in a sharp breath. "What happened? Are you all right? Do you want me to come over?"

"Thanks, but I'm getting out tonight. I'm not hurt too bad." I paused. "I fell off my porch roof while talking to Logan."

"Oh."

"When I got home, Gina had changed my sheets back to the red ones, and I didn't take them off. So when he showed up, he was—" I fought to keep the fresh pain out of my voice. "It was bad."

"What did he do to you?" Zachary demanded.

"Nothing." I swallowed the truth—I couldn't tell anyone about Logan's shading, or he'd be locked up forever. "I broke up with him."

"Good. I mean, er—" He stammered a few incoherent syllables. "Wait, what's that got to do with the roof?"

"Logan wanted to talk some more."

"Talk you out of it."

"Maybe. No, I'm getting it out of order. I broke up with him after I was on the roof. Then I guess I slipped."

"And your aunt found you?"

"No, Logan had to get Megan, who got Gina."

"You sure you're not badly hurt?"

"I just sprained my wrist and my knee, and bruised some ribs." I scratched my side through the thin blue hospital gown. "This bandage itches like crazy. Oh, and I blacked out."

"Christ."

"They admitted me so they could monitor my brain for swelling. Which means sadistically waking me up every two hours to see if I feel sick or dizzy. Pretty annoying."

"Not as annoying as dying in your sleep."

"True." I tried to fluff my pillow. The scratchy pillowcase smelled of chlorine bleach. "Have you ever had a concussion?"

"Head-butt at a football match. I won't say who started the row."

He chuckled, but I didn't join him. His reply had jolted my memory, back to a summer day when I was twelve.

Logan had been teaching me how to ride a skateboard on our neighborhood sidewalks. I sucked, but he wouldn't give up. He wanted me to hang out with him and the boys at the park, not sit on the curb with the other girls and watch.

That day, a white delivery truck was double-parked in front of the

Indian restaurant on the corner, flashers blinking. I didn't see the car swerve around it, into the opposing lane, because I was finally staying on the board for three, four, five, six (!!) sections of sidewalk. I was even steering a little by shifting my weight. I was flying.

When the sidewalk ended, I didn't want to stop. I put out my arms and guided the board in front of the van toward the empty side of the street.

"Logan, I'm doing it! Look at—"

I had no time to scream at the oncoming car before something slammed my body backward. Brakes screeched, mixing with my shriek of pain as the blacktop tore the skin of my back. It all ended with a *thunk!* and a groan.

Logan was lying on top of me. His eyes were dazed, and his forehead was red where he'd hit it on the bumper of the parked delivery truck.

"Careful," he said, then slumped unconscious.

If Logan hadn't saved my life that day, I realized now, I wouldn't have become his girlfriend. I wouldn't have called him stupid just after midnight on October nineteenth. If Logan hadn't saved my life, maybe he'd still be alive.

"Aura?" came a new voice in my ear. Zachary's.

"Sorry. What did you say?"

There was a short silence. "I'll be right over."

"Those are beautiful!" Aunt Gina tossed aside her Sudoku book and hugged Zachary as he entered my hospital room. "I'll see if the nurse's station has a vase." She hustled out the door.

"Hello." Zachary shuffled over, his eyes on the aluminum crutch propped against the side of the bed. "How do you feel?"

"Useless." I held up my right hand in the beige splint. "But the doctor said my wrist wasn't too bad, so in a week I should be able to use both crutches." I eyed the bouquet of roses he held by his side. "Are those for me or are you making another stop?"

"Oh, sorry. Here." He offered them to my good hand.

"Thank you, they're gorgeous. The red and yellow look so pretty together." I counted: six of each color. Their sweet scent eased the ache in my head. "I'm so glad I got hurt," I added with a grin.

"Er, yeah." He smoothed the sides of his trousers, then sat in the metal-framed chair my aunt had vacated. "The man at the flower shop said that yellow was for friendship and red was for, well, more than friendship."

"Does this mean we're both?"

He looked down at his hands. "It means I don't know which we are."

I froze, my nose inside one of the red blooms. "But last night—"

"Last night I was less confused."

My stomach flipped. "Confused about whether you want to be with me?"

"No!" Zachary put his palms out. "I know I want to be with you. But not if you're in love with someone else."

"I'm not," I whispered, wishing I could sound more convincing. "I broke up with Logan, remember?"

"And it almost killed you."

"The roof was only ten feet up or so."

"Not just literally." He pointed to the phone. "I could hear it in your voice—it hurts you just to say his name. And I can see it in your eyes right now. You're not over him."

I tried to look straight at Zachary and swear that I was, but the image of Logan shading seared my memory. I ended up staring into the roses. "I'm working on it."

Zachary sighed and sat forward, elbows on his knees. "Aura, I'm really patient, but I'm not a bloody saint."

"Here we go!" Aunt Gina clacked in on her platform heels, carrying a green glass vase full of water, which she set on the tray stand in front of me. She hummed "Deck the Halls" as she ripped open the package of flower food and poured the powdery contents into the vase.

I watched the process as if it fascinated me. Anything was better than looking at the regret on Zachary's face.

Suddenly Gina glanced between us. "Is this a bad time?"

We both shrugged halfheartedly.

She hurried to place the roses in the vase, still in their wrapper. "That's good for now. We'll arrange them better when we get home tonight." She left the vase on the tray stand and picked up her handbag. "I'll be in the cafeteria. You need anything?"

I shook my head. She kissed my cheek, then on her way out patted Zachary's shoulder in a way that said, *If you upset Aura in her weakened state, I will end you.*

After she was gone, I picked at the florist's gold label on the roses' wrapper. "So, back to breaking up with me . . ."

"I'm no' breaking up with you." Zachary intertwined his fingers, elbows still on his knees. "How can I, when we're not really together?"

We're not? "It's complicated."

"I know it's complicated. I've had a front-row seat for two months, and it still hasn't been enough time. I want to give you that time, so that when you're ready, we can just be the two of us." Zachary sat up straight and put his hands on the chair arms. "Time and space."

"Space?" My head started to pound worse than ever. "So we can't even see each other?"

"At least not until after the trial. Then you can decide."

"But I already decided." My hazy mind fumbled for proof. "I could've switched the sheets back to purple last night, but I didn't. I chose you."

"It wasn't you choosing me. It was circumstance choosing me for you."

"Whatever! I'm glad about it." I wanted to reach for him but knew he would turn away. "What are you so afraid of?"

His fingers curled as his green eyes bore into me. "I'm afraid that someday you'll hate me for making you take a shortcut."

"No shortcuts. I'm ready to move on." At least, I wanted to be ready.

"Moving on doesn't mean moving on to me." He tapped his chest. "I don't want you to want me just because I'm here and alive."

"What if I never saw Logan again? What if he leaves forever? Would that be enough for you?"

"If he left now, he'd take a piece of you with him."

My life force seemed to drain out of me. Exhausted, I sank back onto the flimsy pillow and closed my eyes.

Zachary was right. I wanted to move on, but I couldn't ask him to settle for half of me.

"But that piece won't be gone forever." Zachary came to stand next to my bed. "One day you'll be ready. We'll both know when that happens."

I noticed he said "when," not "if." It reminded me of his favorite song, his confidence that he would possess my heart.

"You're not staying forever," I said. "You're going home in June."

Zachary reached out and laced his fingers with mine. "Well, then, there's your deadline."

When I got home that night, I settled on the living room couch—my temporary bed until I could use both crutches to get upstairs. Beside me on the coffee table lay my stack of books for our history thesis. Now that classes were out for two weeks, I finally had time to explore the mysteries of Newgrange, and meeting Ian Moore had whetted my appetite for answers. Zachary had offered to do this month's star map alone—partly because of my injuries and partly, no doubt, to avoid me.

As always, I lingered on the photos my mother had taken. Their edges were wrinkled and their corners nearly rounded from the dozens of times I had handled them.

But my favorite one I never touched at all. I kept the candid Polaroid of my mother in a sealed plastic bag.

In the picture, Mom stands on a hillside, squinting off into the morning sun, which casts a long shadow behind her. A breeze flaps the tails of her open gray raincoat and fans her long dark curls.

The sticky note on the back read, "Taken by some Irish guy who claimed I looked 'mystical' gazing out at the River Boyne. (Really I was just trying to figure out which road would take me to a breakfast place.)"

As always, I gave the photo a quick kiss through the bag before returning it to the folder.

My second favorite picture was the one of the dark burial chamber doorway, surrounded by blinding white quartz and fronted by a large threshold stone carved in swirling spirals. Above the door sat a smaller rectangular opening that allowed light in only once a year—at the winter solstice sunrise.

I flipped open my mother's journal—what was left of it. After the December 26 entry, more and more pages had been torn out, leaving only mundane details about what she'd eaten and where she'd stayed. Based on these bits, I could trace her dwindling budget.

The last entry was complete, for all the good it did me.

> Monday, April 20
> Going home tomorrow. My work here is done. Not "done" as in finished. But "done" as in, I can't stay one more minute, not like this.
> No way I'm going back to Philly, though. Maybe I'll move to Baltimore. I do love crabs.

"About time Gina went to bed."

I almost dropped the journal. "You scared me!" I hissed at Logan.

The lamplight was so bright I couldn't see more than his vague violet outline next to the couch. I switched off the lamp. The white lights of the Christmas tree cast the room in a soft glow.

"Sorry I didn't come earlier," Logan said. "Your aunt was freaked enough without finding out I was here." He sat on the coffee table. "I was afraid to come at all, after the way I was last night. I could've killed you."

"I forgot I was wearing that necklace." I picked at the orange lint on the afghan blanket. "No wonder you got so shady."

"I'm sorry. The red sheets and the obsidian and . . . that guy—" Logan spied the vase of roses on the end table across the room. His fists tightened, then slowly released. "But that's no excuse. I should've held it together." He gestured toward the front yard. "And then when you fell, I thought I'd died all over again. I couldn't pick you up. I couldn't call for help."

"But you did get help."

"If Megan hadn't been home—"

"If Megan hadn't been home, one of the kids across the street would've woken up and gotten their parents. You saved me. It's you I'm worried about." I lowered my voice to the softest whisper. "Did you really turn—I mean, all the way?"

He hesitated. "Yeah. For a few seconds, I was a total shade."

I put my hand to my mouth, trying not to show my horror at his temporary monstrosity. "What was it like?"

"It's hard to describe. The closest I can come is riding a roller coaster in the dark—like Flight of Fear at Kings Dominion? It was terrifying and thrilling, and I had no control whatsoever. I couldn't even see what was coming next. Something else was pushing and pulling me."

"Like a person?"

"No, a force outside of me—like gravity."

Logan was more subdued than I'd ever seen him. I wondered if he was worried about shading again.

"If this force was so powerful," I asked him, "why didn't it keep you a shade? How did you turn back into a ghost?"

"That was the most amazing part. When you fell, I was so afraid you were hurt, it was like you filled up my whole head, so there was no room for any of my stupid crap. Next thing I knew, I was like this again." He held up his glowing violet arm. "Pretty wild, huh?"

"Logan, this is incredible. It means shades can come back." My mind boggled.

"But I was only a shade for three or four seconds, and it took something huge to snap me out of it. And when I did, it was like skateboarding through quicksand. Uphill."

"Wow."

"I don't know if I could turn back into a ghost if I shaded again, so I gotta be careful, or I might never pass on. That force might suck up what's left of my soul." He lowered his head. "Speaking of passing on, I need to tell you something."

"Get out!" Aunt Gina loomed on the stairway. "Logan's here, isn't he?" She came down a few steps, scanning the living room. "That's who you're talking to?"

Logan stood up. "No, you don't get it," he said to her, though she couldn't hear him. "I was about to—"

"Haven't you done enough damage?" Facing his general direction, she stalked forward and pointed to me. "Look at her!" She was in front of him now, but she couldn't have known it. "You did that!"

"I know," Logan said softly, then turned to me. "I'm here to say good-bye."

I thought my chest would cave in. "Aunt Gina, please give us a few minutes."

"No." She reached into the pocket of her robe and brought out the obsidian pendant. "Not one more second."

Logan moaned and backed away, through the coffee table, straight for the glowing Christmas tree. The edges of his image crackled and snapped, and I clutched the sofa cushion to steady myself.

Then he disappeared.

"Get out!" Aunt Gina advanced across the room.

"He's gone," I whispered. Ignoring the ache in my ribs, I rolled onto my side away from her. "He's gone for good."

Chapter Twenty-one

After my fall, we stayed home for Christmas instead of traveling to see my grandmother. Aunt Gina tried to cook a turkey herself and spent half the day on the phone with Grandmom getting tips. I guess it turned out okay, but I couldn't taste much of anything.

It felt like Logan had died again. My body was heavy and numb, even after I stopped the painkillers. I had no idea where he'd gone or when and if he was coming back, despite scouring the Internet for rumors. No one had seen him or heard from him in almost three days. Zachary had been right—I wasn't really over Logan, not by a long shot.

I was sitting at the table finishing my (store-bought) pumpkin pie while Gina did the dishes, when the phone rang for what seemed like the fortieth time that day. I tried to think which cousin hadn't called yet to wish us a Merry Christmas.

Gina came out of the kitchen. "Honey, it's Dylan."

I took the phone. "Hello?"

"Hey." Dylan fell silent. For a moment I wondered, with my heart in my throat, if he was holding out the phone so Logan could speak. "Remember how you guys always used to come over on Christmas night after you got back from your grandmom's?"

"Yeah." The Keeleys would play music and serve yet more food, and then we'd all watch *It's a Wonderful Life.* "What about it?"

"Nothing. Just . . . that was cool."

It hurt to remember exactly how cool. "How is it over there?"

"Everyone's crying. Do you wanna come over?"

"Does your family want me there?"

"Siobhan does. My dad sort of does. So I guess if we had a vote, it'd be tied, two and a half each."

"Why don't you and Siobhan come here? We could drive through Hampden and look at the lights."

"Aw, that'd be awesome! Hang on."

Dylan dropped the receiver. He was gone for several minutes, and I wondered if he'd forgotten I was on the phone. Maybe he'd gotten wrapped up in one of his new games.

Then suddenly he was back. "Okay-we'll-be-right-there-bye!" He hung up.

In less than an hour, Siobhan was driving Dylan and me down 34th Street, a tradition Gina and I had missed this year, between her obsession with Logan's case and my obsession with, well, Logan.

The Chieftains' Christmas CD played on the car speakers as we crawled with the heavy traffic, under rows of lights that stretched above the narrow street.

Elaborate displays covered every surface of the shops and row homes. It was an unwritten law in Hampden—you had to put up Christmas lights, even if you didn't celebrate the holiday. Which just proved that there were forces in this world stronger than religion.

"He's not here in the car with us, is he?" Siobhan asked.

"No," Dylan and I replied in unison, knowing she meant Logan. Then again, the light displays made the street too bright to see ghosts.

She lowered the volume. "Last night Mom and Dad were up late wrapping presents. They were talking in their bedroom, and I guess Mom was in and out getting supplies, and she left the door open." Siobhan paused. "They want to move away."

"What?!" Dylan grabbed the back of her seat. "Move where?"

"Anywhere—" Her voice faltered. "Anywhere Logan's never been."

"I'm not going!" He pounded on his knee. "I finally have friends at that lame-ass new school."

"Dylan, you don't have a choice," Siobhan said.

"But you do. You and Mickey are eighteen. You could get an apartment and I could live with you."

"We're going to college."

"So go to college here!"

"You don't get it, do you?" she snapped. "Mickey and I want to get away as much as Mom and Dad do, if not more. Too many memories. Even driving here . . ." Siobhan flapped her hand at a Christmas tree made out of hubcaps. "Logan used to love Hampden."

"He still does," I told her. "He can come here any time he wants." Although maybe not at the moment, with all these red lights and giant Santas.

She wiped her eyes, smudging mascara onto the side of her forefinger. She rubbed her thumb against the stain. "Maybe if we move, if he doesn't have us to haunt, he'll pass on."

"Um, I got news on that," Dylan said.

I spun to face him, provoking a sharp pain in my bruised rib. "From Logan? What did he say?"

"If we win the case, he wants to move on in public. Starting tomorrow, he wants me to spread the word so everyone can come."

"Everyone?" Siobhan said.

"Post-Shifters. Especially those with cameras."

I let out a harsh laugh. "Logan is passing on as some kind of performance?"

"A grand finale." Siobhan snorted. "Classic."

"'Blaze of glory,' he says." Dylan looked at me. "It might be kinda cool if Logan and I find the right place. It has to be somewhere near the courthouse, somewhere he's been before."

"The Green Derby," Siobhan said. "The pub where Mickey and I are playing next month. Logan's been there, and it's only a block away." She slapped the knob of the gearshift. "I can't believe I just helped him in his diva-ness."

"You want to see it as much as we do," Dylan told her. "I mean, you can't see it. But you can see all the people who *can* see him. Does that make sense?"

"Yeah. It'll be nice to hear one last crowd screaming his name."

I laid my head back and stared through the windshield, until my eyes lost focus and the street became one wide blinking sun.

Logan's love affair with the world would have one last good-bye kiss. If only we could have that too.

"What if you guys lose?" I said. "What's Logan going to do? Won't he disappoint the crowds if he doesn't pass on?"

"He thought of that," Dylan said. "Says he'll do a short concert."

"And he'll expect us to play for him?" Siobhan sniffled, then her breath hitched into a sob. "Why couldn't he just go to begin with? Why does he have to make it so hard?" Her voice stretched to the breaking point. "Why does he have to be such an asshole?"

I pulled a bunch of fast-food napkins from the door pocket and handed one to Siobhan. "He's not being an asshole," I said quietly. "He's just being Logan."

"Same difference." She covered her mouth. "No, I don't mean that. He was a good brother. He was a sweet guy."

"He still is," Dylan and I said together.

"Shut up!" Siobhan tore another napkin from the stack in my hand. "You people are such freaks, you know that?"

"*We're* freaks?" Dylan said. "That guy over there built a Christmas tree out of Natty Boh beer cans and Old Bay seasoning jars."

Siobhan laughed. "Okay, good point." She dragged the napkin under her nose and across her cheek. "I wish I was a freak too."

* * *

My aunt went back to work after Christmas, once I'd mastered the crutches enough to get myself to the bathroom and kitchen and back to the sofa. I stayed home, since I couldn't drive with a sprained knee, and I did not want to share her twelve-hour days at the office (though I really could've used the money).

Logan didn't come over anymore. I lay awake each night in the living room, waiting but never calling. He kept his vow to stay away, and even though I knew it was for the best, each moment without him felt darker than the one before. The uncertainty and fear robbed me of sleep, until I felt like a shade myself—scattered, staticky, and in a very pissy mood.

Zachary called once, but only to discuss our research project. I knew he was giving me space, but his absence felt more suffocating than his hovering ever could.

Two days before Logan's trial, I tried to distract myself by studying for midterms. Megan was supposed to come over to keep me company and share my calculus misery, and then we were going to her house for New Year's Eve.

The doorbell rang half an hour before she was supposed to show up, which was odd. Megan was never on time, much less early. I made my way to the door and pulled the curtain aside to look onto the porch.

Two men stood there. The tall one in front, with a head of dark, bowl-cut hair, faced the door. His partner was slightly shorter, with light brown hair in the same odd style. The second man had his back to me, scanning the street. They were dressed like DMP agents, but instead of white uniforms, theirs were solid black.

Obsidians.

I stepped back, almost losing my balance on the crutches. Before I could move again, the dark-haired man held a badge up to the door's window.

"Ms. Salvatore," he called. "We need to speak."

I checked the deadbolt to make sure it was locked. "Can you come back later when my aunt's here?" I hated admitting I was alone, but there was no way I was letting them into the house.

The agent leaned close to the window. "There are some things she's better off not knowing, correct? Things about Logan Keeley?"

My blood turned to ice. They must have known he'd turned shade, if only for a few moments. Did they have detectors? Would they hunt him down, trap him in a box and keep him on a shelf forever?

I unlocked the door and opened it. "Just for a minute."

The dark-haired man gave a slight bow before entering. "I'm Agent Falk. It's a pleasure to make your acquaintance." The other agent followed him in, but didn't introduce himself. He stayed at the door, watching the street, as Falk walked into the dining room.

"May I?" He pointed a small laptop case at the table.

"What do you want from me?"

Agent Falk quirked his chin. "We want nothing but to help you achieve your potential."

"Potential for what? Seeing ghosts? I'm not exactly unique that way."

"No, not in that way at all." Without sitting down, he laid the laptop on the table and opened the lid. The computer was already on, with some sort of database program running. Falk pulled down a list of numerical files. He selected one, and the hard drive hummed.

The picture that resolved in the center of the screen squeezed my heart to the size of a grape.

Logan, as he was in life. As he was the night of his death, onstage, on one knee. The photo was professional quality, capturing him with the mic at throat level, sending his brilliant blue lust-for-life gaze up above the camera.

Up into eternity.

I sank into the chair closest to the computer and let my crutches fall against my lap. "Where did you get this picture? Were you there that night?"

"Not personally. We have operatives who would blend in at a punk concert much better than I would."

"Why were you following him before he died?"

"Ms. Salvatore." Falk slid into the seat across from me. "You know you're the First. We know you're the First. By definition, there's only one First. Therefore, everything you do, everyone you know, is of interest to us."

I squeezed my hands between my knees, as my fingers had suddenly turned cold. "You follow me."

"Not all the time. God knows we don't have the resources. But as you come of age, our curiosity grows."

"Why? Am I going to sprout wings when I turn eighteen? Grow a second head or an eleventh toe?"

Falk didn't laugh or even smirk. "Honestly, we don't know." He shifted the computer in front of him and tapped the screen with both index fingers. "Things have grown more interesting since the death of your boyfriend."

My fist clenched, wanting to smash this guy's nose. *Interesting.* He was talking about the worst thing that ever happened to me like it was a science project.

"Logan's pre-Shift," I said. "What do you want with him?"

Falk signaled the other agent, who slipped his hand out of his pocket. In his palm he held a small disc made of ice-clear crystal.

Falk spoke. "Do you recognize this device, Ms. Salvatore?"

"It's a summoner. It can call a ghost who's tagged by the DMP. We use them in"—my tongue stuttered along with my pulse—"in the courtrooms. To get ghosts on the witness stand. It lets a ghost go somewhere they never went during their life."

"Correct. Summoners are made of clear quartz, which acts in opposition to obsidian. A tagged ghost must appear anywhere the summoner is activated."

"Logan is tagged." I tried to take slow, deep breaths to calm my racing pulse, but the bandages on my ribs wouldn't stretch far enough. "His tag gets removed after the trial. That's the law."

"Of course it is. Any basic social studies class teaches that state and federal laws apply to ghosts as well as the living. After all, they're people too." Falk tapped his nails on the tablecloth. "However, the law becomes rather fuzzy when applied to shades."

"Logan's not a shade." My voice cracked on the last word. "You can't hold him."

"Actually, we can. According to the readings from his tag, he's exhibited the metaphysical signature of a shade on several occasions, including Saturday night at this address. Coincidentally when you took an injurious fall. It's more than enough evidence to hold him.

His parents can sue to release him, but most of these cases are tied up in legal limbo for . . ." Agent Falk put a thumb to his sharp chin, as if calculating. "Forever, actually."

I gripped the edge of the table. "They never get out?"

"Shades are far too dangerous to set free. Therefore we've decided that the only feasible solution is indefinite detainment."

"They disappear," I whispered, then turned to the other agent. "Is that what happens?"

He regarded me with eyes as clear and cold as the crystal in his hand. "We must protect the children."

His voice slithered down my spine, twining between each vertebra.

"I know shades are dangerous," I said to Falk, "but what if we could help them turn back into ghosts?"

"Rehabilitate them?" The arch of Falk's eyebrow screamed his skepticism. "It would be like training a rabid dog to guide the blind."

My anger surged at the comparison. "What do you know about shades, or ghosts, or anything? Without us post-Shifters, you wouldn't even know that they exist."

"But we do know, and we've developed ways to learn more, with or without the help of post-Shifters." The agent narrowed his close-set brown eyes. "If Logan Keeley moves on, he will cease to be a threat, so we would appreciate it if you would do everything in your power to make that happen."

"I don't have that power. If his family wins their case, he'll move on. If not—"

"If not, he'll be what we consider an 'at risk' ghost. Too near to shading to allow his freedom."

I pictured Logan locked up in a BlackBoxed room or on a shelf in some DMP vault for years, maybe decades. Maybe forever. My own mind seemed to shade at the thought.

"Please . . .," I whispered. "Logan's a good guy. He just gets a little excited sometimes." I turned to the shorter agent. "What if he were your son? Or your brother? Wouldn't you want to give him a chance?"

"That's what we're doing with this visit," Falk snapped. When I looked at him, he smoothed his hand over his throat and down the front of his black uniform. "So you can warn him. Encourage him."

"Why?" I twitched my shoulders, which prickled with fear and confusion. "Why not collect him now, if you think he's a risk? And why help me keep his secret?"

"Ah." Falk closed the laptop. I wanted to grab it back to see Logan's full-color photo again. The agent folded his hands on the computer's silver lid. "The Keeley case has garnered a lot of media attention. Detaining him prior to his trial would create a public relations nightmare and throw a spotlight on our indefinite detention program. We can't afford to look bad just as you post-Shifters are coming of age. Recruitment is the department's number one priority, so that we can better understand ghosts."

"Better control them, you mean."

Falk spread his thumbs and shrugged, as if to say *Whatever* without actually saying *Whatever*.

Not breaking eye contact, I reached out and slid my calculus textbook in front of me. "I need to study."

"Of course." He placed the laptop back in its case and zipped it.

"Best of luck with all of your endeavors, especially in the courtroom." He joined his partner at the door. "And please give our regards to Logan, along with our message."

My brain felt jumbled with all the new information. "What message?"

"Get out." He tilted his head and offered a joyless smile. "Or we'll take you out."

I spent the next half hour calling for Logan, but he wouldn't appear. When my throat started to hurt, I phoned Dylan.

He picked up on the second ring. "Hey, Aura."

"Tell Logan to leave."

"Why? When?"

"Whenever. After the trial at the latest. If not, the Obsidians are going to lock him up for being a shade."

There was a long pause. "How do they know?"

"His subpoena tag must have a detector on it. I've been trying to reach Logan, but he won't answer me. So you have to warn him." I hurried through a shortened version of Agent Falk's spiel.

When I was finished, Dylan said, "Um, what did these Obsidian guys look like? Black uniforms, haircuts like Moe from the Three Stooges?"

"Yeah, why?"

"They just pulled up in front of our house."

My heart thumped. "Is Logan there?"

"No. I'm by myself."

"Then let them in. They won't hurt you, but don't piss them off, okay?"

"Got it." His voice held a quiet strength, giving me a twinge of pride.

"And please—tell Logan I love him."

Dylan hung up. I clicked off the phone, set it on the table, and stared at it, like I used to do while waiting for Logan to call me. Some nights he'd forget, consumed with his music, and I'd go to bed wondering if he would ever be all mine.

Soon he would be no one's.

Chapter Twenty-two

I sat on the witness stand, resisting the urge to scratch the maddening itch under my knee bandage. I'd looked out at this courtroom from the adjacent translators' seats countless times over the last few years.

But this time I was speaking for myself.

A red light above each door showed that the BlackBox had been deployed. Logan would stay away until it was his turn to testify. Then he would be summoned with the quartz disc connected to his subpoena "tag." My toe slid over the notch on the floor where the disc would be inserted.

Dylan had passed on the Obsidians' warning to Logan, who apparently had fallen very quiet, then spent the rest of the night alone in his old room. He knew that as long as he was tagged, the Obsidians could detain him at any time.

Gina approached the stand in her periwinkle suit, her eyes bearing the usual kind chill. The judge and jury knew I was her niece, so she had to be careful not to look like she was coddling me. I'd seen her compassionate-crusader courtroom routine many times, but had never been the source of her ammunition.

"Let's begin with the events early in the evening of Friday, October eighteenth. Did you see Logan Keeley immediately after the concert?"

I took a deep breath, trying not to think about the reporters and bloggers in the packed courtroom. I vowed not to look at the smug CEO of Warrant Records, sitting at the defense table in an expensive suit.

"Yes," I told her in a clear voice. "I saw him go backstage with Mickey to meet with the A and R reps from the two record companies."

"When did you see him again?"

"About half an hour later." I folded my hands in my lap to keep them from fidgeting with my blouse.

"And then where did you go?"

"Back to the Keeleys' house for a party. It was his seventeenth birthday." Aunt Gina had asked me to mention that fact, to add sympathy. A murmur from the jury box confirmed that this had been a good ploy.

"How would you describe Logan's demeanor at the party?"

"I'd never seen him happier."

Gina bowed her head for a moment to let my statement sink in. A soft blond curl fell over her cheek.

"How much alcohol did you see him consume?"

"I saw him drink three pints of Guinness, plus part of a fourth pint. Then he had about half of a mixed drink called Liquid Stupid."

The crowd reacted to this with scattered titters.

"Your Honor, a sample of Liquid Stupid was left on the deceased's nightstand." My aunt retrieved a sheet of paper from her table. "A previous witness, a forensic expert, has authenticated this exhibit, already admitted into evidence. The Liquid Stupid substance was estimated to be one hundred eighty proof. Ninety percent alcohol, more than ten times the strength of beer. There were also traces of codeine found in the solution. The forensic expert concluded that this concoction would have severely impaired the judgment of a one-hundred-fifty-pound man such as the deceased, especially one who had already consumed more than fifty ounces of beer."

The judge peered through his reading glasses at the sheet of paper. "Yes, this has been admitted already. Please continue."

Gina asked me, "What did Logan do after he drank the Liquid Stupid?"

"We went to his room."

Her voice was gentle but firm. "For what purpose?"

My stomach fluttered, and I took another deep breath. "For the purpose of sex."

I heard a tongue click. One of the jurors, an older woman, shook her head. For the most part, though, the crowd seemed unsurprised.

Gina was unfazed by my semi-smart-ass response. "And did you achieve this purpose?"

"No." I tried not to sound defensive.

"Why not?"

I hesitated, hoping that the roof would cave in or aliens would vaporize the courthouse in their effort to conquer the planet. Anything to keep from saying it.

"Aura? Tell us what stopped you from consummating your relationship."

"The alcohol had made him . . . um . . . He couldn't."

The snickers spread throughout the courtroom. I gritted my teeth, hating Mr. and Mrs. Keeley for making me tell the world. Instead of being famous for his music, Logan would go down in pop culture history as the Ghost of the Guy Who Couldn't Get It Up.

"Then what happened?"

My gaze dropped to the floor. "I was mad at him. I told him he was stupid."

Gina upped the urgency in her tone. "How did he respond?"

"He almost passed out, but then he said he knew how to fix it. He said he was going to take a shower and wake up." The words came fast now, tumbling over one another. "So he went to his dresser and got a package of something he said was shampoo. And then he left, and the next time I saw him, he was—he was a ghost." My voice halted. "He was dead."

I hadn't cried during any of our rehearsals, though Gina had told me that tears would be a nice touch. I'd obsessed over choosing the right words and emphasizing the right syllables. In rehearsals, this testimony had been a performance.

But now it was real. Logan was gone. And I was standing in his bedroom all over again, with my shirt backward and inside out, seeing him in violet, feeling my world shatter into so many pieces that seventy-six days later, I was still picking them up.

Even now, each eye released only a single tear. They dribbled down my cheeks, so slowly they seemed to be having a reverse race, seeing which could take longer to fall.

"No further questions, Your Honor."

"Your witness," the judge said to the defense attorney.

Harriet Stone approached from my right, spiked heels clicking on the hardwood floor. Twice before I'd translated for cases involving Stone's clients. She didn't even try to hide her disdain for ghosts, which meant translators got a dose of it too.

I wiped my cheeks and faced her with my last bit of strength.

"Thank you for testifying, Ms. Salvatore." She glanced at my aunt, then at the jury, as if to remind them I was related to the plaintiff's attorney. "The death of your boyfriend must have been a difficult ordeal."

I said nothing, since it technically wasn't a question.

Stone buttoned her suit jacket, a scarlet that brought out the blush on her sharp, pale cheeks. She was from that older generation of women who thought wearing red—and shoulder pads—made them look masculine and therefore powerful. At least tomorrow she'd have to put on another color, since Logan would be in the room.

"Prior to the night in question," Stone asked, "had Logan Keeley ever consumed alcohol to the point of unconsciousness in your presence?"

"Yes."

"How many times?"

I cringed inside at the hurt this would cause his parents. "Four times."

"What were his last words to you?"

I gripped the smooth wooden arms of the witness chair. That memory belonged to me and Logan, and this woman wanted to steal it. Taint it. And what would it prove?

Then I remembered something Aunt Gina had once told me: A good lawyer never asks a question she doesn't already know the answer to. Logan must have been asked this same question during his deposition.

"Ms. Salvatore? What did Logan say to you just before he walked off to the bathroom?"

I spoke to the far wall of the courtroom. "He said, 'Wait for me, Aura.'"

Stone crossed her arms and tapped her pen against her side as she paced. "And have you?"

My pulse surged. I hadn't expected these questions. "Have I what?"

"Have you waited for him? Have you been involved with Logan since his death?"

"In what way?"

She stopped pacing. "Have you spent time with him in your bedroom?"

"Yes." I was *not* getting into specifics.

Stone approached the witness stand, close enough that I could smell the hair spray keeping her black bun sleek against her scalp. "What did you do with him on these visits?"

Blood rushed to my face. *Logan, you didn't.* Not that he would've had a choice. Ghosts can't lie.

I opened and closed my mouth, then said, "We talked. Listened to music."

"That's all?"

"Sometimes we would read."

Gina stood. "Objection, Your Honor. I fail to see the purpose in this line of questioning."

Stone spoke directly to the judge. "I'm trying to establish the fact that the so-called victim has led anything but a tragic existence since his death. According to Logan Keeley's deposition, he has walked the streets of Dublin, attended numerous concerts for free, and spent many a night indulging in sexual play with his living, breathing girl-friend."

The crowd gasped. Even Megan put her hand to her wide-open mouth. I couldn't look at Logan's parents.

"Please continue," the judge said, speaking loudly to restore order.

"Isn't this true, Ms. Salvatore?" the lawyer asked me, arms folded in what looked like triumph.

My hands had gone cold and my face red-hot. I steadied my breath and slowly drew my palms over my cheekbones to cool them. They could try to humiliate me, they could try to sully my memory of Logan, they could try to turn what we had into something sleazy.

But I wouldn't let them.

"That's correct," I said in a strong, steady voice. Before she could ask for details, I threw them at her. "I took off my clothes and I touched myself. We spoke to each other, we pretended, we made it as real as it could be."

The lawyer unfolded her arms and tugged down her jacket as she strutted away from the witness stand. "Thank you. No further questions."

"Logan's not suing you," I blurted out. "His family is, so even if he's having a good time—and you might want to ask him about that—"

Stone turned quickly. "Your Honor—"

"—they're in more pain than you can imagine."

"Your Honor, I ask that these remarks be stricken from the record as nonresponsive."

The judge banged his gavel. "The witness may step down."

Using the edge of the witness box, I dragged myself to stand. Then I pointed to the Warrant CEO. "You took him from us! Ghost or not, he's still dead."

"Step down now, miss," the judge barked. "You are released."

I almost scoffed at his choice of words. *Released into what? A deeper level of hell?*

Instead I straightened my suit and said, "Thank you," before retrieving my crutches.

"Furthermore," the judge said, "the jury will disregard those remarks."

"Thank you, Your Honor," said the defense attorney, with a fake sweetness that almost made me choke.

As I hobbled away from the witness stand, I held my chin straight and high, meeting no one's gaze—not Gina's, not even Megan's.

I was truly alone now, so I might as well get used to it.

By the end of the day, the news and rumors had spread to every corner of the Internet, or so it seemed. I thought about checking a few

Japanese websites to see how they translated the phrase "ghost fucker."

"By the time school starts again next week," my aunt said on the drive home, "they'll have forgotten all about it. There'll be some new scandal, you'll see."

I looked out the side window at the heavy white clouds and prayed for a nationwide blizzard that would knock out all power and phone lines. Or at least close school for another two weeks.

Then I sent a text message to Zachary.

ALL OUT OF PATIENCE YET?

"I'm proud of you, kid," Gina said. "For the way you stood up for yourself. And the way you told the truth. I'm sure it wasn't easy."

"You knew, didn't you? Both sides get to look at the same evidence, right?"

"I read Logan's deposition. I never imagined they would use"— she waved her hand like she was swatting a gnat—"that part of it."

"Any other surprises I should know about before the defense starts their side tomorrow?"

"I don't think so. You don't have to come. Your part is over."

"I want to hear Logan speak." I ran my finger along the rubber seal of the window. "It might be my last chance."

"God willing," she said under her breath.

I pretended I didn't hear her as my phone vibrated with a new message from Zachary. I opened it, my pulse skittering.

NOT EVEN CLOSE.

That night I lay on the couch, staring at the darkened Christmas tree. Aunt Gina always insisted on leaving it up until Epiphany on January 6, but we never turned the lights on after New Year's Eve, so it might as well not have been there. It looked sad, with all its decorations slightly off balance. Even its plastic branches looked wilted.

I was finally drifting off to sleep when a violet glow filled the room.

I kept my eyes closed to see how long he would stay. His light grew brighter as he came nearer, until it enveloped my entire world.

"I don't know if you can hear me," Logan whispered, "but I came to give you something. Something I shouldn't have kept."

I almost opened my eyes then, but he shifted to my right, kneeling or sitting on the floor by my side.

He took a deep breath, which still sounded so real I could almost believe he was alive. "Here goes. It's called 'Forever.'"

Logan began to sing, a lilting tune I didn't recognize. At first I wondered if we'd seen the band in concert together or had listened to it on one of our first dates.

Then he reached the chorus, and the words were us.

All my insecurities, all his excesses, all the ways we fought and pushed and pulled. And how it all didn't matter. Those things that tore us apart were no match for forever.

Tears flowed from beneath my closed lids and tickled as they trickled down my cheeks. Logan must have seen them, but he didn't let on. He just kept singing his last encore—his grand finale, all for me.

I'd been so wrong about us. If he'd lived, we would've been happy. Not every day, but over the span of time that made up forever.

But he hadn't lived.

A hole opened up inside me, so raw I had to curl up on my side away from his light, pulling my good knee to my chest to ease the ache. The hole gaped so big it seemed like I could crawl inside, let the darkness swallow all thoughts of the future that once stretched before us. We had lost forever.

When Logan finished my song, he remained for several silent seconds. I heard nothing but my own shaky breath.

Then he said, "That's all."

And disappeared.

Chapter Twenty-three

Megan sat with me the next day in the courtroom, in the back row, away from the Keeleys.

"I'll be so glad when this is over." She fanned herself with the magenta flyer for Logan's "Passing On" party. "Mickey's a total mess. I wish his parents hadn't dragged out everyone's pain with this trial. Greedy little mofos."

"It's not about the money." I dabbed my runny nose with a ragged tissue. "Gina says they want to make sure it never happens again." I looked at the clock. Two minutes to nine.

"Right. They'll change the world with one lawsuit. Record companies will all become saintly and nonprofit and stop destroying the lives of starry-eyed dumb shits like Logan."

"He's not dumb. He had good grades."

"Being smart doesn't make someone undumb."

I sighed, too tired for one of Megan's rants. I'd stayed awake most of the night after Logan left, wondering whether to call him back to my side. To make matters worse, the courtroom was overheated today, increasing my exhaustion.

The bailiff entered, and we all stood for the judge. With my bad knee, by the time I stood, everyone else was sitting down.

Before my aunt took her seat, she turned to find me. I gave her a weak thumbs-up. From where I was sitting, I couldn't see her opponent, Harriet Stone, but I knew the defense attorney would be wearing a more muted color today. I hoped her arrogance would be similarly toned down.

The first witness for the defense was the toxicologist who worked for the medical examiner's office. His tests showed that the quantity and purity of cocaine in Logan's system wasn't enough to kill a healthy young man on its own. Even if he'd snorted the entire sample the A and R rep had given him, he should've experienced only a quick, intense high.

Problem was, Logan had a crap-load of alcohol in his system at the time, and the combination had triggered sudden cardiac death through ventricular fibrillation—Logan's "worms in the chest."

Gina cross-examined the witness, pointing out the obvious fact that without the drug, Logan would still be alive. "Isn't it true that any amount of cocaine, when mixed with alcohol, can be deadly?"

"It has been fatal in some cases," the toxicologist said, "especially if the user has an undiagnosed cardiac condition. But the man who gave him the substance couldn't have expected—"

"Doctor, I'm not asking you to read a drug dealer's mind. I'm asking if cocaine mixed with alcohol can trigger sudden cardiac death. Yes or no."

The doctor hesitated. "Yes."

I sagged in my seat, wishing I could box up that testimony and send it back in a time machine as a seventeenth birthday present for Logan. Such a small slice of knowledge could have saved his life.

After a few more witnesses for the defense, we took a quick lunch break; then the trial resumed at two o'clock.

When everyone was seated, someone dimmed the lights. The BlackBox indicator glowed red above the rear door.

Next to the witness stand, two kids sat back-to-back with a blue light next to each. The witnesses would switch off from question to question, each of them answering for Logan in turn.

One of them was a slim African-American boy of about fifteen; the other, a little blond girl who looked about ten years old, though she must have been at least fourteen, since that was the minimum age for this work. They both seemed scared, and I felt a tug of sympathy.

The judge nodded to the bailiff, who hit another switch on the wall. The BlackBox lights winked out.

Logan appeared on the witness stand, summoned by the clear quartz disc. Out of place in his unbuttoned shirt and baggy skate shorts, he scanned the courtroom, astonished.

Megan leaned close and whispered, "The diva in him is totally loving this."

I tried to smile. She had no idea what was at stake. I leaned over the armrest into the aisle so Logan could see me.

When our eyes met, the rest of the room seemed to darken. It felt like a spotlight was shining down on each of us. My chest hurt, just as it had when he'd sung to me last night.

I wrapped my arms around my waist. *Please end this, Logan. Please nail this case so you can leave.*

Harriet Stone walked up to the witness stand. She spoke softly to the kids, then hit the switch under the boy's blue light, making it glow. Finally she faced Logan, though she couldn't see him.

"Please state your name for the record."

"Logan Patrick Keeley."

The boy repeated what he'd just said. Stone asked basic questions like Logan's age and hometown, which he answered with an edge of boredom in his voice. After each response from the translator, the kid who hadn't translated would nod to confirm.

Finally the lawyer progressed to the matter at hand. "Please tell us how you became personally acquainted with Warrant Records."

"The A and R rep called us," Logan said. "A friend of his had seen one of our shows in September."

"When you say 'our shows,' you're referring to the band the Keeley Brothers, correct?"

"Yeah. So he comes to our gig at the community center on my birthday. And since we totally kicked ass—" He stopped and spoke to the girl, whose turn it was to translate. "You can say 'kicked butt' if you want."

Megan laughed. She was the only one.

The girl recited Logan's words, and then he continued:

"So afterwards the rep comes up and introduces himself. Says he's dying to sign us right away." Logan waited for the girl to catch up.

"But Warrant wasn't our first choice, and besides, we promised our folks that we wouldn't sign anything without their permission." He beamed at his parents, as if expecting them to praise him. I guess they didn't respond as he'd hoped, because his expression darkened for a moment.

"Anyway, I saw the rep offer the drugs to Mickey, who got so pissed—um, so angry that he told him to, um . . ." Logan seemed to fumble for a synonym for "fuck off." "Well, he said he wasn't interested."

"What about you?" Stone asked. "Were you interested?"

"I was interested in a contract. So I wanted the guy to like me, right?" He waited for the translation, this time by the boy, whose nervousness seemed to be fading. "My parents always taught me that part of making friends is accepting hospitality. It makes people feel good when they can do things for you."

"Are you saying you accepted the cocaine to make the defendant's representative happy?"

"Exactly. I never planned to try it. I've seen enough burned-out musicians. I even stopped smoking pot to save my singing voice. No drugs for me, uh-uh."

I mirrored Megan's *yeah, right* glance. No drugs, other than enough alcohol to drown a whale.

After the translation, Stone stepped right up to Logan's box. "Then why did you take the cocaine?"

Logan kept his focus on the lawyer. "It was supposed to be our night. It was my birthday, but I wanted it to be about us." He pounded his fist into the side of his leg without a sound. "And then I

messed up. Big-time. I guess I lost track of how many beers I'd had."
After the boy repeated his words, Logan added, "Liquid Stupid was
made for me."

Stone began to pace. "Your girlfriend testified yesterday that the
alcohol made you incapable of sexual intercourse. Why didn't you just
wait until another night?"

"I was afraid." He shut his eyes briefly, and when he opened them
again they burned straight at me. "Afraid of losing her."

My mouth fell open. *Logan*, losing *me*? What kind of bizarro universe had he been dwelling in that night?

"I'd let her down before, see. I wanted to make it up to her." He
paused, and I heard the same words out of the mouth of the boy.
"She was the most important thing in the world to me. She still is.
But she was losing faith."

I shook my head slowly, even though I knew he was right. I'd had
so many doubts.

"I couldn't blame her for it. All I ever talked about was playing
music and being famous." He squirmed while the translator caught
up. "I wanted to show her that none of that mattered compared to
being with her. I would've given it all up, Aura, I swear."

My jaw trembled so hard, my teeth started to chatter. "No," I said
in a whisper that verged on a squeak.

"It was the happiest night of my life." Logan gestured to his outfit. "Proof, right?"

After checking with the judge, Stone asked the girl translator to
describe Logan's clothes, which became part of the official record.

Then the attorney spoke to Logan. "Do you testify that you knew what you were doing when you ingested the cocaine, that you under-stood the risks involved?"

My aunt shot to her feet. "Objection."

"Overruled." The judge gave her an odd look. "The witness will answer the question."

"But the witness is in no position—"

"I said, I'll allow it." He nodded in Logan's general direction. "Please respond."

"Honestly?" Logan shrugged. "I didn't know it could kill me. If I'd ever heard that, I forgot it a long time ago. But I knew it was dangerous."

"Then why take the risk?" Stone asked.

Logan turned his head to look at me. "Because she was worth it."

A buzz shot through the courtroom when the translator finished the statement. I covered my face, wanting to drag my skin off with my fingernails. Logan's death really was my fault, and now with every word, he was losing the case and sealing his eternal, BlackBoxed fate.

"Thank you," the lawyer said. "No further questions."

I uncovered my eyes and watched Gina approach the witness stand.

"Logan, you say that being with Ms. Salvatore that night was worth the risk. The risk of what?"

"Becoming a coke addict, mostly. In the long run."

"What did you think the drug would do to you that night?"

"Maybe give me a nosebleed. And insomnia, which was sort of the point." Logan tilted his chin, thinking. "I knew it could make me dizzy and sweaty." He held up a finger. "Oh, and horny."

The girl giggled as she recited the last part.

"Did it ever enter your mind," Gina asked, "that taking this drug would result in your death?"

"No!" Logan's brow creased into several violet lines. "Why would I want to die? I had a great family, I had a future doing what I loved, I had the best girlfriend in the world. And it was my *birthday*, for God's sake." His voice choked with anger. "I had everything, and I lost it."

I clutched my hands together so hard, my sprained wrist sent shocks of pain up my arm. *Logan, please don't shade out.*

Gina stepped closer to the witness box. "But as a ghost, you can have certain experiences. You can haunt."

"Haunting, yeah. So much fun. If I want to be with my family, it means watching them cry. It means knowing that I put those tears in their eyes." He looked at me across the courtroom. "As for Aura, I hung out with her after I died, and even though she made me happy, it killed me not to touch her, it killed me to know we had no future. And now, because I died, I've lost her." He waited for the boy to translate, then addressed the jury. "I can't touch, but I can still feel. And I tell you, if this were my life . . . I wouldn't want to live."

The courtroom was frozen in silence, listening to the translator's halting recitation. My heart felt like it would leak its lifeblood if I looked at Logan another second.

"So did I know I could die?" he said. "Absolutely not. With all I had, with all I could've had—" He gazed at me for what felt like an eternity. "Why would I ever take that chance?"

As the jury deliberated, I stared at the BlackBox indicator light, glowing red again. Logan had left the room, and so had his translators, who

were probably enjoying a couple of pizzas and ice-cream sundaes. That
had always been my post-trial ritual. I never wanted to speak for a
ghost again, now that I knew firsthand the pain that lay behind a case.

"Aura."

Mr. Keeley was standing in the center of the aisle next to my seat.
He'd spoken quietly, not in his usual booming voice.

I scooted over to give him room to sit. He grunted as he eased his
burly frame into the seat, and I worried about his heart. The stress of
the case, on top of losing his son, must have had his cardiologist on red
alert. I remembered last New Year's Eve, sitting in the hospital with
the rest of the Keeleys, waiting to see if Logan's father would survive
his first heart attack at the age of fifty.

Mr. Keeley used a handkerchief to wipe the sheen of sweat from
his ruddy face. "I don't know what to say, other than I'm sorry."

My throat thickened. "That's plenty."

"I wanted to say it right, but I don't know how." He sat perfectly
still, as if one wrong move would collapse him.

"I guess that makes two of—"

"I don't blame you for what happened."

"Uh, thanks." I noticed he didn't say "we" didn't blame me, thereby
not including Logan's mom. "I don't blame you, either."

He flashed me a shocked look, then smiled in a way that reminded
me so much of Logan that I couldn't help but return it. It hit me that
Logan would never have Mr. Keeley's thick silver hair, or the laugh
lines at the corners of his blue eyes.

"Touché." Mr. Keeley smoothed the creases of his trousers, relax-
ing a bit. "I miss him. I'd give anything to speak to Logan directly. Or

even indirectly. He won't talk to us anymore, or at least Dylan won't tell us what he says."

"That might be for the best."

"I know Logan's angry with me," he said in a low voice. "But he'll see, all this pain will be worth it if we win."

"And then what?"

"Then Logan will move on." He folded his hands. "And maybe, one day, so will we."

I stared at the scuffed-up rubber knob at the bottom of my crutch and thought of everything that had happened since Logan's death. "Mr. Keeley, one day we're all going to move on, even if he doesn't."

Nodding slowly, he sat back in the seat, eyes fixed on the red BlackBox light. "That's what worries me the most."

Megan came back down the aisle from visiting Mickey. She stopped when she saw Mr. Keeley. "Oh. I thought you went to the men's room. No, don't get up!" she added as he stood to leave.

He motioned for her to sit. "I should get back to Kathleen and the kids." He patted Megan's shoulder. "Please, the next time you come over, bring Aura with you."

She watched him shamble toward the front of the courtroom, then slid past me as I moved back into the seat beside the aisle. "I just talked to Mickey," she said. "Mr. Keeley and Siobhan think they won, but Mickey and his mom are sure they've lost."

"What about Dylan?"

"He didn't say." She sat with a sigh. "He looks almost as freaked as you."

Of course. Dylan knew that if the Keeleys didn't win, and Logan couldn't pass on, the Obsidians would lock Logan up forever.

I slumped down in the seat so I could rest the back of my head. The fear was sucking all the oxygen from my brain.

A hand smoothed my hair. It was Aunt Gina, who had just re-entered the courtroom through the rear doors.

I sat up straighter. "Did they do it?"

She nodded. "Logan's subpoena tag was taken off. He's a free man." The corners of her mouth turned down. "He needs so much to be at peace. If we lose this case, I don't know how I'll live with myself."

A door in the front corner of the courtroom opened, and the jury began to file back in after less than an hour's deliberation. Gina squeezed my arm, then hurried to her table.

My muscles wound themselves into double and triple knots as the court proceeded through its final formalities. By the time the defendant stood to receive the decision, I was on the verge of a full body cramp.

The foreman opened the envelope.

Liable.

As in, guilty.

Logan was free.

I sank forward, head in my arms, and wept. As the courtroom erupted with shouts of wonder and jubilation, Megan wrapped her arms around my back and rocked me, the way she had when Logan died.

It was over, almost. Logan would escape this world, escape everyone who wanted a piece of him. And we would all begin to heal.

Chapter Twenty-four

L ogan zoomed up to me the moment I hobbled through the door of the packed and raucous Green Derby pub.

"We did it!" He enveloped me in a violet-bright hug. "Dylan told me you were amazing on that witness stand." Then he whispered, "And now they won't put me in a boring little box for the next sixty years."

I rolled my eyes. "Don't even joke about that. I was so scared."

"Me too. Talk about a fate worse than death. But it's over now, and time to party." He waved to Megan as she came through the door. "Hey, they're selling five-dollar pitchers of Harp."

"My aunt is here," I told him, "so I better stick to soda."

Megan pushed over to us. "Logan, look at you, all bright and shiny."

"Do I look different?" He straightened his shirt. "I feel different.

Here, we saved you guys seats up front with my family." We moved toward the other end of the bar, the crowd parting for my crutches.

"How do you feel different?" I asked him.

"Like something is calling me." His voice sounded older and deeper than before. "I just hope—" He cut himself off and scratched the back of his head. "I hope it's something good."

His image shone almost painfully bright, despite the flickering lamps on the walls and tables of the pub. Seeing him like this, it was hard to believe he had ever shaded. "I'm sure it'll be good," I told him.

On the stage, Mickey sat tuning his acoustic guitar and Siobhan her fiddle.

"So you convinced them to play," I said to Logan.

"It's good exposure. See the flyers people are passing around? Their first gig will be so jammed." He watched his brother and sister for a few moments. "I'm glad I could do something good for them, after all the pain I caused."

I decided not to derail his self-inflicted guilt trip. I stopped next to an empty chair at the end of the front row. "What's your last song?"

"You'll see." He knelt beside me as I sat. "It's not the one I wrote for you. I wanted that to be for us and nobody else."

"You knew I was awake, didn't you?"

He smiled and shrugged. "I wouldn't waste a stellar performance on an unconscious girl."

Siobhan tapped her bow on the side of her chair. "Is Logan here? We're ready whenever you are." She bit her lip. "No rush."

"I better go," Logan said to me. "I don't know how long before this peace-through-justice thing expires." His face more solemn than ever,